Bill Knox began his writing career as a young Glasgow journalist. Now a full-time author, he has been a crime reporter, motoring correspondent and news editor. He makes many contributions to radio and television and is well known to Scottish viewers as writer and presenter of the Scottish Television police liaison programme Crime Desk.

Witchline is Knox's twenty-third adventure thriller, the seventh to feature marine insurance investigator Andrew Laird. Knox has also written some thirty crime and sea stories with Scottish backgrounds. His work is published in the USA and translated into ten languages, with world sales exceeding four million copies.

WITCHLINE

An undercover trip to Jersey to investigate a case of maritime insurance fraud involves Andrew Laird in a trail of blackmail, casual violence and finally murder as he fights the Channel Islanders' inbred, traditional code of secrecy to undercover the truth about Mehran Holdings, an old-established company which operates like a buccaneering throwback to the eighteenth century. Mehran have a deathlist way of keeping their secrets. Laird's name could be the next on the list.

BILL KNOX

WITCHLINE

Complete and Unabridged

ULVERSCROFT
Leicester

First published in Great Britain
under the name of Robert MacLeod

First Large Print Edition
published 1999

British Library CIP Data

Knox, Bill, *1928 –*
Witchline.—Large print ed.—
Ulverscroft large print series: mystery
1. Detective and mystery stories
2. Large type books
I. Title II. MacLeod, Robert, *1928 –*
823.9′14 [F]

ISBN 0–7089–4102–8

Published by
F. A. Thorpe (Publishing) Ltd.
Anstey, Leicestershire

Set by Words & Graphics Ltd.
Anstey, Leicestershire
Printed and bound in Great Britain by
T. J. International Ltd., Padstow, Cornwall

This book is printed on acid-free paper

For Mark and Catherine

'*Every wreck under the sea belongs to someone*'

An international
marine insurance expert

This story is about marine fraud.

Marine fraud exists, deals in millions, and is alive and growing right at this moment. This story is fiction — but the real thing is even bigger.

Ask the marine insurance companies who have to pay out.

B. Knox

Prelude

The last straw was the evening Mary Litarna came home from work, opened the door of her apartment and was met by a flood of water.

Mary Litarna was a schoolteacher and unmarried. She taught English and Health Care at a village school near Almeria in southern Spain. She had had a long, hot, tiring day; she had been close to knocking hell out of those Garcia twins when they tried that damned fool trick with a dead lizard.

Now this. Kicking off her shoes, she paddled barefoot across the apartment's terrazzo floor, reached her little kitchen, and called on several Saints for support as she saw the cause. The damned washing machine had gone wrong again. Water was flooding out from underneath it in exactly the same way as before. In the two months since she'd bought it, using carefully scrimped savings, that white and chrome monster had already broken down three times. The last time it had also chewed up three pairs of pants, her best bra, and that white nylon *blusa* with the indecent neckline which was the best mantrap she'd ever owned.

Abandoning the Saints and cursing, Mary Litarna turned off the water supply, spent the next couple of hours with a mop and pail drying out her apartment, hung dripping rugs over the little balcony, then poured herself a stiff gin and collapsed in a chair. The Garcia twins were forgotten. What was she going to do about that damned appliance?

So it had been a bargain at the cut-price discount store outside Almeria. So she'd even been given an extended guarantee, serviced by the discount store's own *technico*. What the hell good was that when she couldn't turn her back on the thing without something happening? Had anyone ever been drowned by a washing machine?

When Mary Litarna had graduated from teacher's training college, she'd gone to England for six months of what she liked to call postgraduate studies. Part of that time she'd worked as a maid in an hotel. The manager had been Swiss, his wife a jumped-up English bitch. But if anything went wrong with the hotel's equipment or supplies they didn't waste time or money. They wrote direct to the errant company's managing director at head office. They usually got results.

Mary Litarna got a pen and some

damp-smelling notepaper — it had been in the bottom drawer of her dressing table. She found the washing machine's instruction book, found the maker's head office address, then began writing. Every word had a carefully chosen, stabbing edge.

Finished, she put the letter in an envelope, addressed the envelope, then poured herself another stiff gin. She felt much better. Sipping the gin, she had happy thoughts about how she could make life suitably miserable for those Garcia twins over the next couple of weeks.

Mary Litarna posted the letter on her way to school the next morning.

Through her action, a man she didn't know and would never meet had just been sentenced to death.

Though she would get her washing machine fixed. Eventually.

1

It was a Thursday afternoon in early September, one of those afternoons when pale yellow sunlight made London's skyline glint like gold. It was a magic which made people brighten and put a new spring in their walk. At Buckingham Palace, tourist cameras clicked like machine-pistols at the Changing of the Guard. Outside Harrods, a police-woman in uniform was propositioned by a very small drunk and was too busy laughing to arrest him.

It was that kind of day.

Andrew Laird looked out at it from a third-floor window in the big, stone-fronted office block which formed one side of a quiet, hidden Victorian square not far from the shopping bustle of Oxford Street. He had his tie loosened and his shirtsleeves rolled up. Down below, in the square, there was still late blossom on some of the trees. A young street busker sat at the bottom of a statue to some forgotten hero and played his guitar while he watched the girls go by. A small dog that seemed to be with him lifted its leg on a parked Rolls-Royce Corniche.

The office block was the headquarters of the international Clanmore Alliance Assurance and the third-floor window view belonged to Osgood Morris, Clanmore's marine insurance claims manager. Laird had been summoned through and was waiting for Morris to finish a telephone conversation, one Morris didn't seem to be enjoying. Laird grinned as he heard Morris's shrill voice make a new protest. A Swedish cruise liner had grounded briefly and unsensationally off the Florida coast, her owners were presenting a damage claim which was a blend of Scandinavian charm and sheer brass neck.

'No, positively not!' Morris's voice rose sharply. 'Read the policy conditions. That's specifically excluded. Specifically — '

Down below, the busker's dog had transferred its attentions and was sniffing at the wheels of a black Cadillac. More girls were walking under the trees. Morris was still talking on the 'phone, but tomorrow would be Friday, then came the weekend.

When, among other things, Andrew Laird would be celebrating his thirtieth birthday. He caught a glimpse of his reflection in the window and gave a slightly wry grimace at what he saw. Stockily built, just over medium height, he had been one of Clanmore Alliance's team of ten marine claims assessors for close on three years. It was, in some ways, an easier life than he'd had earlier. Sometimes he still felt out of place in an office setting.

He had a feeling some people in Clanmore, including Osgood Morris, might agree.

Andrew Laird had grey-green eyes framed by faint crow's-foot lines, a nose that had been broken and reset. He had thick dark hair that was prematurely grey at the temples. The rest included long, strong-fingered hands, a voice that still held a wisp of a Scottish accent, and a smile which could be surprisingly boyish. He didn't ruffle easily.

But another part of his story was the tattoo marks on his arms. On one, a stylish Chinese dragon crawled from wrist to biceps muscle. On the other, a foul anchor with elaborate chain was equal in colour and length.

That had been in Hong Kong, when he'd been too young to know better.

'Goodbye,' snarled Osgood Morris, ending his call.

Laird turned as the telephone slammed down. Morris, a small, thin, weasel-faced man with a sharp nose and sparse hair, sat like a petulant gnome behind his executive-size desk. It had its own built-in VDU terminal. The marine claims manager wore a three-piece dark-blue business suit with a striped shirt and a plain black tie.

'Damn them,' shrilled Morris, glaring at the telephone. 'Do I look like I run a charity?' He didn't, even when he bared his teeth in an attempted smile at Laird. 'My worry, not yours. Sit down, Andrew.'

'Thank you.' Laird settled in the chair placed opposite. It was well out of reach of the desk. Someone had once tried to grab Morris by the throat.

'Our Swedish friends can wait.' Morris pushed one file of papers aside and fingered another, much slimmer. He sucked his lips. 'How much do you know about the Channel Isles — Jersey in particular?'

Laird raised an eyebrow. The Channel Islands were British and Jersey was the largest of them. From Jersey, on a clear day, you could count the houses on the Brittany coast of France. They were tourist islands, but to a seaman the Channel Islands meant fierce rocks and tides and Admiralty chart number 2669, speckled with warnings to mariners that were hard to forget.

'Well?' Morris was waiting.

'I've been, that's about all.' It was a mild lie. His ship had berthed in St Helier harbour for several days. After the first night and a near riot in a harbour bar, there had been no more shore leave.

'I see.' Morris sighed. 'Some local contacts

might have been helpful. Do you remember the loss of the cargo ship *Rosewitch* off the Portuguese coast about two years ago?'

'Yes.' It had been a hefty insurance claim. Laird had been glad he hadn't been involved. The *Rosewitch*, a small but modern cargo ship, had sunk in deep water soon after sending out a frantic Mayday call. All but one of the crew had survived, reaching the Portuguese shore by lifeboat.

'Clanmore Alliance paid out close on £3 million sterling. We carried the hull insurance, of course — but we also covered some of her cargo.' Morris's thin mouth tightened. 'The *Rosewitch* was owned by Witchline Shipping, the major component of the Mehran Holding Group — they're based on Jersey. She was sailing from Southampton for Genoa, with a mix of general cargo. But she stopped off at Jersey on the way, to unload some building materials the Mehran people wanted brought over.'

Laird nodded, remembering something else. The *Rosewitch* had been the last case handled by Frank Harrison, Clanmore's senior claims adjuster, before he retired. Harrison had been a golfing fanatic. Six weeks after he left, he'd dropped dead from a heart attack after sinking a long putt.

'Clanmore still insures five hulls for

9

Witchline, we've handled their business for more than a decade.' Morris paused, tapping the file with his fingertips. 'Witchline has always had a reasonable reputation. There was the usual formal inquiry after the sinking, no awkward questions.' He paused deliberately. 'There is one now. Why has some of the *Rosewitch*'s cargo turned up in Spain?'

Laird's mouth shaped a silent surprise. 'No doubts?'

'It doesn't look that way.' Morris shrugged. 'So we have an apparent case of barratry.'

Barratry — an old-fashioned word for marine fraud. Laird could hear the sound of the guitar in the square still filtering into the drab functional office. But Osgood Morris was talking about a different kind of world, and, whatever Morris's faults, he was one of the sharpest marine insurance men in London.

'How do we know?'

'In a damned stupid way. Some Spanish woman bought a new English-made Paladin washing machine from her local cut-price store. When it gave her problems she wrote direct to the Paladin factory, kicking up hell.' Morris shifted unhappily. 'She gave the machine's serial number. The Paladin stock computer says it was one of a consignment lost on the *Rosewitch*.'

Laird raised an eyebrow. 'Computers aren't perfect.'

'Agreed.' Morris considered the VDU terminal beside him with a jaundiced eye. It was only a week since the Clanmore computer had suddenly and unexpectedly gone down, causing two days of chaos. 'But that particular Paladin washing machine isn't sold in Spain — never has been. Paladin have a wholesaler in Malaga who handles other products for them, and they were curious enough to ask him to visit the woman. She'd given the correct serial number, and he located other Paladin washing machines which should have been among the *Rosewitch* consignment. The cut-price dealer apparently bought a truckload from a stranger — no questions, because they were cheap.'

'Meaning he thought they were plain ordinary stolen,' murmured Laird. 'I've a stupid question. Any sign of seawater damage, as if they'd been salvaged or — ?'

Morris shook his head.

'What about the ship's crew?'

'Scattered to the winds. Her master, Captain Daniel Shelton, has vanished to South America — he faded from the scene a month after the official inquiry. The body of the man who allegedly drowned was never

11

found. Even the Shipping Federation can't trace any of the rest.'

Laird frowned. 'How many are we talking about?'

'Ten men. Various nationalities, no firm backgrounds.'

'But seamen. Maybe with union cards?' It was another possible source for background.

Morris shook his head. 'Witchline Shipping are non-union, always have been — they're Liberian registered, flag of convenience style. The National Union of Seamen say none of the crew were members.'

'Tidy.' But that kind of checking took time. It fuelled Laird's growing suspicion. His grey-green eyes narrowed and he leaned forward. 'Osgood, how long have you known?'

'A few days.' Morris avoided his gaze, looking at the old print of a paddle steamer which hung on the wall. 'Certain — well, certain aspects had to be considered, hasty action had to be avoided. Then, naturally, our chairman had to be consulted.'

'Naturally,' said Laird stonily.

Osgood Morris lusted after a seat on the Clanmore Alliance board and would happily have consulted the chairman every time it rained. But 'certain aspects' — that was different. Laird knew what it meant. The marine claims manager was a member of the city's unofficial middle-management mafia. They formed an invisible web spread through insurance and banking investment houses, government departments and big business. They were contact book names and telephone numbers; they traded in gossip, information and rumours. They protected their own backs by helping one another. A favour given was an investment for the future.

'Anyway, there is now a distinct smell of corruption around the *Rosewitch* sinking.' Morris pushed the file towards Laird. 'This will show you how the insurance payout took Mehran Holdings through a very bad financial patch, one they hid very nicely at the time.' He sucked his teeth, the weasel look back on his face. 'They may be in continuing financial trouble, they've done some very strange things lately, and we're still insuring the Witchline fleet.' He sat back. 'I want you to go to Jersey.'

'I see.' Laird wished he did. 'Then I knock on the door and say I've come to get our money back?'

'I don't think I'd recommend that.' Morris built a little prayer-like steeple with his fingertips. 'We have to know more about Mehran Holdings — anything that might be useful, including gossip. Mehran Holdings grew from Witchline, which was founded by two brothers Mehran — both dead. Two cousins, offspring of the founders, are directors of Mehran Holdings. Their names are Paul and Diane, they're still youngish by my standards — the woman in her forties, Paul a little older. Tell a few suitable lies and they should be glad to meet you.'

'Arranged lies?'

Morris nodded. 'Arranged and justified. Mehran Holdings has become involved in arranging a major round-Jersey international power boat race for next summer. The Mehrans have been dropping heavy hints they're looking for sponsors. They should welcome a stranger bearing gifts.'

'Like money.' Laird frowned. 'How much?'

'Up to a maximum of £100,000 from our publicity and advertising budget,' said Morris calmly. 'The money exists, the approach is we're examining possibilities. It should be enough bait to allow you to ask questions.'

'It should.' As a deception, it was typical of Morris's twisted thinking. But it was good. 'Have they been told?'

'Not yet.'

'Then don't rush things.' Laird was fighting for his weekend, his birthday, but also being practical. 'They'd expect some kind of first approach, before I arrived.'

'True.' Morris wasn't totally pleased, but considered it. 'I could make an initial 'phone contact this afternoon, follow it up with a telex tomorrow — '

'Then I could arrive Monday.'

'Monday.' Osgood Morris sighed in reluctant agreement. 'All right. I'll explain the delay to our chairman, then make the arrangements.'

'It'll look a lot better,' said Laird cheerfully. Rising, he collected the file.

'Before you go, there's one thing more.' Morris gave a critical frown which took in Laird's loosened tie and rolled-up shirtsleeves. 'The Chairman tells me he's not happy about the standard of dress of staff in this department.'

'That's rough,' protested Laird. He lowered his voice confidentially. 'Still, Osgood, maybe you could smarten up a little — even change your socks more often.'

He was out of the room while Morris was still trying to splutter.

★ ★ ★

Clanmore Alliance's team of ten marine claims assessors was housed in a large open-plan office at the far end of the third-floor corridor. Mostly they worked away

15

from base and the five desks were a reasonable allowance between them. They had two computer terminals and the usual scatter of telephones. The word processor in the far corner was regarded as personal property by Nancy Andrews, the young Jamaican girl who had the vague title of general assistant. Nancy ran most things, including the message board by the door.

Laird found her sitting on one of the desks, sewing a button on a jacket for Tony Dello, another of the claims assessors. Dello was still wearing the jacket and didn't look happy.

'She's a damned bandit,' complained Dello, scowling at Laird.

'I'm a dam' black bandit,' corrected Nancy, winking. She kept a sewing kit in her drawer, an animals' charity box beside it, and it was a case of money in the box before she'd thread a needle. She paused from her task. 'What did The Man dump on you, Andy? Something faraway and glamorous?'

'No. Near, and the Channel Islands — Jersey.'

'That's where I met my wife,' grunted Dello. 'I wouldn't — ' He broke off with a yelp as the needle flicked again. 'For God's sake, Nancy, watch it.'

Laird shook his head and went past them. Dello was divorced. Nancy was still friendly with Dello's wife. Dello was just back from settling a claim against a tanker which had spilled oil off the coast of Malta and should have known better than to talk so much about the new woman he'd met out there.

He reached his own desk, dumped down the *Rosewitch* file, then went over to the message board with its list of where people were and when they might return. Halliday and Balfour were both due back, Halliday from Finland, and Balfour from a genuine, old-fashioned case of piracy off Singapore. With Dello due some time off, the other two would have to cover Laird's existing workload — or keep it on the back burner until he was finished.

A telephone rang. Laird left the call to Nancy, settled down at his desk, and opened the file.

First came part of the original Clanmore report drawn up by Frank Harrison two years before. He had interviewed the *Rosewitch*'s captain and some of her crew, he'd talked to management and to the Portuguese authorities. He'd done a thorough enough job, though here and there Laird sensed a man who had been more or less counting the days until he started drawing his pension.

Well equipped, well maintained, the 2000-ton cargo ship had been fully laden with a mixed cargo which included a thousand cases of whisky bound for the Italian market. The Paladin consignment of 200 washing machines was far down the list, along with containers of vehicle spares, several hundred cases of tinned jam, and some drums of chemicals. The whisky, he noticed, had been a twelve-year-old malt. It didn't come better.

Until disaster struck, there had been no problems on the voyage. When it happened, weather conditions had been reasonable with a moderate sea and only a hint of fog. The *Rosewitch*'s position had been approximately eight miles off the south-west tip of Portugal, near Cape St Vincent. She had been travelling at a modest ten knots.

Captain and crew spoke of a sudden impact shortly after midnight, of a massive inrush of sea below the waterline. There had barely been time to send out that Mayday message then launch a lifeboat. The man who had been lost was believed to have been trapped below, probably in the crew quarters. The lifeboat filled with survivors had landed at dawn at a tourist beach on the Algarve. A few days later, wreckage from the *Rosewitch*, including some splintered whisky cases, had been washed ashore.

The court of inquiry's formal verdict was that the ship had been lost as 'the consequence of collision with an unknown submerged object.'

Laird shrugged to himself. All fair and reasonable — if the Spanish woman hadn't complained about her washing machine. Nobody could blame the court of inquiry for its verdict, or Frank Harrison for accepting it. Every day, somewhere, the sea took its inevitable toll. Five hundred ships a year were casualties — some simply disappearing without survivors.

That was cruel fact, just as a 'submerged object' was a common enough cause. It could be an old wreck or a previously uncharted rock. A new menace had been suspected in recent years, the vast, prowling bulk of a nuclear submarine patrolling just under the surface. A few cases had been established, usually involving fishing trawlers, and nuclear submarines didn't come up to apologise if they were the wrong nationality.

But there was another side to the coin, a side where there were other suspicions which couldn't be backed with proof. Every marine insurance office knew of cases where it was suspected a ship's cargo had been secretly landed then the heavily insured ship taken out and scuttled in deep water.

Suspicions weren't good enough. Usually the insurers still had to pay out.

Visitors to the room came and went but, thankfully, left him alone. At last, he decided to take a break and went over to Nancy. She was tapping at her word processor, stopping now and again to sip at a mug of coffee.

'Thirst can be a terrible thing,' he said sadly. 'I feel like a dried-out camel.'

'You look like one.' she said tartly.

Abandoning the word processor, she ambled into the small storeroom she used as a kitchen. When she came back with another filled mug, Laird was studying the latest additions to the muscle-man pin-ups decorating the wall behind her desk.

'Here.' Nancy handed him the coffee, then grinned at the pin-ups. 'Hot and strong, Andy, the way I like my dream men. What do you think of that big hunk on the right?'

Laird looked. The muscles went with long, fair hair and a simper. He shook his head. 'I've seen sexier-looking hamsters.'

'I'd take my chance.' She lingered, watching him sip the coffee, and became more serious. 'I helped Morris's secretary gather some of the data for the *Rosewitch* file. Shouldn't you start in Portugal?'

'Not when the roots have to be in Jersey.'

'I suppose.' She frowned, not finished. 'A man drowned.'

'Maybe he did, maybe he didn't.' Laird felt

a momentary guilt. He'd seen the man's name, he couldn't remember it. 'There was never a body. It could be a piece of window-dressing to make the rest more authentic.'

'Suppose it did happen,' she persisted. 'It could be murder, right?'

Laird took a moment before he answered. He hadn't got that far with his thinking. 'Yes, it could be.'

He left her and took the coffee back to his desk and the file. The man listed as drowned had been a forty-year-old Australian deck-hand named Francis Heeney, with no known next of kin. Like the rest of the *Rosewitch* crew, apart from her captain, he'd only signed on for that voyage.

That happened. Laird took another gulp of coffee and thought about it. There was nothing unusual about signing on a new crew that way. They could be good men or they could be dockside scrapings, and a seaman never asked a shipmate about his past. He waited until he was told, because it was the best way to stay friendly. All the signs were that Francis Heeney had died a stranger among strangers.

Once she left port, a ship became a separate world. He'd seen it happen, knew what it could mean.

21

Grimacing a little, Andrew Laird read on. The next section of the file concentrated on finance, not the scanty details given in Mehran Holdings' published accounts but the very different picture put together by Osgood Morris's city mafia. There were signs that the pooled information had alarmed more than a few of them.

But it began with names. Mehran Holdings had four directors. Paul and Diane Mehran were listed as executive directors, an Erick Roder had the title of financial director, along with an associate named Raymond Garris.

Witchline Shipping was the firm's main asset, but Mehran Holdings also owned two medium-sized hotels, a travel agency and a car rental franchise, all on Jersey. A lot of money seemed to have gone into a proposed marina development on the island and there were minority share-holdings in two British mainland cargo warehousing companies.

But everything was overshadowed by a well-concealed shortage of hard cash, by a catalogue of bank overdrafts and loans. Things had been bad at the time of the *Rosewitch* sinking; the £3 million insurance payout from Clanmore Alliance was dryly described by one merchant banker as 'most opportune'.

This was not the end of it. Laird shaped a

whistle at the next paragraph. The Witchline fleet still had five vessels — *Woodwitch* and *Tidewitch, Cloudwitch, Ladywitch* and *Starwitch*. But the first three were old, almost at the end of economic operation. *Ladywitch* and *Starwitch*, more modern, had been quietly sold to a Greek shipping company on a lease-back basis.

He stopped there, pulled a telephone over, and dialled a number. When it was answered, the man at the other end of the line had a gruff east coast accent. His name was John Lewnan, he was a full-time official with the National Union of Seamen. He had been bo'sun on Laird's first ship.

'Surprise, surprise,' said Lewnan when he heard Laird's voice. 'First your boss asks us favours, now we get the office boy.'

'Just an old shipmate, John.' Laird grinned as a rumbling oath came over the line. 'Remember when I lanced that boil on your backside?'

'You mean stabbed,' grunted Lewnan. 'I'd have been safer with a vet. So what do you want?'

'Anything extra your people know about Witchline Shipping but Osgood Morris didn't ask about? I don't care how small.'

'Small is all it will be,' warned Lewnan. The union official paused for a moment.

Laird heard him speaking to someone else. Then he came back on the line. 'All right, usual time, usual place. Now sod off — I've work to do. We're not all capitalist lackeys.'

'Up the revolution,' said Laird mildly, and hung up.

Another of the marine claims team had arrived in the office. He gossiped with Laird for a few minutes then went to collect his mail from Nancy. Alone again, Laird used the telephone for two more calls — neither to do with the *Rosewitch* but, between them, enough to ensure that another claim could tick over for a few days. The ship was the *Textilla*, a Dutch freighter which had been carrying a cargo of frozen meat to West Africa. The ship's refrigeration system had broken down, the meat had been a stinking putrefied mess by the time the *Textilla* had docked, and Clanmore Alliance had been handed a headache. The local People's Committee government wanted their money back for the meat before the *Textilla* as much as moved again; it had been hard enough to have her captain released from jail.

Finished, Laird rose and stretched, then went across to the big grey metal cabinet on the other side of the room. Opening it, he searched among a racked collection of rolled-up charts and located Sheet 2669

'Channel Islands and Adjacent Coast of France'. He had it spread out on a table when Tony Dello joined him.

'Brushing up on detail?' Dello stood at his elbow, looked down at the chart, and gave a cynical chuckle. 'It's a good place to be — if you've got the right credit rating.'

'I've been,' said Laird. 'And your ex-wife is showing.'

'I know. I suppose Herself and I had some good times there.' His fellow claims assessor had the grace to sigh. 'Half an hour's flying time from London and it's all change — rules, laws, money. Hell, they even have their own postage stamps.' He grinned to himself. 'Happy days, happy nights — for a spell.'

'I could use a contact in Jersey,' said Laird. 'One I could trust.'

'All right, but no guarantees when it comes to brains,' warned Dello. He shook his head. 'He's a distant cousin to Herself, though that's not his fault. His name is Chris Newgrange, he's young, too keen to be true, and as thick as three planks.'

'What does he do for a living?'

'Do?' Dello was embarrassed. 'He runs a little hole-in-the-wall insurance agency in St Helier. I fixed it so he does some fringe business for us — small boat insurance cover, that kind of thing. He's clean — every way. But don't ask him to try joined-up writing.'

Laird chuckled. 'He'll still do. Let him know I'm coming. No need to tell him why.'

'Will do.' Dello looked down at the chart again and made a noisy business of sucking his teeth. 'You know, if these islands were French, the way they probably should be, instead of British, I probably wouldn't have met Herself — or be having to pay alimony.'

Laird grinned.

But Tony Dello was right. The Channel Islands were accidents of history. The French still called them the Iles Normandes and still had toehold ownership of a couple of small islands and some offshore rocks. But the main islands, 100 miles from the nearest British mainland, only seven miles from the French coast, rated as British Crown dependencies — close enough to self-governing colonies.

They were small, they were prosperous. They shared a three-pronged wealth based on cattle and agriculture, useful tax laws, and a booming tourist trade. Jersey, the largest and the nearest to France, had a 60,000 population that increased five times over during the summer months. All because they'd been won in a confusion of long-forgotten Anglo-French wars, so forgotten

26

that even twentieth-century France had stopped mourning her lost Iles Normandes. True, the islands had been the only British territory to be occupied by Germany in World War Two. But for most people that was fading history too. Tourists were the new invaders. From France, for instance, a fleet of ferry boats brought French families across on duty-free day-return shopping sprees.

'Andy.' Dello was still persistent at his elbow. 'Look, I know what I'm talking about. Play it cool down there — they've still some damned near feudal ideas, even if you don't need a passport to get in.'

'As long as you're British with credit cards — I know.' Laird soothed him down. 'When you were there, did you ever hear of the Mehran family?'

'Mehran like in Witchline Shipping?' Dello gave a lugubrious grin. 'Now you're really talking feudal. They've been in Jersey so long that they wouldn't let Noah land when he arrived with his ark. They didn't want all those funny animals.'

'Maybe they lost out,' said Laird seriously.

Dello blinked. 'How?'

'Now they've got tourists.'

★ ★ ★

27

Andrew Laird shared a London basement apartment with an English oil engineer. It was off the Bayswater Road, tiny, with two cupboard-sized bedrooms, but the arrangement cut the rent in half and months could pass without them meeting. He went there once he'd finished work and packed two bags — one for the weekend, one for Jersey. He followed that by stealing a drink from one of the oil engineer's carefully hidden bottles of whisky, then he went out and ate dinner at an Italian restaurant along the street. Afterwards, he spectated briefly at the non-stop poker game the proprietor ran in the back kitchen.

He left at nine, flagged down a taxi, and had the driver take him to Charing Cross. From there, it was a walk of a minute to Mary's House, a small, shabby-fronted bar hidden away in a side street. The landlord was an ex-soldier who had named the bar after his wife, and Mary's House, busy with customers during the day, was usually quiet after dark. It was a place for a meeting that could be denied later.

John Lewnan was sitting in a corner booth, studying a racing sheet. The seamen's union official was a small, thickset man with close-cropped greying hair. He wore a blue pin-striped suit with a white shirt and a knitted red tie. Two stubbed-out cigarettes lay in the ashtray in front of him.

'Still trying the horses?' asked Laird, sliding into the seat opposite.

'I'm trying, they're not.' Lewnan tossed the racing sheet aside. He had three fingers missing from his left hand, torn off when they were caught in a deck-winch. That was when he'd become a union official. 'Usual for you?'

'My turn.' Laird signalled the sleepy-eyed barman, who knew them. Lewnan drank brandy with a beer chaser, Laird usually stuck to whisky. 'Thanks for coming.'

'I'm feeling charitable.' Lewnan scowled. 'But I could have done without you — and Witchline Shipping. How bad is the smell around the sinking?'

'It solved a few financial problems they managed to hide. The wolves were scraping at the office door, getting ready to come in through the window.'

'Two years ago.' Lewnan sighed. 'As I remember, that wasn't a good time to try to sell a ship.'

'The market was rock bottom, at give-away prices,' agreed Laird dryly. 'At insured value, Witchline probably doubled what they'd have got if they'd sold.' He shrugged at Lewnan. 'Then there was a bonus. It looks like they sold off her cargo.'

'Bastards,' said Lewnan softly. He left it

there as the barman brought over their drinks and Laird paid. Then he took a swallow of brandy, rinsed it round his mouth, and sat back as he swallowed. 'She had a new crew for that last trip — except for her captain.'

'Captain Daniel Shelton,' murmured Laird. 'I've got the court of inquiry details.'

'Captain Daniel Shelton.' Lewnan grinned. 'Married, lived in a nice little cottage outside Brighton. He must have a personal crystal ball for forecasting the future. The day before the *Rosewitch* sailed he put the cottage on the market, for sale. Date of entry three months later.'

'You're sure?'

Lewnan nodded. 'We've a secretary who lived near him. But he wasn't the only one with a crystal ball, Andy. What do you know about the deckhand who was supposed to have drowned?'

'Francis Heeney, Australian, no next of kin.' Laird shook his head.

'He was having dental treatment. The dentist knew he was a seaman.' Lewnan raised his mutilated hand and scraped a thumbnail along his chin. 'Three months after the *Rosewitch* sinking we got a letter from the dentist. His late patient Heeney owed him close on £200 for dental treatment, and would we pay it? We wrote back, telling him to go to hell, that Heeney hadn't even been a union member.' He paused, lowering his voice. Two tourist couples had wandered into the bar and were settling at a nearby bench. 'I dug out the letters again after you called. I seemed to remember something odd, an' I was right. This dentist mentioned that Heeney had insisted all the treatment was done in a rush, before he sailed — though none of it was urgent.'

'Like maybe he knew he wouldn't be back?' Laird sipped his whisky, then swirled the rest of the liquor in the glass. 'John, her new crew were hired at Southampton. If we're thinking crooked, who'd do the recruiting?'

'You mean crimping,' grunted Lewnan. 'Garbage collecting.' He finished his brandy at a gulp and washed it down with some of the beer. 'Our union branches keep tabs on them, the best they can. Southampton now — there was a nasty little swine down there. Had himself some back-up muscle too. We used to call him the Crab, because he scuttled around so much.'

'What do you mean, 'used to'?'

'He's dead. He was found floating in one o' the harbour basins.'

Laird stiffened. 'When?'

'When?' Lewnan looked puzzled for a moment then swore softly. 'Eighteen months back, I suppose. But — '

'But that could make him worth asking about?'

'Yes,' said Lewnan. He looked sadly at his empty brandy glass, then shook his head quickly as Laird made to signal the barman. 'My turn.' He winked. 'That keeps it sociable — no capitalist bribes, right?'

'Right,' agreed Laird solemnly. He waited until Newnan had ordered. 'So tell me about the Crab.'

'His real name was Pete Varrick.' Lewnan shrugged. 'Small and greasy, ran a dockland betting shop, made his real money crimping — you know what it's like. You'll always have somebody wanting out of the country fast and ready to pay, somebody else wanting some extra crew, no questions asked. Your average decent shipping line would disinfect the office if someone even mentioned his name — and he'd sense enough to steer off the Chinese and Lascar trade. The Triad gangs have that side sewn up. They damned near do their own hiring and firing.'

'Who took over when he died?'

Lewnan shrugged. 'I could ask.'

'Leave it for now.' Laird stopped while the new order of drinks arrived. Lewnan paid for them with money from a worn leather purse. 'I could drive over tomorrow.'

'Tomorrow?' Lewnan scowled. 'I've a union executive meeting tomorrow. If I'm not there, I know somebody who'll try an' stab me in the back. If you could leave it till Monday —'

'I'll be on my way to Jersey.'

'Swimming with the sharks?' Lewnan tasted his new glass of brandy almost absently. 'Could you maybe do me a favour there — say hello to someone for me? He might even be useful to know.'

'Who?'

Lewnan gave a half chuckle. 'An awkward old devil, but Jersey born and bred. He was captain on my last ship, he was pretty good to me when I got my fingers chopped. He's retired now, but we've kept in touch. Could you — ?'

Laird nodded. 'Anyone you call awkward is worth meeting.'

'Good. I've something you could take out to him, something I know he wants. I'll get it to you tomorrow.' Lewnan settled back. 'Now, what's been happening to you, Andy? You know, important things, like women.'

★ ★ ★

It was late before Andrew Laird got back to the basement apartment. But he rose early on the Friday morning and was at the Clanmore Alliance building by 8 a.m. He left his two travel bags at his desk in the empty assessors' office, then caught Osgood Morris as the marine claims manager arrived for work.

'Going somewhere?' asked Morris, glancing at his wristwatch.

'Southampton.' He told Morris why and drew a petulant frown.

'What do you expect to get? A graveside interview?' asked Morris acidly.

'Someone may remember something, Osgood. It's worth a try.'

'I suppose so.' Morris sucked his teeth, then nodded. 'All right. You're expected on Jersey on Monday. I made that 'phone call to Mehran Holdings before I left last night. The follow-up telex will be with them this morning.'

'And?'

Morris gave one of his weasel smiles. 'I spoke to Diane Mehran. She sounds — ah — a forceful female. But very happy when I told her why you'd be coming, and our sponsorship interest. You should get the red carpet. For now, anyway.'

'That's nice,' said Laird sarcastically.

He left Morris, stopped at the cashier's department, signed for some money, then went down to the basement and collected one of the Clanmore pool cars. It was a Ford coupé, grey and nearly new, and he checked that the tank was full.

Five minutes later he was driving out of London, making for the Southampton motorway. There was cloud and some rain around in place of the previous day's sun, but traffic was reasonably light and he made good time. In two hours, he was steering the Ford towards the seaport city's dockland area with the blue stretch of Southampton Water and its skyline of cranes and shipping growing around him. He caught a glimpse of the great, graceful bulk of the *Queen Elizabeth II* lying at her berth, loading another batch of tourists for one of her millionaire-style cruises, but he was more interested in the blue 'Police' sign which marked the dockland area police station.

Laird parked the Ford beside a mix of police vehicles and walked in.

Some talking and several minutes later, he was shown into a small office in the CID area. The man who rose to meet him was young, thin, and weary-faced. He had nicotine-stained fingers and wore denim trousers with a rollneck sweater and a suede jacket.

'Laird?' He gave his visitor a cautious handshake. 'I'm Detective Sergeant Edwards — Bob Edwards. Identification?'

Laird showed his Clanmore identification for the fourth time since he'd entered the police station. Glancing at it, Edwards nodded, returned it, then gave a slight grin. 'Sorry, I've a boss who says we go by the book.'

'And do you?' asked Laird mildly.

'That depends who's asking.' Edwards waved him into a chair while he perched on the edge of his battered desk. 'For instance, people like you usually make a 'phone call, say they're coming.'

'That way, it can become official.' Laird tried to gauge the CID man and hoped he'd be lucky. 'This isn't — yet.'

'But?' Edwards raised an eyebrow.

'It's a possible loose end of a marine fraud. Well outside your territory.'

'On a Friday?' Edwards sighed. 'I've got the weekend off.'

'So have I,' said Laird. 'I want to keep it that way.'

They grinned at each other. Reaching behind without looking, Edwards scooped up a pack of cigarettes and lit one with a match.

'What's your problem, Mr Laird?'

'How long have you worked the dockland stretch?'

'Too damned long.' Edwards drew deeply

on his cigarette and let the smoke out slowly. 'Go on.'

'A man called Pete Varrick.'

'The Crab?' Edwards showed surprise. 'He's dead. There were a lot of happy people when it happened — some of them cops.'

'I'd like to hear about it,' said Laird simply.

Edwards looked at him thoughtfully, then nodded. 'There's no harm in that. I'll dig out the file.'

The detective left him. After a few moments a young, very young constable brought in two massive mugs of coffee on an old tin tray, then left. Laird was sipping at one of the mugs when Edwards reappeared with a manila file in one hand.

'Pete Varrick — our Crab.' He opened the file and handed Laird a photograph. It had been taken in a mortuary and showed a bloated, naked male corpse. Edwards handed over a second photograph. 'That's the live version.'

Laird considered the head and shoulders shot of a broadfaced, greasy-haired man of about forty who had had a thin moustache, heavy eyebrows and a fleshy nose. He had been smiling when the photograph was taken, and that hadn't helped.

'How did you feel about him?'

'How do you feel about vermin? He was

into every dirty little dockland racket going, including girls.' Edwards lit another cigarette, tossing the used match into an overflowing ashtray. 'The story according to his widow is he left home one night saying he had to meet someone. He didn't come back. About a week later his body surfaced beside a Panamanian tramp ship in one of the inner docks. No cement waistcoat, everything still in his pockets!'

'But nobody went into mourning.' Laird nursed his coffee mug. 'Cause of death?'

'The coroner called it accidental drowning, like he'd fallen off a quay.' Edwards shrugged. 'We couldn't prove anything else — and before you ask, we tried. My boss doesn't approve of murder, whyever. The postmortem said Varrick had been drinking, but the alcohol level wasn't dramatic. There were some post-death injuries, like he'd been nudged by a ship. That was all.'

There was a date on the back of the mortuary photograph. It was four months after the *Rosewitch* sinking.

'What did you think?'

Edwards gave a slow shake of his head. 'If you mean did he fall or was he pushed — hell, I don't know. There would have been a queue of candidates. You could have sold tickets if there had been a spectator area.' He paused. 'My turn. What's your interest in Varrick?'

'Some people who maybe employed him to scrape up a crew who didn't ask questions.'

'That's all you've got?'

'Here.' Laird nodded.

'Then forget it,' said Edwards with a disappointed grunt. He tapped a finger against his forehead. 'This is where our Crab kept his records. Nothing on paper, payment in hard cash. We pulled him in a few times, we always had to let him go again. Not enough evidence.'

'Who took over, after he died?'

'A couple of thick locals.' The detective's thin, tired face showed amusement. 'Laurel and Hardy would love them — they can't play it like the Crab did.'

'You said he left a widow,' mused Laird. 'I'd like to talk with her.'

'Try it, and she'd scream harassment, maybe rape,' warned Edwards dryly. 'You wouldn't like our holding cells. The beds are fine but room service is pretty hellish.'

'But you know her?'

Edwards nodded his head. He looked at Laird for another long moment, then sighed and swore under his breath. Turning, he stubbed his cigarette in the ashtray.

'Come on,' he said resignedly. 'I'll show you

where. Her name is Ethel, and you'll be on your own. I like being a sergeant.'

They went in Laird's car. It was a short drive, still within the dockland area, then they turned into a street of small single-storey terrace houses. Each had a tiny strip of garden in front, some of the strips neatly kept, others thick with weeds.

'Coming up, but keep going,' said Edwards, slouching further down in the passenger seat. 'Number forty-seven, the door with the vomit-pink paintwork.' He waited until they'd driven past the distinctive door. 'Why does she matter? I told you, Pete Varrick never let anyone know the kind of hand he was holding — and that included Ethel.'

Laird shrugged. 'I can try. Why has she stayed around here?'

'Money. One way and another, Varrick didn't leave much cash behind. Or if he did, no one can find it.'

Laird stopped the Ford round the first corner. Edwards lit a cigarette and watched him open the door.

'Good luck,' he said sadly. 'You'll need it.'

Going back down the street, Laird walked up the short pathway to the pink door, knocked, and waited. After a moment he heard someone coming, then the door opened. The woman who glared out at him was thin and sharpfaced, with a beehive of heavily lacquered blonde hair. She was probably in her mid-forties, her mouth was a slash of heavy lipstick, and she was wearing a grubby button-front blue dress and old slippers.

'Yes?' A pair of narrow, calculating eyes looked him over. 'What do you want? If you're selling anything, goodbye.'

'I'm not selling. You're Mrs Varrick?'

She nodded suspiciously.

'I'd like to talk. About your husband.'

She looked Laird up and down again, the lipstick slash tightening. 'And who the hell are you, mister? Police?'

'No.' He shook his head. 'But the people I work for have an interest in how he died.'

Her eyes narrowed. Then she stood back, thumbing him into the house. The door slammed behind him as he entered a stale-smelling little lobby and she led the way into the front room. A large man was sprawling back in an armchair. He had a can of beer in one hand, he was dressed in trousers and a faded orange tee shirt, and his heavy face needed a shave.

'Somebody asking questions about Pete,' said Ethel Varrick bleakly.

'Why?' The man stirred, laying the can of

41

beer beside him on the carpet. 'She doesn't want bothered, mister.'

Laird shrugged. The room was well furnished but hadn't been tidied for a long time. One of the window curtains was half off its hooks, some used glasses and empty bottles littered the top of a once-polished table.

'It won't take long, Mrs Varrick.' He ignored the man. 'I won't cause you problems with anyone — including the police. I just want to ask you about a job of work Pete did.'

She stiffened and glanced at the man in the chair. He raised an eyebrow.

'See him off, Arthur,' she said curtly.

Arthur shoved himself out of the chair and lumbered over. Suddenly he swung a clenched fist at Laird's face. Laird dodged the blow, the unshaven face twisted in a snarl, and Arthur came in again, both fists flailing. Swaying clear, Laird tripped him as he lumbered past. The man crashed down, then started to haul himself up, grabbing for one of the bottles on the table. Laird kicked him hard in the stomach and, as Arthur gave an agonised belch of pain and doubled up, he followed that up by slamming the edge of his hand to the side of the man's neck.

Arthur slumped to the carpet again, moaning, cowering like a frightened child.

Ethel Varrick stood open-mouthed, the thin face beneath that monstrous beehive of hair suddenly pale.

'I still just want to talk,' Laird told her unemotionally. 'I was going to say it could be worth your while.'

She swallowed and nodded. Picking up a jacket lying on the chair, she tossed it across to Arthur.

'Take a walk,' she ordered. 'That was pathetic.'

Swallowing, rising painfully, the big man took his jacket and retreated from the room. The outside door opened, then slammed shut again.

'You fight dirty,' said Ethel Varrick, her eyes not leaving her visitor.

'Most people do, Ethel.' Laird thumbed at the window. Arthur was shambling off down the street. 'What's his interest?'

'He's — he's a friend. A person gets lonely.' She moistened her lips. 'What did you mean, it could be worth my while?'

'Let's say you give me five minutes.' Laird reached into a pocket, brought out the wad of notes he'd drawn from the Clanmore cashier, and counted ten of them out on the table. 'Call that half in advance.'

She came over, one hand touched the money as if to make sure it was real, then she looked at him again and shrugged.

'Pete never told me what he was about.' Her voice was bitter. 'He didn't trust anyone, not even me, mister.'

'That's what I heard.' Laird smiled at her. 'But he'd drop the odd hint, wouldn't he?'

'Depends what you mean.' Her eyes were back on the money.

'You know, Ethel.' Laird said it casually. 'Something big under way, or he'd pulled off a good deal, right?'

'Maybe. Not often.'

'He pulled one off not too long before he died, didn't he?' persisted Laird. 'A rush order for enough men to crew a ship?'

'It wasn't a — ' She stopped short.

'It wasn't a rush? He had time?'

She gave a reluctant nod.

'That would be about four months before he died,' said Laird softly. 'Big money?'

'I didn't see much of it,' Her mouth formed an angry line. 'Maybe someone else did.'

'Another woman?'

She didn't answer.

'How long were you married, Ethel?'

'About twenty years.' There was a sudden weariness in her voice.

'Happy enough?'

She shrugged. 'Mostly. As long as I didn't ask questions and kept him fed.'

44

'Then what happened?' Laird saw her hesitate. Deliberately, he added two more notes to the pile on the table.

'It was about two weeks before he died.' She drew a deep breath. 'Look, I knew he sometimes chased after another woman. But this time — damn him, he'd promised me we'd go away somewhere, for a holiday. He had that money, he'd been buying drinks for anything that moved.' She shook her head. 'Then, no — just like that. He couldn't. He had to go away for two or three days, because a deal had turned up.'

'Did he say what kind?'

'I told you, I didn't ask questions. He said he'd make it up to me, that we'd be in the money again. But when he comes back, when I'm sorting out his dam' dirty washing, what do I find? The stubs of two air tickets, that's what, mister. He'd been off with another woman. You know something?' Her voice trembled with anger. 'He laughed when he admitted it. He'd even taken her where I wanted to go — down to the Channel Islands.'

Laird stared at her. 'Jersey?'

'Jersey. Where we had our honeymoon.' For a moment, her defences were down. She wasn't a thin, hard-faced woman with an out-of-date hairstyle and a house that needed cleaning. Ethel Varrick was just female and vulnerable. 'I don't even know who she was, mister. I never will.'

'This deal he talked about. Did it happen?'

'He said it was going to — or someone was in bad trouble.'

'Nothing more?' pressed Laird. He swore under his breath as she shook her head. 'How long was that before he died?'

'A week or so.'

'But you didn't tell the police?'

'Why the hell should I?' She glared at him. 'I'm the Crab's widow, mister. Think I want to be known as the woman the Crab didn't need?'

He nodded a silent understanding. 'Tell me about that last night, the night he drowned.'

'That's easy enough.' Ethel Varrick took one of the used glasses and poured the dregs of an almost empty gin bottle. She took a quick gulp, 'We watched television, then he said he had to go out, that he had to meet someone. He didn't come back. I thought he was maybe with her.' Suddenly she laughed. 'But that time I was wrong. You know something else, mister? The Crab couldn't swim — not a stroke.'

Laird tried, but she knew nothing else. The airline ticket stubs had been destroyed a long time before. He added another note to the money on the table then left. She didn't bother to see him out.

Detective Sergeant Bob Edwards was smoking yet another cigarette, still lounging in the passenger seat, when Laird reached the Ford. Edwards greeted him with a quizzical eyebrow as he got aboard.

'Anything useful?' he asked.

'Yes.' Laird started the car but let the engine idle for a moment. 'You know he was murdered?'

'I know we could never prove it,' said Edwards carefully. 'Unless you've come up with something new.'

Laird told him. Edwards sighed and stubbed his cigarette in the dashboard ashtray.

'Prevention of Terrorism Act,' he said unhappily. 'They keep some kind of record on all passengers to and from the Channel Islands — I know that much. It would mean some digging. How about after the weekend?'

'Who's going to complain?' said Laird mildly, and set the car moving.

* * *

Andrew Laird thought about it most of the drive back to London. Pete Varrick had to have been the crimp who had gathered the

47

Rosewitch's crew from the human flotsam around Southampton's dockland. He'd been well paid. But then, later, suppose the Crab had read of the *Rosewitch* sinking and had become greedy, greedy enough to think of blackmail?

But who should he try it on? Did he know names — or had he gone to Jersey to make sure who had been paying him, to put a name to a face? Laird nearly drove the Ford into the back of a suddenly braking truck while he pondered that one.

Suppose Varrick had found a name. The next thing would have been to make his pitch at blackmail. Except that the Crab hadn't realised the kind of people he was up against, had been fool enough to go to that late-night rendezvous at the docks. In his case, a rendezvous which would be the last he would ever keep. With death waiting in the greasy, oil-scummed water lapping below.

A scuffle, a shout, a splash, even a scream — the odds were against them being heard. Or how many people would want to investigate? How many people would prefer not to know?

Lunch was a cheeseburger and a cup of coffee at a motorway service station. He reached central London in more rain, then battled his way through worse than usual traffic chaos. Some streets were closed because a visiting president of an obscure country was making a state visit to Buckingham Palace.

He wasn't in the best of tempers by the time he dumped the Ford in the Clanmore Alliance basement garage. He almost groaned when he arrived at the marine department floor and was immediately confronted by Osgood Morris.

'How was the Southampton safari?' asked Morris, baring his teeth in what was meant to be a pleasant smile. 'Useful?'

'It looks that way,' nodded Laird. 'Enough to have the local police checking a few things. They'll be in touch.'

'Oh, joy unfettered!' Morris reacted sarcastically. 'A couple of them gave me a parking ticket over lunch.' He beckoned, and they went along to his private office. When he heard what had happened at Southampton, the marine claims manager gave a nod of cautious approval. 'It's helpful, I suppose. If we — ah — dissect your Crab a little more, we might get something of value. He seems to have been no particular loss to humanity.'

Andrew Laird thought of a woman with a beehive hairstyle and wondered. But Morris had a meeting scheduled and they parted a moment later.

There were two envelopes lying on his desk in the assessors' office. One held his Monday morning flight ticket to Jersey, his hotel reservation, and the usual warning that all items claimed as expenses should be backed by receipted bills. The day that happened, Clanmore Alliance would grind to a halt. The other, a fat brown envelope, had been delivered by hand. When he opened it, there was another fat envelope inside.

It was from John Lewnan. The union man had attached a brief, scribbled note to the envelope. 'Get this to Captain Jacob West at Marfleur Cottage, north of St Catherine's Bay, tell him from me that he's a damned old fool, and you might do yourself some good. Or you might not.'

He tucked Captain West's envelope away without opening it, then was dictating a report on the Southampton trip on tape when his telephone rang. Switching off the recorder, he answered it.

'Just checking,' said a woman's voice. 'I'll be clear inside half an hour. Got your toothbrush packed?'

'Not much else.' He grinned at the telephone mouthpiece.

'Geriatric bighead,' came the scalding retort. Then he heard a chuckle and the call ended.

She was a red-haired consultant anaesthetist in a London teaching hospital. She owned a tumbledown thatched and beamed cottage in Shakespeare country, near Stratford-on-Avon, with only one bed. She made the rules when they were there. It was the kind of understanding two people could reach when they'd been close friends for a very long time.

Still smiling, Laird replaced the receiver. It had been her idea to get two tickets for a night at the opera as his birthday gift. Except that the opera performance was in Paris. They were flying out Air France, she had the tickets and had made the weekend reservations.

His smile twisted a little. Seven years had passed since he and the red-haired consultant had been final-year medical students in Edinburgh, with Laird favourite for the class gold medal.

But then had come the night when his mother had died, released from terminal pain, holding his hand, thanking him for doing what she'd asked. There had been too little evidence for the police — but enough to banish him from the medical world. No final examinations. Andrew Laird had gone to sea. Partly to earn a living, partly to hide. Discovering that a skill in stitching wounds or setting broken bones afloat, sometimes in the teeth of a gale, had its own value with no questions asked.

Then, eventually, he'd come ashore again and taken the Clanmore Alliance job. When fate and chance meant he'd collided with the red-haired one-time student on a crowded London Underground platform. That same night they'd agreed she'd still make the rules.

'Mr Laird — ' A deliberate, throat-clearing noise brought him back to the present. Osgood Morris's secretary, a stern-faced, middle-aged woman with a regal manner, frowned down at him. She had a slip of paper in her hand. 'Yours, I think.'

She placed the slip in front of him and had gone before he could thank her. He read it and sighed. It was a telex message, short and to the point, from Paladin Products: 'ADDITIONAL WASH MACHINES, SERIAL NUMBERS EX *ROSEWITCH* CONSIGNMENT, REPORTED MADRID AREA, SPAIN. APPRECIATE COMMENTS.'

Laird swore, shoved the telex to one side, and began clearing his desk. Thirty years of age was a watershed in anyone's life. He was going to finish early.

He was ready to go when Nancy Andrews came over from her word-processor corner. The young Jamaican girl sat on the edge of his desk and swung her long, slim legs for a moment, almost embarrassed.

52

'Andy.' She placed a small package in front of him. 'Happy birthday, when it happens.'

Laird blinked at her. 'Who told you?'

'There's a way I can access the personnel data on the computer.' She chuckled and lapsed into the mock-Caribbean accent she used to cover awkward moments. 'Like I tol' my boy friend, he be dam' lucky yo' is too dam' old for a nice, innocent black gal like me.'

'Thank you.' He looked at her, she nodded and he carefully opened the little package. Her present was a small, beautifully finished pocket knife with his initials on the casing. He was touched. 'Nancy — '

She shrugged aside his thanks. 'No sweat, Andy. I know someone who sells them cheap. But will you do me a favour?'

He nodded. He should have known better.

'Man, yo' listen an' yo' start taking it more easy, yo' hear? Anyone turns thirty — man, that's them practically over the hill — '

She fled before he could grab her.

2

Andrew Laird found Paris, his birthday, and the weekend went past in a whirl. Somewhere along the way he had the inevitable quarrel with the red-haired consultant. Some time later he inevitably asked her to marry him and she fell about laughing. They flew back on the Sunday evening laden with bottles of duty-free champagne and spent the night at her thatched cottage. Next morning, under grey skies, she drove him to Heathrow for his flight to Jersey.

There were the usual security checks but no passport control. He filled in one of the special Prevention of Terrorism boarding cards, thinking of Southampton and Detective Sergeant Edwards as he wrote. Checking back, locating Pete Varrick's card, would be a plodding piece of police work. Edwards wasn't the plodding kind and would hate it. But it had to be done.

The aircraft was a British Airways Boeing 737, filled with a mix of business commuters and tourists. The cabin staff announced they'd only have time to serve coffee.

Laird had a window seat and the people

next to him in the row were a middle-aged couple who held hands and wouldn't have noticed if he had sprouted horns. He sat back, eyes half closed, yawning to himself, mentally tuning out the steady pulse of the Boeing's jets.

Jersey. As far as Mehran Holdings were concerned, he was a prospective £100,000 sterling flying in. That should be enough to guarantee a welcome mat. It was a deception and he didn't like playing that kind of game. But the *Rosewitch* background justified the tactic. The main question was, what exactly was he going to do? Osgood Morris didn't want trouble, but that could be hard to manage.

Given the choice, Laird would have settled for being on another flight, back to Paris for another thirtieth birthday. He chuckled at the notion. Could he have survived it?

★   ★   ★

The 737 arrived over the Channel Islands from the northwest, with the French coastline a solid curve of land to the east and south. Losing height over the sister islands of Alderney and Guernsey, passing tiny, medieval Sark where the private car was still banned as a modern abomination, the aircraft

55

banked round. Jersey was ahead, a rich green shape edged by a thin white embroidery of breaking waves.

Flaps rumbled. Laird saw fields, villages, and an occasional patch of woodland. The sea was clear, the coastline a mix of shallow, sandy bays and sudden harsh cliffs; there were narrow inlets guarded by savage dark reefs. Then, sudden and startling, they were over St Helier, the only town on the island. It had a large, busy harbour and streets of high-rise buildings. There was a glimpse of a passenger hydrofoil creaming out to sea, heading for France, cutting past one of the big vehicle ferries coming in from the UK.

Moments later, they touched down at St Peter airport, then taxied in past parked clusters of private aircraft and a stopover line of commercial jets. The Boeing stopped outside a small, old-fashioned terminal building mostly composed of added-on huts and fluttering flags.

It was warm and sunny when Laird left the aircraft. The scent of banks of flowers battled with the smell of aircraft kerosene, and a tanned airline hostess smiled as if she meant it while she shepherded the new arrivals towards one of the terminal entrances. Two airport police were leaning beside the entrance. One had a baton at his hip, the other was unarmed; both had red and white chequered bands around their peaked caps.

A tall, gangling man stood beside them. He looked in his mid-twenties. He wore a crumpled grey suit with a white shirt and tie, and the piece of cardboard he was holding had 'Laird' written on it in large letters.

Laird went over and the stranger's face brightened.

'Hello. Uh — Mr Laird?' He showed relief at Laird's nod. 'I'm Chris Newgrange. Tony Dello 'phoned to say you were coming over. Welcome to Jersey.'

'Tony talked about you.' Newgrange topped him by several inches, had short fair hair, a beak of a nose, and more neck than chin. 'Did Tony say to meet me?'

'No, that was partly my idea.' Newgrange gave a cheerful bray of a laugh. 'Anything he said about me was a lie, but I've a sort of Clanmore connection, and there aren't too many Monday morning flights from London.' He thumbed at Laird's battered travel bag. 'Any more luggage?'

'That's all.' Laird smiled. Tony Dello had said his ex-wife's relative was a harmless innocent and it looked that way.

'I've a car outside.' Nodding amiably to the two airport police, Newgrange led the way into the terminal building, then along a corridor towards the main arrivals area.

The corridor was busy. Halfway along, two more airport police were questioning a thin, unshaven youth at a security desk, and one paused to wink at Newgrange. The youth wore a greasy buckskin jacket over jeans and a grubby shirt and was being made to empty his pockets. He looked frightened.

'Trouble?' asked Laird as Newgrange ambled on.

'There's a system,' said Newgrange placidly. 'If the pair outside don't like someone, these two grab him for a talk.'

'Then what?'

'With that one, they're probably looking for drugs.' Newgrange shrugged. 'We don't like drugs, Mr Laird. Even if they don't find anything, they may — well, advise him to go back where he came from.'

'Kick him out?'

Newgrange winced. 'Well, something like that. Jersey isn't the mainland.'

They crossed the busy little terminal lobby, went out through another door into the open again, and walked over to the car park. Newgrange's car was a bright red Volkswagen and he opened the passenger door first, heaving Laird's travel bag into the rear seat.

'I gave her an extra clean this morning.' He gave another of his cheerful grins. 'Being seen with you could be good for business.'

Laird raised an eyebrow. 'Why?'

'I know why you're here — the powerboat interest.' He held the door open while Laird got aboard. 'Then I had Diane Mehran on the 'phone over the weekend. When she calls, I jump!'

Laird waited until Newgrange had gone round to the other door, and was behind the wheel. 'Diane Mehran. You know her?'

'She puts some insurance business my way.' Newgrange started the Volkswagen. 'So she matters. She wanted to make sure you'd be met — she also switched your hotel reservation and advised your London office this morning. You're at the Leecom now. Mehran Holdings own it, you're their guest. It's further out, but it's good.'

'Thanks for telling me,' said Laird stonily. He watched Newgrange as he put on a pair of dark sunglasses and then set the Volkswagen moving. 'Do we go through St Helier?'

Newgrange nodded, squeezing the little car past a large incoming coach.

'Then go round past the harbour. I haven't seen it for a long time.'

'No problem.' The Volkswagen jerked forward as Newgrange tramped happily on the accelerator. Their way out of the airport was past a tarmac area scattered with small private aircraft, and the lanky young agent nodded towards them. 'That's the latest Mehran interest. They've got themselves a company plane. I tried for the insurance cover, but didn't get it.'

'Tell me about them.' Laird winced at the way Newgrange cut a corner. His driving style owed more to enthusiasm than skill.

'Mainly, there's Diane and her cousin Paul. They took over about ten years ago, when Paul's father died — he was the last of the original two brothers who built up Witchline Shipping.' The dark sunglasses turned briefly towards him. 'Diane is in her forties, Paul is older, a widower, with two sons in the business. Diane — ' Newgrange grinned a little ' — she's a big woman, in every way. She takes care of the other interests.'

'Like the new marina?'

Newgrange gave a surprise nod. 'That's what I reckon this powerboat race is really all about, a good stunt to publicise the marina when it opens next year.'

'That makes sense.' Already they were nearing the outskirts of St Helier, a growing mass of tall office blocks, hotels and apartment buildings. Only a low wall and a strip of promenade separated the road from the sea and, on the landward side, they were passing a line of boarding houses and restaurants. Laird shifted back to Newgrange. 'There are two other directors, Roder and Garris. Do you know them?'

'Not particularly.' Newgrange shook his head. 'They're outsiders. I'm like the Mehrans — Jersey by birth.'

Laird didn't push it further. The Volkswagen stuck with the thickening traffic on the coastal road, then filtered off to the right. In another minute they were cruising along the edge of the harbour area. It was the way Laird remembered. The tide was out, a mix of yachts, fishing boats and small craft were lying on the bottom mud in some basins, the main deep-water harbour had several large ships moored along its quays. The vehicle ferry he'd seen from the air had berthed and the first of its container trucks was coming ashore.

They stayed with the harbour, with its cranes and its warehouses, for another short distance. Then Newgrange gave an apologetic shrug and they headed up into the town.

'There's my place,' he said proudly. 'Newgrange Agencies. Small but beautiful.'

It was a single-window shopfront in a line which included a used-car showroom and a couple of liquor stores. But the paintwork was bright and a poster in the window declared 'Your Independent Expert'. Laird made an appropriate noise, but Newgrange seemed to read his mind.

'All right,' he admitted. 'It's a crummy hole in a crummy location. But I get along.'

'That's what it's about.' Selling insurance, small agency style, amounted to a blend of luck and hard work. People like Newgrange never made fortunes. Laird looked around as the Volkswagen stopped at a light-controlled junction. 'How far to this hotel?'

'The Leecom?' Newgrange flicked the gear lever as the lights changed. They began to move again. 'Twenty minutes — say that about anywhere on Jersey and you'll get there.'

St Helier amounted to a frantic bustle of traffic, glimpses of long, pedestrianised shopping precincts, then, emphasising the offshore aspect, a thick peppering of banks, finance houses and legal offices. Many of the street signs were still French, every second car seemed to have a registration plate that began with an 'H', marking it as a tourist rental vehicle.

They cut inland again, leaving the town behind, reaching fields and dairy herds, fruit orchards and glassed lines of horticultural greenhouses, which dazzled with reflected sunlight. Tractors and farm trucks shot out of concealed side roads, signs offered food, drink or souvenirs. Two tourist cars had crashed outside a cemetery and a shirt-sleeved police officer was just arriving on a pedal cycle.

'Nobody hurt.' Newgrange gave a quick glance. 'Hire jobs, but I know the firms. I don't have their business.' He grinned. 'One worry less.'

'Mehran Holdings give you business,' mused Laird. He shielded his eyes with one hand as the Volkswagen squealed round a curve and the sun's glare hit from a new angle. 'How did you make the connection?'

'I knew Paul Mehran's sons when we were kids. Matt, the younger one, was a friend. Big brother Simon used to kick me out of his way — still does.' Newgrange gave one of his milder brays. 'Anyway, Matt talked to Aunt Diane, she remembered the kid whose parents used to work a market garden along the road and she feeds me a few crumbs.' The sunglasses turned. 'What I'm hoping for is a slice of some of the insurance action for the marina.'

'It's going to be big?'

'For me. I'd have a happy bank manager. He'd maybe give me a new overdraft.'

Laird left it there. The lanky, fair-haired figure beside him might be more help than Tony Dello had imagined. But that couldn't be rushed.

The road came down to the coast again near some low, dark cliffs fringed by trees and scrub. The beach was a mix of rock and shingle. He saw a couple of cottages, then a white four-storey building showed ahead. They turned into the Leecom Hotel parking lot, stopped beside a few H-plate tourist cars and a couple of delivery vans, and got out. The Leecom was built in the concrete shoe-box style of architecture, with a swimming pool to one side. A few guests lounged around it, there were flags hanging limp from a line of poles around a garden area, and a collection of empty metal beer kegs were piled outside a service door.

'It's not mainstream,' admitted Newgrange. 'In fact you've hit the tail end of the season, so you'll find it quiet. But the Leecom has a good reputation — and any Mehran guest will get the full treatment.'

It seemed that way when they arrived at the reception desk. A sleekly groomed manager in a black jacket swooped in, smiling, summoning a porter to take Laird's bag, making welcoming noises, giving Newgrange the barest of nods.

'We've been told to take good care of you, Mr Laird,' beamed the man. He snapped his fingers. The girl behind the reception desk quickly handed him a small envelope.

'Compliments of Mehran Holdings.'

Laird opened the envelope. A set of car keys tumbled out, and Newgrange gave a wry smile.

'Okay if I leave you?' he asked.

'It looks that way.' Laird winked at him. 'Thanks Chris, I'll be in touch.'

'Good. Well — uh — ' Newgrange hesitated uncertainly. 'I've some calls to make.'

He made a swift retreat. The Leecom manager fussed around Laird for another moment, then the porter led him to a small steel box of an elevator. They got out at the top floor, and Laird's door was along the corridor to the right. It opened into a small suite, a sitting room and separate bedroom, with a bathroom off. He had a private balcony with a view out towards the sea and a trolley in the sitting room offered a well-stocked bar.

The porter laid down the travel bag, pocketed Laird's tip, and left. Glad to be alone, Laird prowled his new quarters, tried the bed, then was unpacking his bag when the telephone rang. He found it on a wall-mounted shelf in the sitting room, and lifted the receiver.

'The hotel called me to say you'd arrived, Mr Laird,' said a woman's voice, husky but brisk. 'I'm Diane Mehran. They said young Chris managed to collect you at the airport.'

'He did.' Laird kept the surprise from his voice. For the moment Mehran Holdings were doing the chasing. 'Thanks for the accommodation change — the hotel looks good.'

'There would be trouble if it didn't.' Diane Mehran gave an amused, confident chuckle. 'And you've got the car?'

'The keys, so far.'

'And you're wondering if we're trying to soften you up?' Diane Mehran stayed amused. 'Yes, of course we are. We want that money your firm is waving. We want you to feel sure we should have it. How soon will you feel settled in?'

'Any time you want.'

'Good.' She was pleased. 'I've cleared my desk for the morning. I'm going out to our marina development. Why not meet me there?'

'When would suit?'

'Any time you're ready. From the Leecom it's only a few minutes' drive.' Diane Mehran wasn't finished. 'My cousin Paul wants to meet you — he had to go over to France today, but he'll be back by evening. Will you join us for dinner tonight? We're informal people.'

He made a brief show of hesitation, then agreed. Satisfied, Diane Mehran said goodbye and the call ended. Replacing the receiver, Laird shook his head. The way Mehran Holdings were doing the chasing, Osgood Morris's carefully created sponsorship story could end up an embarrassing success.

Unpacked, more at home with the few things he'd brought now scattered around, he went into the bathroom, splashed some water on his face, and used one of the 'His and Her' towels. Then he went out on the balcony. The view was across the sea. The water was a sparkling blue, with a lazy swell running, and a small yacht with a red sail was tacking round beyond a patch of rocks. A French tricolour flag flapped at her stern, the French coast was clear in every detail along the horizon.

He stayed on the balcony for a few minutes, leaning on the rail, just watching the yacht and the sea. Then he returned to the room and put John Lewnan's envelope into a pocket. His fingers touched the Mehran car keys, then he glanced around. It was sheer habit. Even if the room was searched, he had nothing that would damage the sponsorship story.

The box-shaped elevator took him down to the lobby where he went over to the reception desk. The girl on duty was a tall brunette. She greeted him with the kind of smile which meant she'd been told about him.

'Needing help, Mr Laird?' she asked.

'I'm meeting Diane Mehran at the marina site.' Laird gave her a whimsical grimace. 'Tell me how not to get lost.'

'That's easy.' She gestured towards the door with her left hand, a chunky diamond solitaire ring glittering on her engagement finger. 'Head north along the coast road. Keep on until you come to the first T junction, then take the right. Pass a tumbledown old farmhouse and you'll see a construction sign for Witchlove Haven.'

'I like the name,' mused Laird. 'Any parking for broomsticks?'

'I only work here.' Her smile twitched and became more genuine. 'Ask Diane Mehran, she might know.'

He grinned, left her, and went out. There was a registration number tag attached to the car keys. It matched a white two-door Ford Fiesta. The luxury Ghia version, it had a light blue coachline, blue upholstery, and an 'H' on the registration plate. Opening it up, he got behind the wheel.

The Ford had clocked less than a thousand miles from new. The fuel tank was full, documents and a map of the island were lying on the passenger seat. He checked the control layout, then saw the combined radio and cassette player had a cassette already fitted. Someone liked Antonio Carlos Jobim. Switching on, letting the music murmur from the speakers, he looked at the map. Things were the way he'd hoped. Once he'd been to Witchlove Haven, he could go on to deliver Lewnan's envelope. The address for Captain Jacob West was Merfleur Cottage; there was a Merfleur Point marked about three miles along the coast from where the marina should be.

He set the Ford moving, put it through its paces on the main road, then eased back on the accelerator and let the other traffic zip past.

He was more interested in the coastline. It was that same mix of sand, black rock and shingle he'd seen from the air. A long stone finger of breakwater with a lighthouse sheltered a variety of small craft and marked the north end of St Catherine's Bay. Beyond it, the sea was scarred with reefs and he saw lines of orange pinheads which had to be floats marking lobster pots.

Suddenly, the road left the sea, swung inland, and climbed into woodland and fields. He came to the T junction with the main route going left. Laird took the right hand, the road dipped again, then he saw a large green and white construction sign.

Witchlove Haven. An arrow pointed at a lane and he followed it. The lane showed every sign it was being used heavily and often. The surface was rutted and broken, hedging had been damaged, some entire bushes had been uprooted. The ruts became worse, the Ford lurched and thumped on its suspension, then a painted barrier pole blocked the way ahead. A man in overalls emerged from a hut, looked at the car as Laird slowed, then nodded, raised the barrier pole, and waved Laird through.

The hedge ended, the track weaved down through rock and scrub, then Laird had his first view of the Witchlove construction site. It was a small, narrow sheltered bay, the shore mostly rock with low cliffs in the background. A cluster of half-completed buildings were located along one side, the largest building still a roofless shell. The site was busy. Several vehicles were parked outside a prefabricated office hut, a mobile crane was positioning a swaying steel girder, workmen in bright red hard hats were pouring concrete and moving materials.

He stopped the Ford beside the line of other vehicles and a woman emerged from the office hut as he climbed out. She was tall and heavily built. She had short, smartly styled auburn hair and wore blue denim jeans and a matching waistcoat over a white shirt-blouse. Smiling, she came straight towards him.

'I'm Diane Mehran. I'm glad you found us, Mr Laird.' She gripped his hand briefly, looking him over, still smiling. Then she gestured around. 'How do you like our Witchlove Haven?' She winced and raised her voice as a cement mixer started up nearby. 'At least you can see the potential.'

'It seems good.' Laird glanced around again. 'Who thought of the name?'

'My nephews.' She chuckled. 'The locals call it Grunt Bay. That's not the image we want.'

'Confusing.' Laird met her sharp green eyes with a matching smile, then indicated the Ford. 'Thanks for the loan.'

'We had a new rental batch arrive last week.' She beckoned. 'Come over to the office, out of this din.'

Laird followed her. Diane Mehran walked with the easy stride of a big-boned muscular woman. As Chris Newgrange had said, she was in her forties with just a trace of grey in her auburn hair, and a few early lines around her mouth. A good-looking woman, obviously nobody's fool. But as she led the way up some steps into the hut he decided someone should have the courage to tell her that, from the back, she didn't look her best in jeans.

Two men were waiting in the office beside one of several trestle tables and desks, and she made the introductions. 'Mr Laird — my nephew Simon and our associate director, Ray Garris.'

The elder of Paul Mehran's two sons was in his late twenties, a thin, tall man with dark hair and a tanned complexion. He had Diane Mehran's green eyes, but with a hawk-like face, high cheekbones, and an impatient mouth. He was wearing khaki overalls, the trousers' cuffs caught inside lace-up boots with heavy rubber soles. Ray Garris was different. Small, thickset, almost bald, when he grinned he showed a couple of gold-filled teeth. He had a pug nose, hardly any neck, and he was dressed in a light-weight grey suit with a blue shirt and patterned silk tie.

Laird shook hands with them both, Simon Mehran's grip a challenge, Garris's little more than a touch.

'We've been warned about you — the money man,' said Simon Mehran with an acid humour. 'Well, don't worry about me. But keep your eye on Diane. We've a pirate in the family tree and she's a throwback. Right, Ray?'

72

'Keep me out of it. I'm not family — thank God.' The Mehran associate director was frosty. Swinging round, he gestured to a line of plan drawings pinned to one wall of the hut. 'Laird, these are more likely to interest you.'

'Admire,' murmured Simon Mehran.

'Simon.' His aunt gave him a warning glance. 'Go ahead, Mr Laird.'

Laird went over. The largest drawing was an architect's pen and ink sketch of how Witchlove Haven would look on completion. Yachts and powerboats would be berthed along a curve of quay partly carved out of the living rock. Close by, the main building would be a large club-house with a swimming pool and a full-length balcony restaurant. Other buildings would include boat stores and repair facilities, and there would be a quayside bar. Further back, the drawing showed a motel-style row of small apartments.

It would be a major development; it would cost a lot of money.

'I'm impressed,' he told his audience. He meant it.

'Good.' Ray Garris came to join him. 'We're spending enough.'

'Not spending, investing,' said Simon Mehran indignantly. Then he shrugged, his

73

manner soothing again. 'I know how Ray feels. We've put most of the finance together, we've got a lot riding on it.'

'More than a lot,' grunted Garris.

Laird propped himself against the nearest trestle table. 'So Witchlove Haven has to win a place on the map through your power boat race?'

'Yes. If we get the sponsorship we want, that means the prize money we want — then we attract the biggest boats, the fastest boats, the top names.' Simon Mehran stabbed a finger for emphasis. 'Names, Laird. Power boat racing is like a travelling circus — get a few top names, and you get them all.'

'Isn't the Channel Islands on the power boat calendar?'

'Yes.' Mehran brushed that aside. 'But there's always room for another event if it happens to be big enough.'

'Simon is our expert there,' murmured Diane. 'He and his brother race their own boat.'

'Junior league, until Matt and I can buy a new boat — '

'You mean until you can get someone to pay for it.' She stopped him and switched to Laird again. 'We can talk about the race tonight. Why don't we show you over the site while you're here?' She glanced at Garris.

74

'About tonight, Ray — you're still welcome if you can make it.'

'No chance.' Garris shook his head. 'But I'll stay for the tour. I like seeing where the money is going.'

They left the hut, Simon leading the way with Garris, Laird following them with Diane Mehran. He found both of the men ahead a puzzle. Simon Mehran's almost abrasive attitude seemed to be accepted as normal by the other two. Yet, in a quieter way, Garris might have an even harder streak. Which left Diane Mehran. Laird gave her a sideways glance as they passed another growling cement mixer. The big, brisk woman was working at soothing things down, but he had a feeling that if and when her patience ended the results would be spectacular.

They moved on along the site, still as a group, stopping now and again to point out some feature to Laird. Then Simon Mehran came to an unexpected halt. He was cursing, staring out into the bay. A small fishing boat had nosed in from the sea and was passing a buoy which flew a red warning flag.

'Where's Jody?' Still cursing, Mehran glared around, then shouted, 'Jody, where the hell are you?'

One of the workmen came hurrying over. He had ginger hair and a drooping moustache and was already scowling.

'Seen it?' demanded Mehran.

The man nodded. 'They're the people we chased yesterday, boss.'

'They need a lesson,' grated Mehran. 'A real lesson — have we anything ready to blow?'

'There's one charge just laid, boss.' The man hesitated. 'The one for that spur of ledge near the entrance. But — well, it could be risky.'

'It'll scare the hell out of them, that's all.' Mehran's lips tightened. The fishing boat had come down to little more than steerage way. There were two men aboard, one lounging at the outboard motor at her stern, the other floating out a baited line of hooks. 'Do it.'

'Simon — ' Diane Mehran's voice cut like a knife. 'Have you gone mad?'

'No.' Mehran scowled at the boat again. 'They've been warned off, like plenty of others. They've been told to stay out, they ignore us.' He drew a deep breath. 'That red flag says we're using explosives. That's exactly what we're going to do. Jody — '

The ginger-haired workman shuffled his feet and gave a worried glance at Ray Garris.

'No risk?' asked Garris softly. 'You're sure?'

'None. Just a noisy little bang.' Mehran was confident.

Garris gave a slight nod. The workman turned and trotted off.

'What are you using?' asked Laird slowly.

'Cordtex.' The little boat was still bobbing out in the bay, a long curve of floats in the light swell now marking the line with its baited hooks. Simon Mehran gave a cold grin. 'We're clearing rock to improve the berthing approach. They'll get a nice little surprise.'

Cordtex. Laird knew it well. An underwater explosive which looked like thick rope, it could be wound round anything, anywhere. It was one of the most powerful underwater explosives commercially available. He moistened his lips at the thought. Nobody with sense played games with Cordtex.

Moments passed, then a warning siren screamed its note across the site. Workmen stopped what they were doing, the mobile crane backed into shelter. One of the men in the fishing boat rose to his feet, staring.

The siren screamed a second time. An instant later a whole section of sea and shore exploded with a flat roar. White water and black, broken rock boiled skywards; the force of the blast swept over everything like a sudden gale. Laird felt spray on his face and saw lumps of rock pepper the foam-lashed sea like shrapnel, some of the smaller pieces landing around the fishing boat — and though his ears were still dulled by the blast he could hear Simon Mehran laugh.

'Bloody hell,' said Ray Garris softly. 'Diane — '

She was still staring, saying nothing.

Already, the fishing boat had abandoned its line of floats. Still being tossed by the waves from the explosion, her outboard engine began a noisy hammering. Her crew of two were crouching low, as if terrified of what might happen next. The wake beginning to churn at her stern was probably more than she'd ever achieved before. Making a tight turn, she began streaking out towards safety.

'Lesson learned,' said Simon Mehran confidently.

'Maybe.' Garris stood with hands jammed in his pockets, his pug-nosed face a stony mask. 'Suppose they run straight to the police?'

'They know better,' declared Mehran. 'We had a warning flag, we sounded a warning siren.' He gave a calculating grin towards Laird. 'Hell, we've even got an independent witness!'

'You'd better be right, my son,' said Ray Garris very deliberately. 'Little bangs I don't mind, big bangs are for idiots.' He paused, glaring at the younger man. 'That was what I call a very big bang. You understand me, my son?'

Simon Mehran's face flushed red. His mouth shaped as if he was going to answer. Then, instead, he shrugged. Without a word, he walked back towards the office hut.

'Sorry, folks.' Garris stepped over to Laird and Diane Mehran, his voice dryly apologetic, his face empty of emotion again. 'Diane, you're going to have to talk with Paul when he gets back and make sure that son of his gets his tail kicked in. Either that, or I'm voting for a new project manager.'

'I'll speak to Paul.' She moistened her lips, regaining her composure, suddenly laying a hand on Laird's arm. 'I'm sorry. Don't judge us too harshly. I think — well, maybe you should come back another time. This won't happen again. I guarantee it.'

'Leave the rest till later,' agreed Laird. He saw the fishing boat, now clear of the bay, beginning to vanish from sight round a headland. 'I'll come again. I'll be on the island for a few days.'

'Good,' said Garris. He glanced at his wristwatch, which had a chunky gold bracelet, then looked at Diane Mehran. 'I'd better get going. I've things to do — that business we talked about.'

'Yes.' She pursed her lips. 'I'll speak to

Paul, then call you.'

'Do that.' Garris switched to an amiable mood and turned to Laird. 'We should get together for a drink. I'll be in touch. Forget young Simon's little exhibition — now and again he plays to the gallery, that's all.'

Nodding goodbye, Garris left them and ambled over to the parking area. His car was a dark blue BMW. Gravel spat from the wheels a moment later as he accelerated away.

Diane Mehran sighed to herself, then stood with her hands on her hips, a wry, undoubtedly angry Amazon of a woman.

'There are times I wish Simon had been drowned at birth.' She shook her head as if clearing the thought away. 'Anyway, about tonight. Can you come about seven? The house is called Mehran Gate. It's inland a little from St Helier. I'll make sure the hotel desk gives you directions.' She gave a slight laugh. 'Don't be too late. We eat early.'

'I'll be there.' Laird nodded, sensing the woman wanted him to leave. That suited his own plans. 'I'm going to disappear for the afternoon. I've got the car, it's a chance to explore around a little. But if you hear from Clanmore Alliance — '

'Of course.' She nodded her understanding. 'I'll tell them you're researching. Why not?'

'It sounds better.' He let her lead him in the direction of the cars. All around, the construction site was getting back to normal again, the only signs of what had happened some broken pieces of wet rock lying along the shore. Out in the bay, the red warning flag flapped as before. 'Then tonight, I can hear your race plans.'

'You will. And we want to hear what Clanmore Alliance would want for their money.' Diane Mehran slowed. 'It was a surprise. We didn't expect them to be so friendly.'

'Why?'

'We cost your firm a lot of money not so long ago. There was a ship — '

'The *Rosewitch*?' Laird played his own part. 'I know about that. But there's a saying we have in the trade — no claims, no insurance companies.'

'I like it. I'll remember it.' She chuckled to herself. 'Yes, I suppose that's right.'

She stayed with Laird until he was back in the Ford. Then, as he put the key in the ignition, she raised a hand in goodbye and went off towards the office hut.

The hut and Simon — Laird had plenty to think about as the little car began lurching along the track again, back towards the road. He grimaced as the steering wheel bucked in

81

his hands. Simon Mehran's explosion had blasted more than some underwater rock. It had lifted a corner of the Mehran background, giving him a glimpse of some of the tensions underneath.

But he was glad of something else, the way Diane Mehran had, deliberately or otherwise, been the first person to mention the *Rosewitch* claim. Now that had happened, he had one less problem.

The evening at Mehran Gate was going to be interesting. He smiled to himself, switched on the cassette player, and Antonio Carlos's music began washing around again as the same guard waved him past the barrier pole.

★ ★ ★

Any last trace of cloud had been burned out of the sky and heat shimmered from the tarmac road as the Ford purred towards Merfleur Point. There were apple orchards and fruit-laden pear trees. A trio of girls in minuscule shorts and halter tops waved at Laird as they pedalled past on cycles. The northeast was one of Jersey's peaceful corners, a total contrast to St Helier.

He reached a junction marked by a Norman church. Merfleur Point was to the right, along a minor road. It led briefly through fields where cattle were grazing, skirted the foot of a low escarpment of rocks, then he had reached the sea again. Merfleur Point was a long reach of weed-covered half-tide reef projecting out to a small, elevated hammer-head island. A fragile steel lattice tower on the little island was topped by a warning light, island and tower were both speckled white with nesting gulls.

The road ahead ended at a crumbling curve of a fishing harbour and a few dilapidated cottages. A short distance away, on a rise of ground, an old granite tower stood overlooking Merfleur Point. The seaward side of the stonework had been painted in broad bands of red and white, a marker for coastal shipping.

Laird stopped the Ford at the cottages, got out, and looked around. Some of the little buildings were derelict, a few still had their slate roofs — though one was a ruin with empty gaps for windows. Another, with part of a wall knocked down, sheltered a small, yellow speedboat mounted on a trailer. But the next cottage in the row had been rebuilt and modernized. It had bright paintwork, lace curtains behind the windows, and a garden path made from white beach pebbles. A carved wooden sign beside the open front door said 'Merfleur Cottage.' A short walk away, one cottage which directly faced the tiny harbour's quay was also definitely in use. It had been converted into a chandler's store, complete with display window.

The air felt clean and salt fresh as he went over to Merfleur Cottage, where a mass of dark red butterflies were fluttering among the blue splash of a bank of hydrangeas. As his feet crunched on the pebble path, a dog gave a furious bark. A second later, a Labrador-sized black mongrel charged out, showing its teeth.

'Benny, you brute! Cut that out!' came a shout from inside the cottage. 'Don't be an idiot!'

The dog paused in mid-bark, looked round and wagged its tail as a young woman appeared in the cottage doorway. She had long, raven-black hair tied back by a ribbon, her feet were bare, and she wore a man's faded red shirt over denim shorts.

'It's all right — ' she smiled at Laird ' — he's never sure of strangers.'

'That's sensible enough,' said Laird mildly. The dog watched him, still giving an occasional throaty growl. 'Any notion where I'd find Captain West?'

'He's around.' She was in her late twenties, with a nut-brown tan, dark-brown eyes, and a face as fine-boned as an Egyptian carving.

'Try the store, he's probably in the back shop.' She made a clicking noise with her fingers, directed at the dog. 'You. Back inside. Now!'

She returned into the cottage, the dog following her, and Laird walked towards the harbourside store. The shop window had a starred chip like a bullet hole near its centre and the display behind it was an array of boating gear, cans of beer, and island-made red clay pottery. A bell chimed as he opened the door, and he went into the cool, dark interior. The shelf space was mostly filled with small-boat ironmongery and fishing tackle.

'Through the back,' hailed a gruff, cheerful voice.

Following the sound, Laird pushed aside a curtain made from short lengths of fine, knotted rope and went through into a room laid out as a workshop. A light above a bench shone down on a bulky, white-haired man in a short-sleeved grey shirt and patched grey trousers. Peering at whatever he was working at, he kept his back to the door.

'I'll be right with you.' The white-haired man used a small screwdriver, picked up what he'd been working on, then turned. 'As soon as I check this.'

The light glinted on the blued metal of a

heavy, long-barrelled pistol. The man took two limping, almost lurching steps away from the bench and the pistol came up, the barrel pointing away from Laird. A soft, flat cough came from the weapon, followed by a sharp smack. A target on the opposite wall jerked.

'Better.' The man grinned and lowered the weapon. It was a highly lethal-looking air pistol, with a ringed foresight and screw-adjustment rear sight. 'The trigger pull needed easing a shade.' Beckoning, the man limped back to the workbench, cocked the pistol with one smooth lever movement, loaded in a waisted lead pellet, and handed it to Laird. 'Go on, have a try.'

Smiling, Laird raised the heavy pistol and pointed towards the target. The air pistol kicked as he pulled the trigger, he saw the target quiver on the outer left, and he smelled burnt gun oil.

'Captain West?' he asked, handing back the weapon.

'That's me.' Captain Jacob West placed the pistol on the workbench. 'And that's a Webley .22, fully rifled barrel, one hundred metres per second velocity — worth respecting.' A pair of pale blue eyes twinkled as they studied Laird. 'Where did you get that trouser belt, mister? Karachi?'

'Yes.' Laird looked down, surprised. The

plaited leather belt at his waist, with its heavy metal seaman's buckle, was styled for fighting or ornament as desired. With Clanmore Alliance, a spare ballpoint pen was now more important.

'I had one the same, but I outgrew it, boy.' Jacob West slapped his paunch, grinning. 'Johnny Lewnan telephoned me. You're Laird?'

Laird nodded.

'Got something for me?'

'Yes.' Laird produced the bulky brown envelope.

'Thanks.' West deliberately checked the envelope was still sealed, stuffed it into his hip pocket, then picked up a thick stick which had been propped against the workbench. 'Right, you've earned a beer. But no drinking on the premises when the weather is good.'

They went through to the front shop. Jacob West picked two cans from a stack on the floor, gave one to Laird, then thumbed towards the door. Laird followed him out. Leaning on his stick, West led his visitor to a wooden bench overlooking the tiny harbour. Sitting together on the bench, they opened the cans and tasted the lukewarm beer.

'Did Johnny tell you what this is about?' asked West.

Laird shook his head.

'It'll keep.' West grinned to himself. 'What do you think of Merfleur?'

'It's peaceful,' said Laird diplomatically. The little harbour was badly silted, littered with driftwood. The only other thing floating was a black rubber inflatable Zodiac boat with an outboard engine. A larger craft would have gone aground.

'It's off the map, you mean.' West took another swallow of beer. 'I was born in Merfleur. I can remember half a dozen lobster boats working out of here.' He shrugged. 'Times change, right? When I came back to the island, I bought the whole place for a song.' One hand tapped his right knee. 'That was after this, when I was beached.'

'What happened?' asked Laird.

'Never get in the way of a mooring cable when it decides to snap,' said West dryly. 'I lost this leg, they gave me a tin replacement. So I came back, rebuilt the cottage, fixed the other one up as the shop. Nobody ever comes this way, but it's a hell of a good way to get beer wholesale.' He changed the subject. 'Johnny Lewnan said you were coming to take a look at Witchline Shipping. Seen any of the Mehrans yet?'

'I've come from them.' It was pleasant in the sunlight, Laird felt mellow enough not to curse the seamen's union man for talking too much. 'I was at Witchlove Haven.'

'You mean Grunt Bay.' West chuckled to himself. 'I heard them blasting more rock a spell back. Who did you meet?'

'Diane and Simon — '

'Simon I'd keep in a cage and poke raw meat through the bars. Anyone else?'

'Ray Garris.'

'He's another I wouldn't turn my back on.' West used the tip of his stick to flick a small stone out into the harbour water. 'What did Johnny Lewnan say about me — the truth?'

Laird chuckled. 'It wasn't very complimentary.'

'It wouldn't be.' West was pleased. 'But I can usually keep my mouth shut if it matters.' The pale blue eyes showed a studied innocence. 'So if I remember a ship called the *Rosewitch* — '

'Then, like you say, you can keep your mouth shut,' said Laird slowly. 'Did you know her?'

'I saw her a few times, that's all. Witchline ships don't often visit Jersey.' West shrugged. 'You know how it goes — they're kept out where the money is.'

Laird nodded. The modern merchant shipping fleet, regardless of flag, operated that way. Sometimes years could pass without a ship coming into her home port. New crews could be sent out by air, relieved crews could come back the same way. Repairs and maintenance were carried out at any yard where the price was right.

'I'm interested in the last time she came into St Helier. How her crew behaved, whether anything unusual happened.' He left it at that.

'I'll remember that.' The big, white-haired man finished his beer and threw the can into the harbour, where it floated for a moment. 'It's lunch time. Have you eaten?'

'Not yet,' admitted Laird.

'We'll see what the domestic staff can provide. But call them that and they'll kill me.' West wiped the back of his hand across his mouth, waited while Laird finished his drink, then used the stick to rise. 'Did you look in at the cottage?'

'Yes. A girl in a red shirt — '

'That's Kiri, our sort of house guest.' West chuckled. 'My Belle and Kiri's mother were stewardesses together on one of the old Cunard cruise ships. The pair of them keep in touch.' He gave a good-natured shrug. 'Kiri is working in Jersey for a few months. When she arrived, she needed a place to live till she got settled — we've still got her.'

The arrangement obviously didn't displease Captain West. He was humming under

90

his breath as they started towards the cottage. But as they passed the shop he stopped and used his stick to point towards the star-shaped hole in the display window.

'Take that as a warning,' he said with a dry solemnity. 'Never presume a gun isn't loaded.'

'The air pistol?'

'Yes.' West sighed at the memory. 'I kept one on my last ship. It earned its keep. Get out on a bridge wing in an afternoon watch, see some loafer skulking on deck — zap! Nothing like a lead slug close to the ear to set anyone moving.'

Laird could believe he meant it. The sea encouraged odd behaviour. On his first ship, the chief engineer had gone everywhere with an imaginary parrot on his shoulder. Later, he'd known a captain who thought he was being poisoned and insisted the cook tasted everything before he ate. Then there had been a second mate who wore goggles and moved around the bridge on a make-believe motor cycle, complete with noises.

'How long have you been ashore?' he asked.

'Three years.' West limped on.

'Ever miss it?'

'Miss it?' West stared at him. 'When I sleep with my wife in our own bed every night? Mister, that's a damned stupid question!'

Benny came bounding out to greet them when they arrived at Merfleur Cottage. Barking, the black dog jumped around West and ignored his half-hearted cursing until a small, very plump woman bustled out. Belle West was rosy-cheeked, had her grey hair pinned back in a bun, and wore a light cotton dress which hung around her like a technicolour tent. West greeted her with an affectionate slap on the rump.

'Johnny Lewnan's friend.' He thumbed at Laird. 'I said we'd feed him. Will the rations stretch?'

'There's always a spare crust.' She smiled at Laird, then gave her husband a quick, searching glance. 'Have you got it?'

'Yes.' West patted the pocket where he'd put Lewnan's envelope. 'Where's Kiri?'

'Here.' The young woman appeared behind Belle's ample shape. She was wiping her hands on an apron, and she smiled at Laird. 'Hello again.'

'Kiri Vass, the menace I told you about,' introduced Jacob West, with a wink. 'Call her Kiri, everybody does.'

She nodded, but looked directly at West.

'Yes,' agreed West patiently. 'He's Andrew Laird, he brought it. But I haven't read the thing.'

'Then get on with it,' said Belle West with a

92

degree of irritation. 'Go and hide if you want. We'll look after Andrew.'

Giving her a sheepish grin, West nodded. The dog at his heels, he hobbled past them and vanished into the first room along the hallway.

'That's what he calls his day cabin — where he goes when he wants to sulk or be secretive,' said Belle West. Her plump shoulders straightened. 'But this time I'm going to find out what's happening.'

She bustled off after her husband into the same room. The door closed behind her.

'They're always that way!' Kiri Vass gave an amused, despairing gesture with her hands. 'Let's try the kitchen. It's safe enough.'

Laird followed her through. The hallway had photographs of ships on both walls. A small shelf held a barometer, a ship's brass clock, and a Pacific conch shell. The kitchen beyond it was large and modern in equipment, but with antique copper pots hanging from hooks set in the old wooden ceiling beams. Pots bubbled on a king-sized electric stove, a table in the middle of the floor had been set for lunch.

'Did you have a beer at the shop?' asked Kiri Vass. 'Or is that a damned stupid question?' She saw her answer. 'Could you use another?'

'Not right now.' Laird shook his head. 'But I'd like to know what's in that envelope I brought.'

The raven-haired woman chuckled and shook her head. Opening a drawer she took out some extra cutlery, then turned to set an extra place at the table. Laird watched her. Still barefoot, Kiri Vass was slightly above medium height. Her eyes were dark brown, she had long, slim legs and a neat waist. The way she bent forward at the table and the way not many of her shirt buttons had been fastened gave him a glimpse of the tanned, full curve of her breasts.

'Jacob was talking about you.' He waited until she looked up. 'He says Belle and your mother were cabin stewardesses.'

'True.' She grinned at him. 'Any time those two meet and talk, I listen. They were a right little pair of ravers.'

'Cruise life in the raw?'

'Jacob wouldn't appreciate some of it. Mum and Belle, cabin-hopping!' She grimaced in mock despair. 'Who'd believe it?'

'Why not?' Laird smiled, thinking of Belle's plump, matronly shape. 'You seem to like it here.'

'With Jacob and Belle? They treat me like a daughter.' She guessed his next question. 'No, they've no children. Belle says they tried.'

Laird went over to the window. The view was out towards the old stone tower on the rise. He'd seen others. They were called Martello towers, a Corsican name, but they'd been built in the early nineteenth century when Napoleon was threatening to invade Britain. There were Martello towers scattered around the Channel Islands, another string were located along the south coast of England — all monuments now.

Kiri Vass came over, leaning her elbows on the window ledge.

'Interested?' she asked, looking out at the tower.

'My folks only had a shed at the bottom of their garden,' he said gravely.

'In Scotland?'

He nodded.

'It's in your voice.' She brushed a stray strand of that raven-black hair back from her forehead. 'How long will you be on Jersey?'

'A few days.' Laird turned from the window. 'How about you?'

'I'm counting in weeks.' Kiri Vass shrugged. 'I've been here most of the summer, working at the airport — I'm acting station manager for one of the charter airlines. The female who had the job got married, got pregnant, and took maternity leave.'

'And you got drafted?'

'I was stationed in Paris.' Her eyes twinkled. 'There's a difference — but I've liked it.'

'Including the yellow speedboat?' he suggested.

'The one parked in the old cottage? I just wish it was mine — it belongs to one of Jacob's friends.' She gave a mild frown, considering him. 'I get to use it when I want. If you'd like a trip, maybe we can fix something.'

The kitchen door opened and Belle West came in, followed by her husband. Both were beaming. Kiri Vass went straight towards them.

'Have you got it?' she asked.

'Nearly, girl — nearly!' Jacob West put an arm around her waist and gave her a squeezing hug. When he let her go, he limped over to Laird and shook him by the hand. His grip was like a vice. 'Boy, you brought us some good news. You'll hear it soon enough.' He paused, suddenly more serious. 'I may ask you for some help.'

'You'll get it.' Puzzled, Laird nodded.

'That's what I hope.' West glanced at his wife. 'Belle, how about a drink to celebrate?'

She smiled, opened a cupboard, and produced a bottle of wine.

'That?' West's face fell. 'Damn it, woman,

96

that's battery acid or worse. Where did you get it?'

'The same place you get your beer,' she said calmly. 'From your shop. So sit down and be quiet.'

It was a good medium-dry white wine, whatever the label. Jacob West and Belle sat on one side of the table, Laird found himself seated beside Kiri Vass. Lunch was a thick bouillabaisse, highly flavoured, with thick chunks of fresh white bread, a spread of cheeses, and coffee.

'That damned bouillabaisse happens at least once a week,' complained West, giving a half-suppressed belch. 'Don't ever ask what's in it, Laird. It's French, and you know the Froggies. They say if something moves, eat it.' He thumbed at his wife. 'She's the problem. Channel Islands, yes — she was born on Guernsey. But the Lord help me, she's half French.'

'What kind of label do you put on me?' teased Kiri Vass.

'You? The original mongrel,' said West solemnly. 'And you can do your own explaining to our visitor.'

She shrugged at Laird. 'I've a Maori great-grandmother, my mother came from New Zealand, then married a passenger she met on a cruise — '

97

'A beautiful man,' murmured Belle. 'Not like some I know.'

'From Liverpool,' jeered West. He winked at Laird. 'A university professor who talks through his nose.' He sucked his teeth. 'Still, there's one good, honest thing about Kiri. At least she'll admit she can't cook worth a damn.' He collapsed back, laughing, as Belle grabbed him by the ear and twisted it.

They talked through the rest of the meal, but about nothing in particular. The Wests made it clear they wanted it that way. Eventually, Kiri Vass got up from the table.

'I've got to change and get over to the airport,' she told Laird. 'We've a string of charter flights coming in.'

'I'll be back again,' said Laird. 'Remember that boat trip.'

She laughed and went out. Minutes later, as Belle began clearing the table, Jacob West nodded at Laird and grunted as he got to his feet.

'Forget the washing-up, Laird,' he said heavily. 'That's woman's work, so I'll be made to do it later. I want a private word with you.'

He took Laird through to his 'day cabin'. The black dog lay in a patch of sunlight by the window, a few papers littered a desk, a large globe of the world occupied a corner. There were some home-made shelves on the walls. One had a framed photograph of Captain Jacob West in his master's uniform next to another of him as part of a group of smiling men in civilian clothes. A collection of well-polished trophies, all for target shooting, were also on display.

'This won't take long.' West closed the door, waved Laird into an armchair, and settled in another opposite. His broad face was serious. 'You were with some of the Mehrans. Do they know, does anyone else know, about the letter from Johnny Lewnan?'

Laird shook his head.

'Can you keep it that way for a spell?' West sucked his lips. 'I'm not making a mystery. There's a good reason — only for a day or so.'

'Then it'll be that way.' Laird waited.

'I said I may need your help. I meant it. Kiri knows why — so don't ask her.' West sucked his lips again. 'When are you seeing the Mehrans again?'

'Tonight. By invitation, at their home. Diane Mehran has given me a room at the Leecom.' It was Laird's turn. He leaned forward. 'You said you might get me something on the *Rosewitch*.'

'I'm going to try. I'll be in touch.' West shifted in his chair, enough to make the black dog raise its head. 'I'll give you a warning, mister. You're on shore leave, in a strange port, on your own. You've got to go up a dark alley. What do you do?'

'Go damned carefully.'

West gave a small smile. 'Do that, any time you're near a Mehran. They may give you a line that they're old Norman-French stock, and it's true. But you know about barracuda?'

Laird nodded and West was satisfied.

A few minutes later he said goodbye to the retired captain and his wife and left. Outside, a green Volvo station wagon was waiting beside his Ford. Kiri Vass got out of the Volvo. She wore a dark grey skirt and jacket uniform with a white blouse. Her hair, freed from its ribbon, brushed her jacket shoulders.

'I thought you'd gone,' said Laird.

'I should have, by now.' Her eyes were serious. 'Jacob hinted you're here for a reason — not the reason you pretend.'

Laird sighed. 'Jacob talks too much.'

'He trusts me.' She looked down for a moment, rubbing the toe of one shoe on the ground. 'Does he have to get involved?'

'No more than he wants. I won't push him.' Laird paused. 'That's a promise.'

'It'll have to do.' She twisted a smile. 'He has something of his own to think about — something I started and sometimes wish I hadn't.' A quick headshake anticipated the question on his lips. 'Leave it there, Andrew. All right?'

She got into the Volvo, smiled at him again, in a different, strangely shy way, and drove off.

3

Andrew Laird drove back to where the old, mellow stonework of the Norman church glowed in the sunlight, then turned the Ford in the direction of St Helier. Fumbling among the cassettes, he loaded one at random and the player started on a selection of reissued Beatles' classics. With the volume turned down, it was a low background which helped him think.

He'd been landed with a puzzle, one which made him curse John Lewnan's devious ways. On the one hand, he had the hope that Jacob West could come up with some help on Witchline Shipping's local background. On the other, the sealed envelope he'd delivered from the union official had been important to all three of the inhabitants of Merfleur Cottage . . . yet ask why, and the shutters had politely come down.

West and his wife were likable, amiable, obviously well able to cope with most things. So why the deliberate hints that they might need him? Laird squeezed the Ford past a lumbering farm tractor, then smiled a little. Suddenly, he'd been thinking of Kiri Vass.

The tanned, raven-haired woman, for all practical purposes an adopted member of the West family, was someone he wanted to meet again. She had her own strength of character. He shook his head. She'd been worried too, and he had the feeling that didn't happen easily.

At the next junction, he joined the tree-lined Trinity Road, a busy main route which cut directly across the island to St Helier. The traffic thickened, the Beatles were singing 'All You Need Is Love'. He grimaced. What he needed was any kind of new real evidence about the *Rosewitch* sinking. Meeting the two Mehrans and their friend Garris had shown him that wasn't going to be easy, and had opened up the minor mystery of how the Witchlove Haven marina was being funded.

That was maybe best tackled from outside the island. But the rest was his — and, for the moment, his alone.

★ ★ ★

St Helier's biggest single problem was called traffic. Jersey might be only a small blob of land in the sea between England and France, but it was a blob which was home to close on 70,000 registered vehicles — several

103

thousand more than the resident human population — and on the average day most of them seemed to be trying to fight their way into the town. St Helier's answer included electronically controlled indicator boards on the main routes, constantly updating which parking areas were full and which had spaces. At peak times they winked like Christmas lights.

The Green Street parking area had spaces. Laird left the Ford next to two Rolls-Royce limousines, checked a street map on a notice board, and began walking. St Helier might be near the end of season, but its streets were still busy. Tourists window-shopped outside stores which were jammed with tax-free jewellery, perfume and luxury goods. Locals fought past with baskets filled with groceries. Florists offered to air-mail their bouquets of blossoms anywhere. Every other shop was selling tickets for the next state lottery.

Some of the main shopping streets, filled with branches of mainland multiple stores, had been pedestrianized. Laird made his way through the crowds in King Street, turned off at a corner and found himself in a quieter avenue of office blocks where every other brass plate was an insurance company, a bank or an offshore consultancy. Mehran Holdings had their headquarters halfway along, their brass plate one of several at the entrance to a modern high-rise block which had a uniformed doorman, a small garden in the lobby, and two elevators in the background.

That was all he'd wanted to see. Turning, Laird cut back through the shopping crowds and past the main post office towards the harbour area. It was only a couple of minutes' walk to Chris Newgrange's tiny Newgrange Agencies' office.

Laird smiled. It certainly wasn't the most expensive address in town. A brewery lorry was unloading beer outside one of the neighbouring liquor stores and a stairway entrance next to Newgrange's office led up to a dental technician's workshop. But Chris Newgrange was happy and independent. What else mattered?

A buzzer sounded as he pushed open the agency's door and went in. A girl sat at a desk in a small, slightly shabby reception area where the rest of the furniture amounted to two spare chairs and a filing cabinet. She wore a black sweater and a white skirt, her hair had been dyed a bright henna red, and she looked young enough to be at school.

'Is Chris in?' he asked.

'Yes, Mr Laird,' She beamed at him, gesturing towards a door at the rear.

'You know me?' Laird was puzzled.

'Chris doesn't get his picture in a newspaper every day.' Still beaming, she pushed a newspaper towards him. 'It's page six.'

It was the *Jersey Evening Post* afternoon edition. Laird flicked through to page six, stared, and winced. The photograph had been taken at the airport, the camera had caught Newgrange guiding him through the arrivals' lobby. There was a bold caption beneath. 'Prominent London marine insurance executive Mr Andrew Laird of Clanmore Alliance Assurance arrived on the island today and was met by popular St Helier insurance consultant Mr Chris Newgrange. Mr Laird is on Jersey to negotiate a major new sponsorship for the Witchlove Haven marina development, with Chris Newgrange as local advisor for Clanmore in this important island project.'

An awkward, throat-clearing noise reached him. The other door had opened, Newgrange was standing there.

'Uh — I was going to call you,' said Newgrange warily. His face reddened, and he quickly indicated the girl. 'This is Liz.'

'He hadn't seen the photograph,' reported Liz.

'But he has now,' said Laird acidly.

'I can explain about that.' Newgrange swallowed.

'Good.' Laird pushed him gently into the private office then firmly closed the door. He glanced round. The room had a large, battered desk with two telephones, more filing cabinets and a small TV set. Someone's advertising calendar was pinned on one wall. Turning, he considered Newgrange grimly. 'So explain.'

'I know a freelance who does work for the *Post* — '

'And you tipped him off,' nodded Laird. 'Why?'

'Publicity for my agency,' said Newgrange weakly. He edged back until he collided with one of the cabinets. 'He didn't exactly write what I told him. I — I didn't say that bit about being your advisor — '

'Next time you plan anything like that, ask me first,' said Laird grimly. 'You understand?'

'I'm sorry.' Newgrange gave a meek nod, then brightened a little. 'But we had a 'phone call about it, from someone who wants to talk to you. I gave him the hotel number, he said he'd try there.'

'Did he have a name?'

'I — let me check with Liz.' Newgrange escaped briefly into the other office, then returned. 'Peter Frere — we both think he sounded local.'

'But you don't know, you didn't ask — you

didn't get a 'phone number from him, or an address?' Laird took Newgrange's embarrassed silence at its own value. Publicity was the last thing he wanted, though probably no real harm had been done. 'Chris, next time, if there is a next time — '

'We will.' Newgrange moistened his lips, and saw a chance to change the subject. 'Have you had any contact with the Mehrans?'

'I met some of them, at the marina development.'

Newgrange blinked. 'Including Diane?'

'Diane and Simon.' Laird didn't waste time on details. 'But no sign of Simon's brother.'

'There wouldn't be.' Newgrange recovered a degree of confidence and attempted a laugh. 'He's been exiled, lucky devil. His father sent him out to Hong Kong on a business trip a couple of weeks ago. But he's due back soon.'

'One less to worry about.' Laird saw Newgrange's surprised interest. 'I mean it's always easier when you haven't too many people to deal with.'

Newgrange nodded wisely. 'I know. If I see a husband and wife coming in together on a car insurance claim — '

Laird cut him short. 'I need to make a couple of telephone calls to London.'

'The private kind?' Newgrange understood. 'Be my guest.' He gestured towards his desk. 'The red 'phone is a direct line out. My sort of personal hot line.' He shrugged sadly. 'Not so much hot as lukewarm. But I keep hoping. I'll — uh — be outside when you're finished.'

He left, closing the door behind him. Sighing, Laird settled in the scuffed leather-look executive chair behind Newgrange's desk. The newspaper photograph was something he could have done without, though the risk was small that he'd be recognised by anyone. But who was Peter Frere? The name meant nothing.

Picking up the red telephone, he used the trunk dialling code for Clanmore Alliance in London. While he waited for the connection, he took another glance around the office and smiled at the folding camp bed stowed in one corner. There were probably times when the lanky young owner was glad to use it.

The call connected. In another moment he was speaking to Osgood Morris, and for once the marine claims manager was pleased to hear his voice.

'Any problems so far?' asked Morris.

'Not yet. Not the positive kind.' Laird wondered if he should apologise.

'I hear they've moved your hotel.' Morris paused. 'Is it — ah — suitable?'

'I'm phoning from somewhere else. New-grange Agencies.'

'Tony Dello's kith and kin.' The marine claims manager gave an understanding murmur. 'Good.'

Laird gave him the Newgrange number, then ran through the Mehran situation, including the marina incident. He decided there was no need to mention his trip out to Merfleur Point. He'd given Morris enough to think about.

'So we want to know more about the marina's financial background.' Morris gave a sigh over the line. 'That has to be outside money. It might be worth seeing if there's any kind of Hong Kong link. We'll ask here. You might get something out of Paul Mehran tonight.'

'I can try,' said Laird.

'You weren't sent to Jersey for a suntan,' said Morris acidly. He paused. 'I had a call from a Sergeant Edwards of Southampton Police. He said the late unlamented Mr Varrick, your Crab, did spend a long weekend in Jersey, as suggested. A fairly nubile young woman was with him. No details available yet about where they stayed or — ah — what they did.'

'It helps,' said Laird softly. It did. The Crab had to have come chasing to Jersey for a good reason. The kind of reason that had killed him not long after he got back home. 'I'll keep in touch, probably through this number. But if there's an innocent call or two from your end to the Leecom Hotel — '

'A devious thought,' said Morris happily. 'You're learning.'

Laird said goodbye and hung up. Then, after a moment, he lifted the 'phone and dialled again. This time he tried Johnny Lewnan's number. The seamen's union man was at his desk.

'You've landed me in something,' accused Laird after the basic preliminaries. 'Johnny, what's in that damned envelope I gave Captain West?'

'Nothing illegal,' said Lewnan with a feigned indignation. 'Do you think I'd do that to you?'

'Maybe not, but just about anything else,' said Laird with heavy sarcasm. 'I want to know.'

'You will,' said Lewnan soothingly. 'Give it time, Andy.' He lowered his voice. 'Look, I've got people around. I can't shout details. But I said Jacob West might be able to help you, and I meant it. He happens to have his own separate problems with the Mehrans, but I know Jacob — he's pretty like you. Stubborn. He'll do things his own way.' Suddenly he chuckled. 'Does the old devil still take pot shots at anything that moves?'

'You know about the air pistol?' said Laird.

'Air pistol be damned,' snorted Johnny Lewnan. 'When I sailed with him he used a 9-mill. Luger — or he did until he shot an ear off the cook!' There was a pause. Laird heard a mutter of voices at the other end, then Lewnan came back on the line. 'Look, I've got to go and shout obscenities at a shipping line. So I'll give it to you straight. When you came to me, I already knew West had trouble. You may need each other. Now go away, good luck, and get off my back.'

Laird heard Lewnan's 'phone slam down. Swearing softly, he replaced his receiver, slammed a hand on the desktop in a way that made a saucer filled with paperclips jump, then rose from the chair and went through to the front office. Newgrange was talking to his teenage assistant but stopped when he saw him.

'Everything all right?' asked Newgrange.

'So far.' Laird nodded. 'You may get calls from Clanmore to here, looking for me. Hold any messages. I'll be in touch.'

'Will do.' Newgrange glanced at Liz. She gave an unconcerned nod.

'Good.' There was a small gap that needed to be filled. 'Paul Mehran went over to

France. You told me he had his own private plane. Does he have a pilot's licence?'

'For light aircraft, yes.'

'What about his sons?'

'Simon and Matt?' Newgrange frowned. 'Maybe. I don't think so. Power boats are their game.'

'They've a beauty of a boat,' agreed Liz enthusiastically. 'You should see it, Mr Laird.' She sat back in her chair, both hands clasped behind her hennaed hair, her small breasts making valiant bumps on her black sweater. 'She's the *Devilwitch* over in the yacht basin.' She grinned at Newgrange. '*Devilwitch* and your pal Matt Mehran — that kind of combination I wouldn't fight off.'

'How about Simon?' asked Laird dryly, ignoring Newgrange's disapproval.

'He's an antique,' protested the girl. 'He must be close on thirty.'

'Mature?' suggested Laird hopefully.

'Ancient.' She winced. Laird had a feeling Newgrange had kicked her under the desk. It made no difference. Her nose wrinkled. 'Anyway, I've heard about him. He's a puke. Anyone who'll beat up a woman is a puke.'

'It was never proved,' said Newgrange uneasily.

'So he's an unproved puke,' she agreed.

Laird frowned. 'Who was the woman?'

'Some female tourist he picked up. She left it late saying no, she needed hospital treatment — '

'She denied it later,' protested Newgrange.

'She was paid off,' said Liz contemptuously. 'Everybody knows that.'

'When did it happen?' asked Laird.

'Early summer,' said Newgrange wearily. 'Maybe there was some horseplay.'

'Then the horse got a broken jaw,' said Liz sweetly.

Laird said goodbye and escaped, leaving them still arguing. Simon Mehran and his local reputation at play was background detail. But the timing was wrong for any link that mattered.

The main St Helier yacht basin was only a stroll away from Newgrange Agencies. He walked there and joined the other people who were ambling around the quayside, rubber-necking at the lines of boats floating in the muddy harbour water. The *Devilwitch* was easy enough to spot, a slim scarlet hull moored away from the other craft, heavily protected by fenders, and with a plain canvas hood covering her cockpit area. Laird felt a pang of envy. If the *Devilwitch* was as fast as she looked with those lines and the fat quartet of exhaust pipes at her stern, she had to be exciting to handle.

Beyond the basin, at the main harbour, he could see a grey fleet auxiliary tanker easing out. Her Blue Ensign was barely fluttering in the light breeze, the sea was calm; she should have a landman's voyage. He turned away, then froze, staring. A middle-aged couple collided with him, and he muttered an apology.

Across the basin two men were standing by a large bollard on the opposite quay. They were talking, and they were looking towards the scarlet *Devilwitch*. One was unmistakably Captain Jacob West. The other, squat and stocky, was Ray Garris. Laird eased back to the partial shelter of some empty fuel drums and watched while the two men talked on. They parted with a nod, and West limped off towards the main harbour. Garris stood a moment longer, then turned away. He vanished from sight behind some huts.

Laird moved too, but slowly, tight-lipped. He was thinking of Jacob West and the vehement way the retired sea captain had declared his distrust of Garris. Yet now they had seemed on reasonable terms, talking — talking about what? Laird shrugged and lengthened his stride. That was Jacob West's business. But it was worth remembering.

★ ★ ★

Andrew Laird drove out of St Helier before the parking areas really began emptying for the evening. Once clear of the town he took the east coast route with its tourist beaches and offshore rocks. Horses were being galloped on the long, smooth sands of Grouville Bay. At the north end, where the great medieval sprawl of Mont Orgueil Castle frowned down on a village and yacht harbour, tour coaches were unloading paying customers who wanted to peer over the battlements.

When he reached the Leecom Hotel, the same brunette was on duty at the reception desk. Laird collected his room key.

'Any messages for me?' he asked, thinking of the mysterious Peter Frere.

She glanced at a board behind her, shook her head, then produced an envelope from a drawer.

'Just this, Mr Laird. From Diane Mehran.'

He opened it. The single sheet of notepaper inside contained his directions for Mehran Gate. Thanking the girl, getting her full-treatment smile in return, he took the elevator up to his room, unlocked the door, and went in.

There were fresh towels in the bathroom and other indications that a maid had been tidying. Going over to the dressing table, he opened a drawer where he'd left a folder with a few faked memos and sets of figures provided by Clanmore's publicity department. When he'd placed it there, he'd used the old, old trick of leaving one of the loose sheets of paper protruding slightly from the rest. Now they were all neatly level.

Laird shaped a crooked grin and checked the rest of the room. There were other small signs. Nothing was missing, but even the zipped toilet bag he'd left in the bathroom had been examined. He'd left the cap on the tube of toothpaste loose, liable to come away if touched. It had been tightened.

That left the telephone. When he checked, the instrument hadn't been bugged — and it did go through the hotel switchboard. But he followed the wire to where it plugged into an ivory-coloured wall socket. There were tiny, powder-like traces of disturbed plaster on the carpet underneath. Sitting back on his heels, Laird brought out the pocket knife Nancy Roberts had given him as a birthday present. One of the blades had a screwdriver tip, and he used it on the two screws holding the socket in place.

When the socket came loose, he shaped a silent, appreciative whistle. Tucked into the space behind it was a small cube of advanced electronics, a cube not much bigger than a sugar lump. He knew the type. It was dual purpose: it could monitor the telephone by picking up induction impulses; equally it could listen to any conversation in the room. The receiver would be a taping unit located anywhere within a quarter of a mile.

The best thing to do was leave it alone. It might even be useful. Replacing the socket, he tightened the screws again.

A little later, wearing swimming trunks and with one of the hotel towels over his shoulders, Laird went back down in the lift. A new girl was on duty at the reception desk as he went out to the Leecom's open-air pool.

A few guests were sunning themselves around the poolside area, but only one person was swimming. Laird recognised her as she completed a length of the pool and came kicking round to start another. He waited, dived in, then surfaced directly in her path. She slowed, then floated beside him.

'Hello,' said Laird mildly. It was the brunette from the reception desk. She was in a blue two-piece swimsuit and she had a small, dark mole above her left breast. 'Trying for a record?'

'I do twenty lengths every evening, as soon as I'm off duty. If I don't, I get fat.' Her long, slim legs kicked lazily, bringing her nearer. 'That was seventeen — it'll do for tonight. Liking it here, Mr Laird?'

'So far.' Laird saw her eyes stray to the tattoos on his arms. 'What's your name?'

'Jo — Jo for Joanna.' She adjusted a shoulder strap. 'I'll give you a tip. Don't use this pool early in the morning. It can be like a deep freeze.'

'I'll remember.' They had drifted, he could amost touch her. 'Who dropped off that map for Mehran Gate? Your boss lady?'

'No.' The water swirled as she moved. 'Simon brought it.'

'Does he look in often?'

'He doesn't — and don't ask me to look sad.' She gave a quick frown, as if she'd said more than she'd intended. 'You won't quote me?'

Laird shook his head. She made a sudden duck-dive under, surfaced again, then climbed out at the nearest poolside ladder. Giving Laird a wave, she walked away.

Laird swam around for a few minutes on his own. Then he left, towelled himself down, and went back up to his room.

He dressed in the spare blue suit he'd packed, a cream-coloured shirt, and a blue folk-weave tie flecked with red. Then he had time to spare. He caught the last minutes of a national TV news broadcast, a regional bulletin, and the local weather forecast. The Channel Islands had thick fog scheduled for overnight. But by midday the sun should be back again.

It could be worse. Switching off the set, he left. Down in the Leecom's lobby, the bar was busy and noisy. Outside the hotel, the evening was still warm and bright.

The white Ford Fiesta purred smoothly as he drove out of the car park, Diane Mehran's sketch map on the passenger seat. It gave him an inland route along minor roads, and there was little other traffic. A narrow bridge took him over a partly dried river running through a small wooded valley. The next piece of road snaked and twisted past a farm and a cluster of cottages, then he caught a glimpse of a large manor house ahead, the grounds surrounded by a high wall.

Two old stone gateposts marked the entrance to Mehran Gate. The gates themselves lay open and he drove on along a gravel driveway. At first it was through open parkland, then, as he neared the house, there were formal gardens with carefully tended flowerbeds. He saw the sagging nets of a tennis court.

Mehran Gate was a sprawling three-storey house of creamy-white stone, the walls covered in ivy. The roof was of dark slate; changes in style and lines indicated how the manor house had been extended over the years. Most of the windows were of diamond-paned leaded glass and the woodwork, painted a faded green, showed signs of needing maintenance. A pair of old ship's cannons sat at the foot of a broad flight of stone steps which led up to an archway and the main door of the manor house.

Laird stopped the Ford beside two other vehicles already parked near the steps, then glanced at them as he got out. One was a tan-coloured Range Rover, the other a sleek metallic-green Jaguar coupé, and both had Jersey registration plates.

He passed them, admired the decorative engraving on the cannons, then went up the stone steps. He'd been seen. As he reached for the wrought-iron bell-pull the heavy oak door swung open. Diane Mehran greeted him with the next best thing to an apologetic smile.

'You're on time, I was late getting back.' She was still wearing her denim work outfit. As Laird went in, she lowered her husky voice, dry amusement behind her words. 'My cousin Paul is back. If the atmosphere needs a slow thaw, ignore it. He had that talk with Simon about what happened this morning.'

'Daddy was cross?' asked Laird mildly.

He'd gone too far for Diane Mehran. Her green eyes hardened for a moment. Then she nodded, saying nothing.

A maid with a white cap and apron was hovering in the background. Leaving her to close the door, Diane Mehran led the way along a broad hallway. The floor was polished oak, the walls were lined with a mix of old, heavy-framed portrait paintings, swords and other reminders of the Mehran past, then from there they went to a carpeted stairway with a thick, ornately carved banister rail. A window gave Laird a glimpse of outbuildings and a walled garden. From the stairway they went along a corridor, then Diane Mehran opened a thickly varnished door and led the way into a large, tastefully furnished drawing room. Broad windows were framed by floor-length velvet drapes. The view was to the front of the house and out over the gardens.

A drinks trolley had been placed beside some armchairs and a couch. Simon Mehran, wearing a plaid-check suit, slouched sulkily in one of the chairs. But Laird's eyes went to the man who turned from the window and came towards him.

Paul Mehran shook his hand as Diane made the introductions. Her cousin was medium height and average build, with the same green Mehran eyes and high cheek-bones. His voice was quiet and clipped, his thick dark hair was lightly flecked with grey, and he had a narrow mouth with a small scar on the left side of his lower lip. He wore a navy blue blazer with dark grey trousers and a light grey shirt and tie.

'Simon, fetch our guest a drink.' Mehran gave his son a glance which brought him to his feet.

Laird asked for whisky, then shook his head when Paul Mehran offered him a cigarette from an engraved silver box. It was six months since the red-haired anaesthetist had made him stop smoking. Mehran snapped the box shut without comment, and Simon brought the whisky. It was a peat-flavoured de-luxe malt, smooth to the taste.

'Not drinking, Diane?' asked Mehran.

'Later, when I've changed.' She smiled at her cousin with an easy familiarity. 'Just don't brainwash Andrew too much before I get back.'

'Why not?' Mehran's scarred mouth twisted briefly. As Diane left the room, he retrieved his own glass from a side table and turned to Laird again. 'I heard you visited Witchlove Haven.'

Laird nodded. 'It was interesting.'

'I heard about that as well.' Mehran's eyes flicked for a moment in his son's direction. 'But would you say good investment potential?'

'Given the right publicity. That's why I'm here.' Laird sipped his drink again. The room had an Italian marble fireplace. A framed photograph on the mantelshelf showed Simon and a younger man, both in racing overalls, both grinning at the camera, with the sea in the background. He went over, took a closer look at the photograph, then glanced at Simon. 'Your brother?'

Simon Mehran brightened a little and nodded. 'That was at a race off Guernsey last year. Matt's the mechanic. I drive — mostly anyway.'

Laird took another look at the photograph. Matt Mehran wore wire-framed spectacles and had a broader, slightly fleshy face.

'When does he get back from Hong Kong?'

'Soon.' Simon Mehran seemed surprised.

'Chris Newgrange mentioned he was away,' said Laird.

Simon nodded without enthusiasm.

'I sent Matt out to tidy a business deal,' said Paul Mehran. 'In this family, we don't carry passengers. Correct, Simon?'

His son said nothing.

'So isn't it time you were on your way back to the office?' asked Mehran pointedly.

'I'm going,' said Simon Mehran stonily. He shrugged at Laird. 'We've a ship stuck in a North African fleapit port with a problem.

I'm delegated to sort things out by telex.' He scowled at his father. 'I'll get a sandwich somewhere.'

He made a bristling exit from the drawing room, the door closing hard behind him. Paul Mehran gave a dry grunt which held some amusement.

'It could have waited until morning, and Simon knows it. Call it part of getting his wrist slapped for this morning. He'll be back by the time we need him.' Mehran finished his drink, walked to the trolley, and filled his glass again. He was drinking brandy. 'Diane said no brainwashing — not unless she's around. But do you really have the kind of money you're talking about?'

'Clanmore has — I couldn't sponsor a rowing boat.'

Mehran tasted his brandy. 'So marine insurance pays reasonable dividends?'

'You should know.' Laird met the man's green eyes calmly. 'Weren't you glad you'd paid your premiums when the *Rosewitch* went down?'

'True.' When Mehran spoke again there was an edge of caution behind his words. 'We've had a good record since. She was a good ship — but we learned some lessons.'

'Like going into lease-back and long-term charters.' Laird took a calculated risk. The last thing he wanted was to appear too innocent. 'Now there's the marina. You're spreading your interests.'

'Diversifying,' agreed Mehran. 'These days, anyone who keeps all his eggs in one basket is a fool. You met Ray Garris — he spends a lot of his time making sure we don't make that mistake. We've another director, Erick Roder, who lives in France. He's our European connection.' He shrugged. 'Erick bases himself at St Malo — I saw him today. At the moment, his main job is raising backing for the marina.'

'Who started the idea?' Laird showed his interest.

'That depends on who you ask, or on how well it does once we open.' Mehran laid down his glass. 'Suppose I show you around? We've had Mehrans living here for nine centuries, and according to Diane it's time we did something about the plumbing.'

Either because of the brandy or because he'd accepted Laird, Paul Mehran proved a surprisingly affable guide.

The portraits hanging in the entrance hall were past generation Mehrans in all their particular glories. Some had been soldiers, some had traded abroad. One had been executed in the Tower of London; another, in naval uniform, had been with Nelson's fleet at

Trafalgar. Two obviously twentieth-century works were nearby. One showed two bearded men with the manor house in the background.

'My father and Diane's father,' said Mehran. He turned to the next picture, a young, fair-haired woman seated in a chair, and his voice softened a little. 'My wife. She died a few years after Matt was born. That's when Diane took over.'

He beckoned Laird on, out into the gardens, leading him round the side of the house. There was a walled herb garden, the air filled with its scents. Beyond it was a small orchard and the ruined remains of a medieval dovecote. Walking along, Paul Mehran considered the dovecote cynically.

'When that thing was built, the lord of the manor really mattered. He could hang and flog, imprison — do pretty well what he wanted.' He stuck his hands into the pockets of his navy blue blazer. 'That would have been interesting.'

'Unless you were a peasant,' mused Laird.

'That was what they expected,' said Mehran without a glimmer of humour. 'Now we have to run this place with a handful of people. Some day, when Diane sees sense, we'll knock the place down and build apartment blocks.'

They spent a few more minutes in the gardens, then headed back to the house. As they reached it, Laird noticed a small door set in very old stonework.

'That was once the family crypt.' Mehran led the way over. 'Twelfth century — or that's the story.'

There was no lock on the door. Mehran opened it, and the late evening sunlight poured into a grey, dungeon-like area of stone walls and a low-vaulted ceiling with a central carved pillar. The rusted remains of a motorcycle lay in one corner, cut logs were piled against a wall.

'Seen enough?' Mehran was outwardly patient. 'It's about time we ate.'

They went into the house and through to a wood-panelled dining room on the ground floor. Diane Mehran was already there, seated at a long table and smoking a cigarette. She stubbed it out. Her dress was a flamboyantly styled red and black silk, cut tight around her ample bust and with a long slash of a neckline; her jewellery was a single gold chain around her neck, ending in a blood-red ruby pendant in the deep hollow between her breasts. She wore just enough make-up, and her auburn hair glinted in the last of the sun's rays coming in from the window behind her.

She was still a big woman, but the effect

was dramatic, enough to halt any man in his tracks. More important, Laird sensed that she knew it and liked it.

'Been on the guided tour?' she asked Paul. He nodded.

'Dear God, we're supposed to be nice to him.' She had Laird sit opposite her, then nodded to the maid Laird had noticed earlier. As the maid began serving, she added a warning. 'No shop talk till later.'

It was a good meal, well cooked, the main course a tender saddle of lamb in a herb sauce. Paul Mehran said little, toying with a glass of wine, leaving the conversation to his cousin — and gradually, cleverly, despite what she'd said, Diane Mehran was the one who probed Laird for details around the Clanmore sponsorship story.

It was a strange fencing match for Laird, the overhead lights now on, the two pairs of green Mehran eyes watching him, the ruby pendant glinting distractingly where it lay. He shrugged as another of Diane Mehran's questions went directly back to why he was in Jersey.

'Nobody hands over money on a plate,' he reminded her wryly. 'I go back to London, I make a report, I give an opinion. How much can we get out of it all — media coverage, TV time with our name up front, general impact?

Will Jersey give us value for money?'

'And if we don't measure up?' she asked.

'We look somewhere else.'

The ruby pendant heaved as Diane Mehran took a deep breath. She smiled, but her expression hardened. 'We won't let that happen, Mr Laird. That's a promise.'

They were finishing coffee when Simon Mehran returned. Father and son exchanged a glance, the younger man nodded at an unspoken question, and the earlier tension between them seemed to vanish.

'No loose ends?' asked Paul Mehran.

'The way you wanted.' Simon was confident. 'Clear some space, and I'll get the race plans.'

Within a couple of minutes a chart of the island had been spread on the table. Using a fork as a pointer, Simon sketched the power boat race plan with a brisk confidence. It would include three different class events. It would involve three complete circuits of the island. Witchlove Haven would be race centre and finish point, but the start would be from St Helier to generate maximum visitor interest.

The planning had been thorough. Watching, listening, Laird accepted that much. A buoyed course was marked on the chart. Guard boats, rescue boats, fuel supplied, radio communication had all been scheduled. Timekeepers and marshals, judges and other officials were listed.

One piece of paper gave the kind of start money and prize money envisaged. Laird whistled a soft surprise at the total.

'We're talking international, we want the best.' Simon Mehran frowned at his reaction. 'They come expensive.'

'Simon, I know. But we want to rent these people and their toys, not buy them.' Diane Mehran leaned against Laird, pointing at another item. 'Hospitality — that much? What are we doing? Building a brewery?'

'The boys can go over the figures again when Matt gets back.' Paul Mehran's voice was calm. Once again, that strange glance passed between the man and his son. Then he turned to Laird. 'We've called the winner's trophy the Witchline Cup. Suppose it became the Clanmore Alliance Cup?'

'Once we see your money,' said Simon sardonically. 'In advance. So we know it exists.'

There was a silence. A clock ticking in the background suddenly seemed loud. Then Laird chuckled. 'Good question. I can't give you any kind of answer.' He made a deliberate show of looking at the chart again. 'Will you and your brother be competing?'

'We might.' Simon Mehran's mercurial mood changed again. 'But not with the big boys — not with our boat. At best, we could maybe tail-end in one of the other classes.'

'We might improve on that,' said his father unexpectedly.

'But — ' Simon swallowed.

'I mean a new boat,' agreed his father unemotionally. 'If you've earned it.'

A slow grin spread across Simon Mehran's face. He said nothing, which was an even greater surprise.

* * *

Andrew Laird left about ten-thirty. Diane Mehran walked with him to the bottom of the stone staircase, then stopped beside one of the guardian cannons.

'No problems at the hotel?' she asked.

'None.' He shook his head. 'If I blink, someone jumps.'

'They were told.' She stood in full profile under the glow of the porch lighting, looking out at the night. 'What will you do tomorrow?'

'That depends on London. I'll probably just look around some more.' He had a sudden realisation she wanted to hear something else. 'But I may need some help on

132

details, the kind you could give. Where can I find you?'

'I'll be in our St Helier office for most of the day.' Diane Mehran used a hand to smooth a wrinkle on the skirt of her silk dress. 'I'll expect you — and it's more friendly than Witchlove Haven.' She smiled at him. 'Goodnight, Andrew.'

She turned quickly, went up the stone stairway, and the manor-house door closed. Taking a deep breath, Laird walked over to his Ford. He was glad to get behind the wheel again, glad to set the car moving away from Mehran Gate and the strange, varied tensions that existed inside its walls. A Mehran obviously couldn't be weak and hope to survive.

It was a dark night, very still, and the Ford's lights showed pockets of mist almost as soon as he'd left the manor-house grounds. Remembering the forecast of fog, Laird cursed under his breath and watched his speed. A roadside sign warned of a junction ahead and he eased further back on the accelerator — then, startled, he braked hard as a figure stepped out into the road ahead and waved him down.

It was Jacob West, wearing an old sports jacket, leaning on his stick, some of his white hair escaping from under the hat jammed on

133

his head. As Laird stopped and wound down the window, West came limping over.

'That was a damned fool trick,' snarled Laird. 'What the hell do you think you were doing?'

'Stopping you,' said West mildly.

Laird swallowed. 'It's an easy way to get killed.'

'That's not much thanks for hanging about here, wondering when I'd see your car.' West chuckled, unperturbed. 'Did the Mehrans feed you all right?'

'Well enough.' Laird gave up. 'So you've been waiting. That means you want something?'

'Yes and no.' West gave an irritating shrug. 'I talked things over with Belle. There's someone we think you should meet.'

'You mean now?'

'He's likely to be aboard by now.' The elderly captain saw Laird's bewilderment. 'He lives on a boat. Are you interested — or are you the kind who wants to be tucked up in bed with hot cocoa?'

Laird grinned at the dry insult. 'Does he know I'm coming?'

'If he did, I don't think he'd be there.' West pointed with his stick. 'That's my car.' It was a big, old model Chrysler, parked just off the road. 'Just follow me. I'm no kind of fast driver.'

He hobbled away. Shaking his head, Laird watched as the Chrysler's lights came on. Then, as the car pulled away, he set the Ford moving again and tucked in behind the other vehicle.

The mist thickened and became rolling banks of fog, but Jacob West kept to the same steady pace. He was using short cuts and back roads. Within minutes they were driving into St Helier, cruising through its late-night glitter of lights and neon signs. Music pulsed from nightclubs, wandering groups of locals and visitors clogged the streets, quieter figures waited in shop doorways for trade.

West was heading for the harbour area. Soon the scene had changed and the streets became deserted, dark with shadows. The Chrysler turned left, skirted some dockside sheds, then stopped. Laird halted the Ford behind it, saw Jacob West get out, and did the same as West came over.

'Let me do the talking to start with,' said West.

Laird nodded. 'Who is he?'

'Someone who used to work for Witchline Shipping.'

'You mean here, on Jersey?'

'Until he had an accident,' said West softly. 'He nearly died from blood poisoning.' He looked at Laird. 'That was soon after the

Rosewitch sailed. You might get something out of him, you might not. No guarantees, not the way he is now.'

He beckoned, and Laird followed. They walked a short distance, then reached the drab edge of one of the harbour's smaller basins. The tide was low, salt air battled with the smells of spilled diesel fuel and bottom ooze and lost. The few lights around showed the thin, drifting fog, the silhouette of a dredger, and a scatter of other boats.

All but one was in darkness. She was a large cabin cruiser, berthed against the quay. Chinks of light showed at the edges of her curtained windows, yet she had a strange, neglected air that only a seaman would have sensed. It was something more than the way she lay partly aground, waiting for the tide to free her from the mud under her keel. The name *Emu* was painted on her stern.

'Looks like he's home.' Jacob West gave a satisfied grunt. 'Come on.'

An iron-runged ladder led down to the cabin cruiser. Gripping his stick between his teeth, using his arm and his one good leg, Jacob West clambered down. On the *Emu*'s deck, he waited for Laird.

'I do the talking,' he warned again.

'What's his name?' asked Laird.

'Peter Frere.' In the darkness, West missed

Laird's reaction. He took a few stumping steps along the cabin cruiser's deck, reached a cockpit door which led below, and thumped it with his stick. 'Peter — Jacob West. Open up, I've a visitor for you.'

There was no answer, no sound except the splash of a fish somewhere out in the basin. Peter Frere — the name given by the man who had tried to contact him after that photograph in the newspaper — Laird recovered from his surprise as West thumped on the door a second time, still with no result.

'Damn him, he's usually back by now.' Frowning, West reached for the door's small brass handle. It wasn't locked and he turned the handle, pulling the door open. He looked in, seemed to freeze, then swore in a low, sick way which held no blasphemy. 'Laird, you'd better see what we've got.'

Laird pushed in beside him, saw, and winced. The main saloon cabin below was a brightly lit shambles of overturned fittings, scattered papers, and smashed crockery. In the middle of it all a man lay sprawled, face down and motionless, a dark red pool of blood spreading out around him.

First down into the cabin, kneeling, avoiding the blood, Laird felt for a pulse behind the man's ear. He was dead. Gently, he turned him over as Jacob West arrived. The blood came mainly from a deep, stab-like wound under his ribcage.

'But — ' Jacob West bent over, staring. 'But, hell, man — that's not Frere!'

'No.' Laird drew a deep breath. It was Chris Newgrange. The lanky, fair-haired insurance agent's eyes were wide and staring, his mouth might have been shaping a final puzzled surprise. Using finger and thumb, he closed his eyelids, then lowered Newgrange's body again. 'But I know him. You don't?'

West shook his head almost impatiently, sucking his lips, glancing around.

'He met me when I arrived this morning. His name is Newgrange, he ran a hole-in-the-wall insurance firm.' Ran it with high hopes for tomorrow, except that Newgrange wouldn't have that kind of tomorrow — ever. Laird felt his lips dry, moistened them and looked up at West. 'Frere contacted him, trying to locate me.'

Jacob West was a man trying to grasp what had happened, trying to think; his broad, weatherbeaten face was beginning to regain its colour, his hands clutched his stick for more than support.

'Frere didn't do this.' His voice was hoarse but positive.

Laird shrugged. Newgrange had struggled.

There were deep cuts on his hands, the kind that happened when a man tried to ward off a knife blow; there were other, lesser injuries around his face and head. But all the signs were that he hadn't been dead for long.

'You said Frere would be here.' Laird rose to his feet, facing West. 'So where is he? Why were you so sure?'

'Don't be a damned fool,' said West greyly. 'Peter Frere lives to a pattern. He — ' He stopped, made a sudden low noise deep in his throat and nodded towards a half-open door for'ard. 'We'd better look around.'

They did. The for'ard cabin had two sleeping berths and had been similarly ransacked. It was the same in a tiny cabin aft. Even the cockpit and the cabin cruiser's claustrophobic engine-room space had been searched, lockers emptied, a waste bin's contents dumped and scattered. But that was all: there was no sign of Peter Frere, no hint of what, if anything, had happened to him.

Back in the main cabin, Jacob West prowled around again, avoiding Newgrange's body, peering, muttering. He used the tip of his stick to stir the remains of a broken gin bottle lying in one corner. There were other bottles, some empty, others still unopened. At last, he straightened. 'This Newgrange, did you know him well?'

Laird shook his head. 'I only met Chris Newgrange today. He seemed friendly — and harmless.'

'He'll have family somewhere.' Jacob West's eyes were bleak. 'Do you want to be involved in this?'

'What do we do?' asked Laird sarcastically. 'Walk away?'

'You can — you should. I'll stay.' West leaned on his stick again, his face empty of emotion. 'Anything you've seen, I've seen. You haven't touched anything aboard — I watched.' He paused. 'You came here to do a job. Will it help to have this hanging round your neck?'

'Maybe not.' Laird hesitated, recognising the harsh logic behind the white-haired man's words.

'Humour me,' said West softly. 'Go up on the quay. Tell me if you see anyone — any sign of life.'

He found himself obeying without being certain why. Leaving the cabin cruiser, he climbed the iron ladder again. The fog was thickening. Standing on the quay, he could hardly see where they'd left their cars. There was no movement, no sound except the lapping of water. When he climbed back down, Jacob West was waiting for him in the *Emu*'s cockpit.

140

'Well?' asked West.

Laird shook his head.

'Good.' West gave a grunt to himself. 'Straight question. Do you trust me?'

'Johnny Lewnan reckoned I could.' Laird looked at the older man in the darkness. 'He didn't see you with Garris this afternoon.'

'That?' West sighed. 'I came here to talk with Frere. He wasn't around. He sometimes wanders over to the yacht basin.' His mouth tightened. 'I know Garris. What did you expect me to do, boy? Spit in his eye?'

Laird shrugged. 'Then tell me about Frere.'

'Some of it.' West looked deliberately at the luminous dial of his wristwatch. 'We can't waste time. But Peter Frere didn't do any of this. Since his accident, he's been someone to pity — frail, a nervous wreck. You don't think he owns this boat, do you? He's the caretaker. I got him the job, and he's proud of it.' He nodded down towards the cabin. 'Would he rampage around like that? Would Newgrange?'

'Then what's your version?' challenged Laird.

'I said Peter Frere lives to a pattern. Most nights he goes ashore to one of the bars around the harbour. Usually he can just manage the price of a drink — '

'It doesn't look that way.' Laird remembered the bottles in the cabin.

West shrugged. 'I know. That can wait. But here's my alternative. Somebody — probably more than one of them — came here knowing Frere was ashore. They were looking for something. Whatever the reason, Newgrange walked in on them.'

'And Frere?'

'I don't know. Either he came along in time to see it happen, or he arrived later and was terrified . . . He'd run. He'd hide.' West paused grimly. 'That's presuming he's still alive. If he is, then the quicker he's found, the better — for his own sake.'

Another fish, larger than the first, was jumping and splashing in the basin. Most likely it was trying to find a way out again. Laird half heard it, his mind spinning.

'That's all?' he asked sarcastically.

'No.' Earnestly, West came nearer. 'But make it do for tonight. I'm asking you to trust me. I'm asking you to keep your cover with the Mehrans — and maybe you'd be doing it for Chris Newgrange. Laird, what happened when the *Rosewitch* went down, I don't know. But you've walked into something else that has a Mehran smell.' He drew a deep breath. 'So — yes or no?'

'All right.' Laird gave a slow, reluctant nod. 'There's a girl, Newgrange's assistant. She knows Peter Frere was trying to contact me.'

142

'That doesn't matter. The police will get round to you some time tomorrow, I expect. But tonight didn't happen. Drive back to your hotel, complain about the fog on the roads when you arrive, act shocked tomorrow when you hear the news.'

'What about you?' Laird frowned. 'You'll call the police?'

West nodded. 'There's a public telephone over at the sheds.'

'When they come — '

'I can cope,' murmured West. An odd wisp of a smile touched his lips and he reached into his jacket pocket. When he brought out his hand, a small round lapel badge nestled in the palm. 'They'll probably know me, anyway.'

Laird stared at the badge. In the middle were the enamelled arms of the State of Jersey. Round the edge were the words 'Police Honorifique'.

'What the hell — ' he began.

'We've paid police on Jersey, and we've honorary police — elected parish amateurs.' Jacob West shrugged. 'I'll cope. I'm a dam' constable's officer. Now move, will you?'

'And tomorrow?' asked Laird.

'Tomorrow is tomorrow.' Jacob West laid a hand on his arm. 'Don't come out to Merfleur or try to contact me. Go and see Kiri at the airport — and go carefully, boy.'

143

4

Thick banks of yellow-grey sea fog straddled most of the east coast road. Any traffic moved at a crawl, and Andrew Laird was glad to reach the Leecom Hotel and leave the Ford. When he went into the hotel's brightly lit lobby, it was almost deserted, but the middle-aged night manager saw him and came over from the reception desk.

'Enjoy your evening, Mr Laird? He grimaced at the fog smoking outside the windows. 'At least you made it back.'

Laird nodded. He had his piece of necessary play-acting to carry out. 'I got lost a couple of times. It can't get much worse.'

'I wouldn't bet on it. We've had a couple of guests 'phone in that they're stranded.' The night manager turned to get Laird's room key.

'Any messages for me?' asked Laird as casually as he could.

The night manager glanced at a board and shook his head.

Thanking him, Laird went up to his room. When he got there, he poured himself a large whisky from the drinks trolley, took a swallow, then carried the glass over to a chair and flopped down.

No messages. That finished a slim hope that Peter Frere might have tried to contact him. The rest was a nightmare. If he closed his eyes, he could see Chris Newgrange lying dead in the *Emu*'s cabin. The young, fair-haired insurance agent, so crestfallen about Frere when Laird had last seen him alive, must have had a reason for going to the *Emu* — maybe because he'd heard from Frere again. But what had happened? Why had the cabin cruiser been ransacked?

Then there were the Mehrans, there was Jacob West's attitude to it all, his casual showing of that honorary police badge — however much or however little it meant. Laird took another swallow of whisky, his thoughts in confusion. But what about Jacob West? What had he been doing earlier?

Should he have left the *Emu* the way West wanted? He sighed to himself, having to admit that it made sense. Or looked that way . . .

He finished the whisky, poured another, and took it over to the balcony. Opening the window, he stepped out into the swirling damp. He could see nothing, but he could hear the faint high-pitched bray of a distant foghorn. Somehow it reminded him of the

145

way Chris Newgrange had often laughed. He stood tight-lipped for a few moments, then swore viciously and went back inside.

★ ★ ★

It was a long, troubled time before he slept that night. When he woke it was daylight, but the fog was still thick outside, and he lay on the bed getting used to the fact that what had happened wasn't a nightmare but real. The time was close on 8 a.m. Getting up, he padded naked through to the little bathroom, looked at his red-eyed face in a mirror, then showered and shaved. When he returned, he hesitated, then dressed in the few casual clothes he'd brought. That meant a blue shirt, fawn trousers, a pair of scuffed lightweight moccasins and a loose cotton jacket.

He was pulling on the jacket when the telephone rang. Frowning, thinking of the concealed bug in the wall beneath it, he went over and answered.

Then his hand tightened on the receiver as he heard Diane Mehran's voice.

'Have you heard, Andrew?' she asked without preliminaries.

'Heard what?' He managed to sound almost cheerful.

'Chris Newgrange is dead.' He heard a

sound like a sigh. 'I'm sorry. It was on local radio this morning — there's no mistake. I checked with Radio Jersey before I called you.'

'Dead?' He was play-acting again, hating it. 'How? What happened?'

'I don't know.' If Diane Mehran was acting, she was doing it well. Her normally brisk, businesslike telephone manner was muted, even sounded shaken. 'The radio report said he was found dead at St Helier harbour. The police say he was murdered.'

Laird didn't know how to answer. She misunderstood his silence.

'It's true, Andrew. He'd been stabbed. It was something to do with him trying to stop a robbery. I felt I had to call you.'

'Thank you.' He said it with an effort.

'He grew up with Simon and Matt.' She spoke gently. 'It's hard to believe. I'll let you know if I hear anything else.'

She said goodbye and hung up. Slowly, carefully, Laird replaced his receiver. The fog was still thick outside his window, but brighter, as if the sun was making a try at breaking through. For the moment, until he went to see Kiri Vass at the airport, there was nothing he could do about anything.

Other people had heard the news item. It showed on the faces of the hotel staff when he went down to go through the motions of having breakfast.

'Mr Laird.' Jo, the brunette receptionist, left her desk and came over anxiously. 'There was something on the radio this morning — '

'Diane Mehran 'phoned about it.' He gave her a dried wisp of a smile. 'But thanks.'

Nodding, she hesitated. 'I saw him with you when you arrived yesterday. He seemed — well, nice.'

It was a reasonable word. Laird watched her retreat towards the desk, then he went into the Leecom's restaurant. It was busy, but a waiter steered him to a table in a corner. The way he hovered sympathetically, he seemed to know, too. Laird ordered coffee, orange juice and toast and shook his head at anything more.

He had sipped some of his orange juice and was on his second cup of coffee when he saw Jo weaving through the tables towards him.

'The police are here,' she said quietly. 'They'd like to talk to you. I've put them in the cocktail bar. It's empty.'

Laird abandoned the coffee and followed her out. She left him at the door to the cocktail bar. It smelled of stale smoke and beer, it hadn't been cleaned from the previous night, and two figures were waiting at the bar counter. One was a policewoman in uniform, a stockily built blonde. The other, a thin, balding man in a brown suit, had a horselike face and a small moustache. He left the policewoman and came over.

'Mr Laird, I'm Detective Sergeant Moisan, State Police.' He paused, sucking his lips. 'I — ah — '

'I've heard,' said Laird simply. 'Someone telephoned.'

'I see.' Moisan looked relieved. 'So I don't have to do that part. Can I ask who told you?'

'Diane Mehran of Mehran Holdings. I'm having business discussions with them.'

'We know about that.' Moisan nodded. He had the appearance of a man who hadn't had much sleep. He certainly needed a shave. 'Suppose we sit down?'

They went over to a table. Laird took one of the chairs, the detective sat opposite. The policewoman joined them but Moisan ignored her.

'How well did you know Newgrange?' he asked.

Laird shrugged. 'I only met him yesterday, when I arrived.' Out of the corner of his eye he saw the policewoman had a notebook and was writing. 'He handles some insurance for my firm.'

'Handled,' corrected Moisan bleakly. 'We've

149

talked with the girl who worked for him, Liz — ah — '

'Hatton,' prompted the policewoman.

Moisan gave her a sideways glare. 'Liz Hatton. The girl says you went to their office yesterday afternoon.'

Laird nodded.

'Newgrange told you a man called Peter Frere wanted to contact you. Is it correct he didn't have any way of getting back to Frere, but he'd told Frere you were at this hotel?'

'That's what he said.'

'Had you any reason to doubt him?' asked Moisan unexpectedly.

'No.' Laird didn't hide his surprise. 'I thought Frere might telephone me here, but — '

'He didn't. We checked when we arrived.' The horse-face opposite didn't alter expression. 'This is genuine routine, Mr Laird, checking what the girl told us, mopping up. Do you know Frere? Have you ever met him?' He took Laird's headshake as an answer. 'Did you talk with young Newgrange again?'

'No.' Laird drew a deep breath. He wondered how the man would have reacted to the truth. 'Sergeant, I'd like — '

'Almost finished, Mr Laird.' Moisan stopped him. 'Where were you last night?'

'With the Mehran family at their home,

Mehran Gate. Until about ten-thirty.'

'A hell of a night for driving back here.' Moisan grimaced. 'It was bad enough getting out from St Helier this morning.' He scraped a thumb across the dark stubble on his chin. 'Ten-thirty — they'd confirm it, I suppose?'

'I suppose.'

'Have you any idea why Frere wanted to contact you — any idea at all, apart from that newspaper photograph?'

'No.' Laird saw the man's faint shrug towards the policewoman, the way he visibly relaxed.

'Our police surgeon says time of death was about nine-thirty, not much later.' Moisan lowered his voice a little. 'He was stabbed on the boat where Frere was living. Obviously we want to locate Frere. We can't.'

'What about Chris? Who found him?'

'One of our honorary police.' Moisan's disgust wasn't hidden. 'You're from the mainland, Mr Laird. You don't know about them.'

'He's lucky,' murmured the policewoman. She had stopped writing.

'We've two police forces, Mr Laird.' Moisan ignored the interruption. He tapped his chest. 'I'm paid police — that's our local label, we do the job pretty much like anywhere else. But the honorary police are elected like village councillors — at times they're as big a dam' nuisance. They were the real law on Jersey until not so long ago, they still stick their noses in every chance they get, we can't afford to stand on their toes.' He growled under his breath. 'Anyway, one of them knows Frere, got him fixed up on this boat, looks in on him every now and again. He did, at around eleven last night, and found Newgrange. We don't know why Newgrange was there, or whether Frere contacted him again. But it looks as though Newgrange walked in on trouble of some kind, maybe found Frere having some kind of a fit. When we get Frere — ' He shrugged and left it there.

'What about next of kin?' asked Laird. He rubbed a hand across the table and met a sticky beer stain. 'If there's any way Clanmore Alliance can help them, we will.'

'His father retired from business a few years back. He and Newgrange's mother left the island and settled in the United States — somewhere in Florida. They've family there.' Moisan scowled. 'They're being contacted. We didn't want Newgrange's name to get out before they'd been told, but since when did the media give a damn about that kind of thing?'

'But if we can help — ' repeated Laird.

'I'll pass the word.' Moisan hauled himself to his feet. Quietly the policewoman did the same. 'One thing, Mr Laird. We'll need you to sign a formal statement. Could you look in on us at St Helier, some time this afternoon?'

Laird nodded.

'Good.' Moisan made a friendlier noise. 'Newgrange had no close relatives left on the island and he lived alone — which doesn't help. I'm going back to have another talk with that girl Liz, to see if I can jog anything else out of her memory.'

'She's scared stiff already,' murmured the policewoman.

'Of me?' Moisan made a protesting noise. 'Hell, I'm the fatherly type.' He turned back to Laird. 'Thanks for your time.'

Moisan left, the policewoman followed him. As they vanished, Laird sat back with his eyes half-closed. The policeman had asked the normal questions, had received the answers he'd expected. But that was almost incidental. Chris Newgrange had been murdered around nine-thirty. By that time, Simon Mehran had certainly been back at Mehran Gate. That didn't remove any Mehran involvement; if anything it complicated things even more — and Peter Frere was still missing.

He heard soft footsteps, caught a light whiff

153

of perfume, and looked up. It was Jo from the reception desk; she had an oddly anxious expression on her face.

'You've another visitor.' Jo's eyes showed she wasn't pleased. 'When she heard the police were here, she took the passkey and said she'd wait in your room.' She shrugged. 'I couldn't exactly stop her.'

'Her?' Laird raised an eyebrow.

'Diane Mehran.'

Laird grimaced. For a totally irrelevant moment he remembered Jo in the pool and the mole above her breast and his expression softened.

'What do you want me to do?' he asked mildly. 'Throw her out?'

Jo snorted and flounced off. Sighing, Laird hauled himself out of the chair and headed for the lift. When he reached his room, the door was ajar. Going in, he found Diane Mehran standing at the balcony window, looking out at the thinning fog. She turned, a lighted cigarette in one hand.

'They've gone?' she asked.

'The police?' He nodded. 'It was routine. How long had I known Chris, when did we talk last?'

'That's what I expected. But I decided I had to come over.' Diane Mehran was in a tailored blue two-piece, a frilled edge of blue

154

blouse showing around the collar. She gave a vague gesture with the cigarette. 'What are you going to do?'

'Tell my London office. Then it will depend on how they feel.' Laird shrugged. 'They may say I should leave things for a few days.'

'But after that, life goes on?' Diane Mehran gave a small, humourless laugh, a strange sound from a woman her size. She came nearer. 'What did the police say about it?'

He shrugged. 'They're looking for a man called Peter Frere. He's missing. Chris Newgrange was killed on the boat where Frere was caretaker.'

'That's the gossip in St Helier.' Her green eyes seemed puzzled. 'I know Frere, he used to work for us. But why would Chris be involved with him?'

'You mean be there?' If the Mehran family's connections were as good as Laird thought, there was no sense in being too vague. 'Frere had been trying to contact me through Chris. We don't know why.'

'You don't know him?'

Laird shook his head.

'It just doesn't make sense.' She took a deep breath, the kind that strained the tailored blue jacket. 'Not with Peter Frere. He had a lot of domestic bad luck, then he became ill after an accident — '

155

'At work?'

'No. But he was ill for a long time. He couldn't hold any kind of job afterwards.' Diane Mehran pursed her lips. 'But there was some talk of a robbery. What was that about?'

'I wasn't told much, just that Frere had vanished.'

'Then when did it happen?'

'About nine-thirty last night.'

'I see.' An odd expression, one that could almost have been relief, showed in her face then vanished. Suddenly she stubbed her cigarette in an ashtray. 'I'll have to go. You'll still look in later?'

'This afternoon,' promised Laird. 'Once I've signed a formal statement for the police.'

'Andrew.' She came over and the high-heeled fashion shoes she was wearing brought their eyelines level. 'Maybe you should be careful what you do until Frere is found.'

He nodded. 'I've thought of that.'

'It makes sense.' She reached out as if to touch his arm, but didn't.

Instead Diane Mehran crossed to the door. She looked back as she left and gave a faint smile. Then the door closed firmly behind her, leaving Laird with a strong feeling that Diane Mehran had had more than one reason for coming.

The fog outside was now in definite retreat.

The sun was beginning to break through, the foreshore between the hotel and the sea was becoming a misted outline. Glancing at his watch, Laird knew Osgood Morris would be at his desk and would have dealt with the morning's mail.

Going over to the telephone, Laird punched for an outside line, then dialled Clanmore Alliance's London number. A few seconds later he was speaking to Morris, stopping the marine claims manager's opening greeting.

'We've a problem,' said Laird. 'One you'd better know about.' He paused. 'I'm still at my hotel.'

'At your hotel.' Morris's reedy voice showed he understood the warning. 'I see. What kind of — ah — problem? I thought the Mehran directors — '

'It's something else.' Laird chose every word carefully. 'I've just had the police round. Chris Newgrange was killed last night.'

'Killed?' Morris squeaked his surprise. 'What happened?'

'He was stabbed,' said Laird bluntly.

'You mean murder?' Morris was shocked.

'Yes. The police can't come up with any kind of motive, but a local oddity has vanished from the scene.' It was harsh, it was for the telephone bug's benefit. 'His name is

Peter Frere. He had been trying to contact me for some reason.'

'That's unfortunate — all of it.' Morris spoke slowly, obviously playing the same game of words. 'Are the police friendly?'

'Yes.'

'Obviously we have to be concerned for your safety.' He heard a sigh, then what followed was pure Osgood Morris. 'Then, from the company viewpoint, this could mean unpleasant publicity. Will this be a setback to our — ah — project survey?'

'It might. I don't think so,' said Laird neutrally. 'I'm still talking with Mehran Holdings.'

'We'll have to show sensitivity,' said Morris. 'You know we're anxious to have the matter completed. But — ah — if necessary, as a mark of respect — '

'I'll go along with what seems best.'

'Exactly.' Morris paused. 'Yes, use your own judgement. Offer Clanmore's sympathy wherever it should go. Show we care — but let me know what develops.'

'When it does,' agreed Laird.

He said goodbye and hung up. He'd done what would have been expected. He'd also managed to give Osgood Morris enough for the moment. Morris would tell Tony Dello, Dello would tell his ex-wife. They were two more people who would be touched by what had happened.

He took another glance out of the balcony window. The fog was down to a few clinging ribbons of mist and still fading. The next thing was to get out to St Peter airport and see Kiri Vass. Whatever she had to say, whatever message she had from Jacob West, it would have to be convincing. He had been on Jersey for just over twenty-four hours and already things had become a horrifying mess.

* * *

A night in the open, shrouded in sea fog, had left the white Ford covered in condensation. The damp engine coughed and spluttered as Laird drove away from the hotel, but the road was clear and traffic was back to normal. Then, as the engine warmed, the car resumed its usual throaty purr.

Maybe that was why he had driven about three miles before he became aware of the other white Ford travelling behind him, tucked in two vehicles back and keeping that distance whatever happened. Frowning, wanting to check his suspicions, Laird overtook a small convoy of cars in a single burst of acceleration, then watched his rear-view mirror. Seconds passed, then the other white Ford was there, two vehicles back, as before.

So he was being tailed. He cursed under his breath, watching the road, continuing to check his rear-view mirror. Suddenly the car behind him turned off down a farm lane. Only one car, a large Mercedes, separated him from his shadow and he caught a clear glimpse of the other Ford's driver. It was Jody, the burly explosives man from Witchlove Haven, and he was already trying to drop back again, being balked by a farm truck immediately behind him.

Something had to be done about Jody. Laird saw an innocent tour coach travelling ahead of their little procession, chuckled, then gradually eased back on his accelerator until the Mercedes car was close behind him.

It came down to timing. Suddenly Laird swung his Ford out as if to overtake the coach. Seconds later, giving all the appearance of changing his mind, he moved back in again — then hammered the brake pedal. Rubber squealed. The Mercedes, forced into an emergency stop, seemed to fill his rear-view mirror — but Laird was already accelerating again, pulling away. He heard a crash, the sound of rending metal, then a second bang. But he was intact.

The rear-view mirror showed he could

forget about Jody. The other white Ford had slammed into the back of the Mercedes, then had been rammed in the rear by the farm truck. The last thing he saw was the Mercedes driver out of his car and shaking his fist.

Fifteen untroubled minutes later Laird had parked at the airport. Going into the terminal building, he went to the nearest airline counter and asked for directions. They sent him along a small maze of narrow corridors. The roar of a jet taking off made glass rattle as he reached the charter airlines' administration section, where he asked again, and moments later he was shown into Kiri Vass's office. It was a modest cubicle of a room and sparsely furnished. Kiri sat behind a desk, wearing the dark grey airline uniform he'd seen before.

Jacob West was sprawled back in a chair beside a window which overlooked the main runway.

'Hello, Andrew,' said Kiri quietly, her tanned face expressionless. 'We wondered when you'd arrive.'

'But we knew he would, didn't we?' said West gruffly. He pushed himself up from the chair, ignoring his stick, and hobbled over. 'Everything all right, boy?'

'Couldn't be better,' said Laird with acid sarcasm. 'What did you expect?'

161

The bulky, white-haired figure blinked and frowned. 'I hoped you wouldn't feel that way.'

'Anyone normal would,' said Kiri Vass grimly. 'What did you expect, Jacob?' A rounded sea pebble, pure white in colour but with a thin veining of green, sat on her desk as a paperweight. She fingered it for a moment then looked up. 'Andrew, I'm sorry about Chris Newgrange. Really sorry.'

'Does anyone think I'm not?' exploded West in a hoarse, loud voice. 'Damn it, girl — '

'Keep your voice down,' she told him wearily. 'You're not on a ship, these walls are like paper when someone like you starts bellowing.'

Scowling, West muttered to himself then surrendered. Still standing, he supported himself against a filing cabinet.

'I'm sorry too. Everybody's sorry.' He shrugged. 'Kiri knows about last night — all of it. So does Belle.'

'Probably more than I do.' Laird settled into another chair placed waiting for him. 'One of Simon Mehran's people tried to follow me this morning.'

West's eyebrows rose. 'Tried?'

'I lost him.'

'That's why I wanted you here, not at Merfleur. I don't want you connected with us — not just yet.' West moistened his lips hopefully. 'I could use a beer, Kiri — but I'd settle for a cup of coffee.'

She nodded, still fingering the green-veined pebble, still looking at Laird. Then she opened one of the desk drawers and took out a vacuum flask and some white plastic cups. Silently, she poured coffee into three of the cups. One went to West, who grunted his thanks and went back to his chair by the window. Kiri pushed the second across to Laird. Another aircraft was taking off outside and she waited until the thunder of its jets faded.

'We've talked, Andrew,' she said quietly. 'Jacob, Belle, myself. We've agreed you've got to know our side of things, all of it.' Her dark eyes challenged him. 'But you'll have to do the same. Maybe Chris Newgrange died because of us, maybe he died because of you. Until Peter Frere turns up somewhere — '

'Turns up alive somewhere,' growled Jacob West. 'That's what you mean, girl.'

'Jacob, please.' She winced at the interruption, her attention still with Laird. 'Have the police contacted you?'

'They came to the hotel this morning.' Laird sipped his coffee, looking at her over the edge of the plastic cup. 'They said Chris was killed around nine-thirty last night.'

'Jacob saw the preliminary report this morning.'

Laird turned and frowned. For the first time he noticed that Jacob West was wearing the Police Honorifique badge in his jacket lapel.

'You can do that?'

West nodded.

'What else have they got?'

'Not a lot. Peter Frere was drinking in one of the harbour bars until about nine.' West scowled, shifting his bulk. 'Drinking with his own money. Then he left. What Newgrange was doing is a blank.'

'So where were you around nine-thirty?' asked Laird bluntly.

'Me?' The retired captain's anger flared, and he started to rise from his chair. Then, just as suddenly, he subsided again and gave a short, humourless laugh. 'All right, that's fair. I was on my way from Merfleur to Mehran Gate. By car, alone. I could have made a detour by the harbour, but I didn't. Now call me a liar.'

'And I was here until ten, working — with witnesses,' said Kiri Vass. She gave a small, tight grimace at Laird's reaction. 'That's before you ask. You should, Andrew — I've my own share in this.'

'Which we're going to tell you about,' said

164

Jacob West heavily. 'After you answer this, boy. Can your Clanmore people prove that Witchline Shipping faked the *Rosewitch* sinking — prove it beyond doubt?'

'No.' Reluctantly, Laird shook his head. 'Not the way a court would want, not yet. But some of the cargo was landed.'

'Careless,' murmured Jacob West. 'Very careless. But maybe Peter Frere could help you there — if you got him talking sense and found someone who'd believe him.' Taking out a handkerchief, he made a noisy, time-wasting business of blowing his nose. Then he looked at Kiri. 'Our turn?'

'Yes.' She rose.

A small metal safe stood to one side of her desk. She bent, spun the dials of the combination lock, then opened the safe. Reaching behind some bundles of tickets and papers, she brought out a tiny cardboard box. Laying it on the desk, she beckoned Laird over. As he joined her, she removed the lid. A strange, black lump lay inside, resting on a scrap of dress material. It was roughly the size and shape of a tennis ball. The sunlight from the window glinted on the edge of gold coin projecting from the top.

'This is how we found some of them.' Kiri's voice was level. 'But they're not all that way.' She flicked back a fold of the dress material.

'Most are like this.'

Laird stared at a gleaming gold coin, still clearly stamped with the head of a long-dead king. Sometime, somewhere, maybe in a museum, he'd seen coins like it before. He looked up, saw Kiri and West were waiting, and moistened his suddenly dry lips.

'French?' he asked.

'A double Louis d'Or — Louis the Sixteenth,' nodded Kiri. 'Minted 1778.'

Laird touched the rough, black lump beside it, feeling the edge of gold coin which showed. The black, lava-like substance was called concretion. Part of the strange, underwater chemistry of the sea, it happened erratically on anything man-made which was left submerged. In time, it became like tough, protective scar tissue round an item — yet sometimes something else lying next to it could be unaffected.

'Louis the Sixteenth got chopped in the French Revolution,' said Jacob West helpfully. He grinned. 'Don't stand with your mouth hanging open, boy — anything could fly in. But we've collected a few more like these, not counting silver coins. So far we're just scratching around. There are plenty more waiting for us.'

'That's true, Andrew.' Kiri's mouth shaped a slight, partially sad smile but her tanned,

166

fine-boned face stayed calm. 'We found ourselves a treasure wreck.'

'Correction. Kiri did — Kiri with her father's help,' said West. He scooped up a folder lying beside him and tossed it on the desk. 'You can have a look at these. One of them was in the envelope you brought over from Johnny Lewnan — he has the contacts. He has been handling a few things for us.'

Laird opened the folder and fingered its thin bundle of papers. His mouth felt dry. Some of the papers had embossed seals and sprawling signatures, some were typewritten, others were photocopies of old documents.

'She was the French eighteen-gun brig *Vanneau*. She vanished in a gale back in 1779,' said West almost dreamily. 'What you brought us confirms we've an exclusive five-year salvage licence from the French Ministry of Marine — as far as they're concerned, they still own her. Then we've a non-exclusive clearance from the Board of Trade in London, though we didn't tell them much. We've even written to the US Navy Department — that was Kiri's idea, to keep everything legal. Well, nearly everything.'

'We haven't registered with the Receiver of Wrecks for Jersey,' said Kiri Vass wryly. 'That's basic, that could still be trouble.'

'We'll tell them when we're ready,' West

scowled. 'Not before. We'd have officials swooping in like vultures, we'd have tax men, we'd be fighting off thieving hordes — '

'You'd rather wait until you've cleared out anything that matters,' said Laird stonily. Too many questions were crowding in to take them in any kind of order. 'How do you know she's the *Vanneau*?'

'Her ship's bell, some engraved plate we found, some help from Johnny Lewnan in matching up old records,' said West. He winked. 'When Johnny sent that envelope over with you it also meant you could be trusted.'

'It's nice to know,' said Laird sarcastically. He looked at them both. 'What's the rest of it? What does an eighteenth-century French brig have to do with the US Navy?'

'Not a lot, if we're careful,' said West hopefully. 'You explain it, Kiri. You're better with words.'

'Am I?' She saw Laird was waiting patiently and sighed. 'All right. We know from French records that two brigs sailed from the port of Brest — more or less straight into a gale. They vanished.' She shrugged. 'They must have been blown wildly off course. Probably the *Vanneau* found herself off Jersey and tried to make for Cherbourg or St Malo. Can you remember your history, Andrew?'

168

'You tell me,' he invited.

'The American War of Independence was in full swing, the French loved anyone who was fighting England. You had John Paul Jones and his *Ranger* flying the American flag and creating havoc around the British coast.' Kiri paused, looking down briefly at the gold coin. 'So the French decided to send two shiploads of help across the Atlantic to America. They were carrying muskets, guns, gunpowder, gold, silver — '

'How much gold and silver?'

'At today's values, several million French francs.' The noise of an incoming jet began to challenge her voice. 'Everything was a gift to the Americans. They just — well — didn't get it. They more or less agree they've no claim.'

'That's how it is.' Jacob West slapped a fist hard on his good knee. 'We've got what's left of the *Vanneau* damned nearly in our backyard at Merfleur — ' The rest of what he said was drowned under a roar as a big Swissair passenger jet touched down and swept past outside.

As the thunder faded, the telephone on Kiri Vass's desk began trilling. She answered it, listened for a moment, murmured a reply, then hung up.

'Work.' She grimaced an apology at Laird. 'I'll be right back.'

Laird watched her go, the grey uniform skirt flicking briskly as she walked. The door closed behind her and he turned to Jacob West. The retired master mariner was sitting back, hands clasped over his bulging waistline, his broad face empty of expression, obviously content to wait, showing no curiosity as Laird went over to the window.

The Swissair jet, touchdown completed, was taxi-ing round towards the terminal. A single-engined light aircraft had taken off and was buzzing skyward. An almost ungovernable disbelief in it all came over Laird like a wave. Out there, the big jet with its red and white Swiss emblem represented the most advanced twentieth-century technology. Yet here they were, talking more or less rationally about old wooden sailing ships and sunken treasure. There was that ugly chunk of undersea clinker, that gold coin, those documents, the indisputable fact that there were more known wrecks around the British coastline than anywhere else in the world.

Something else was indisputable. Chris Newgrange was dead.

'Captain West.' The deliberate formality Laird put behind the words made Jacob West straighten. 'When did you find the *Vanneau*?'

'Months ago.' Jacob West scratched his chin. 'A few weeks after Kiri arrived.'

'How many people know about her?'

'Here? On Jersey?' West frowned. 'There's me and Belle, Kiri of course. We've needed some help. There are others, no more than a handful — I know them, I'd trust them no matter what.'

'What about Peter Frere?' snapped Laird.

'Add him.' West sucked his lips and gave a reluctant nod. 'That just happened. He wanders over to Merfleur now and again, and Belle feeds him. He turned up one Sunday and saw what was going on.' He scowled. 'But he's a man left with a child's mind. We swore him to secrecy, he promised to keep his mouth shut.'

'A child likes souvenirs,' said Laird quietly. 'Nice, bright souvenirs. Could he have taken some?'

'Maybe.' West shifted uncomfortably.

'Suppose he found he could sell the souvenirs, or trade them?'

'For liquor? Do you think I haven't thought of that?' asked West bitterly. 'You saw the way the *Emu*'s cabin was turned over — '

'Frere is missing, or on the run. The police are investigating a murder.' Laird's voice sounded like a whipcrack in the little office. 'Did you tell the police any of this?'

'No, I damned well didn't — not last night!' West bellowed his anger, then, just as

171

quickly, lowered his voice. 'I had to think, boy.'

'Think how to protect your investment?'

West flushed red. 'All right, there was that. But how damned cold-blooded do you think I am? Whoever killed Newgrange, there's an equal chance you should blame your hell-sent *Rosewitch*. Have you told that to the police?' He didn't wait for an answer. 'I'd say Frere has something about the *Rosewitch* locked away in his disaster area of a mind, locked away struggling to get out. Otherwise why did he try to get hold of you?'

It was Laird's turn to hesitate, to feel uncertain. He pursed his lips.

'You've got your own running quarrel with the Mehrans. You've never told me why.'

West growled. 'Simple. Before they bought Grunt Cove and turned it into Witchlove Haven they tried to get Merfleur Point. They tried every dirty trick in the book against me, from lawyers to threats and worse.' He paused. 'I had another dog then. You understand? But there was never any proof. I just stuck it out.'

Laird closed his eyes for a moment, then nodded. 'It helps to know.'

'True.' Jacob West nodded grimly and hauled himself out of his chair again. Hobbling over, he stopped when they were face to face. Then he surprised Laird with a grim smile. 'I'll give you this, boy — you speak your mind. It happens I had someone contact the State Attorney-General's office this morning. Your name wasn't mentioned, nor was mine. But there's a heavy hint being dropped to the paid police that Peter Frere may have had something valuable on that boat — and there will be more information to follow that, if necessary.'

'He means it,' said a voice behind them. Kiri Vass had returned. Laird had no way of knowing how long she had been in the room. 'Another thing Jacob hasn't mentioned is that he was out most of last night, looking for Frere.'

Jacob West cleared his throat, embarrassed. 'Just looking, that's all.'

'I'm sorry.' Laird cursed himself.

'Don't spoil it,' said West mildly. 'We're tied together.'

'Could the Mehrans have picked up a whisper about Frere?'

'Frere and gold coins?' West scowled. 'It's possible, as possible as anything else.' He paused. 'Kiri and I had the notion we'd take you out to see the *Vanneau*. The tide should be right when we get there.'

'You do it, Jacob. I can't.' Kiri Vass shook her raven-black hair. 'That 'phone call was about two extra charter flights coming in. I'll have to be here.'

'Our loss.' West gave a dry, sideways glance at Laird. 'He'll just have to make do with me. We'll take my car, he can collect his wheels later.' He went back to pick up his stick. 'Ready, boy? Don't worry, you won't even get your feet wet.'

'Yes.' Laird hung back as Jacob West limped towards the door. 'Kiri, when do you finish here?'

'When it happens.' Her dark eyes looked at him and thawed. 'But I'll be out at Merfleur this evening.'

He nodded, and left before West could grumble again.

★   ★   ★

They travelled in Jacob West's old Chrysler. The upholstery was covered in dog hairs, a half-eaten chocolate bar was stuffed in the ashtray, and the engine sounded rough. But West drove it happily, with little respect for anything else on the road.

They were on the east coast road again, well away from the airport and St Helier, before Laird asked about one of the many things still puzzling him.

'You said Kiri and her father get the credit

174

for finding the *Vanneau*. How?'

'That?' Jacob West removed one massive paw from the Chrysler's wheel and squashed a fly crawling inside the windshield glass. 'He's a geologist — a rock freak, right? Send him a parcel of old stones, and he thinks it's his birthday. You saw that pebble Kiri uses as a paperweight, the white thing — '

'With the green veins.' Laird nodded.

'Kiri picked up some of them on the shore at Merfleur, thought they looked pretty — her word — and sent them off to Daddy.' Jacob West grinned, letting the car wander in a way that made a cyclist swerve for safety. 'Daddy writes back saying what the hell is she playing at, that there's no way pebbles like that belong to Jersey. He likes the joke, but they're from somewhere around the Indian Ocean. You see it?'

'No,' said Laird bluntly.

'Mister, be glad you never served on a ship of mine,' sighed West. 'Look, what did plenty of the old sailing ships use for ballast? Stones, shingle — hell, plenty of builders still talk about ballast when they add gravel to concrete. So you find a lot of pebbles on a beach where they've no right to be — now do you understand? It means a ship had sunk near where Kiri found her funny pebbles, an old-time ship, a ship that might have sailed the Indian Ocean at some time. That could happen easily enough, if she needed repairs, if she took on fresh ballast afterwards — '

'So you went looking,' said Laird with genuine respect.

'We went looking, we found her.' Jacob West blasted his horn and waved a greeting at someone he knew. 'She's not a Spanish Armada galleon, but the *Vanneau* should keep Belle and old Jacob here in comfort for the rest of our lives. Hell, I may even pay for Belle to take cookery lessons.'

He bellowed with laughter at the thought, and began humming under his breath.

★ ★ ★

They reached Merfleur Harbour in another fifteen minutes. Belle West was on the quay, dumpier than ever in a pair of work overalls and cut-down sea boots. The black mongrel dog was with her. So was a stringily built man in a patched tweed jacket and overalls. He was bald except for a clump of ginger hair behind each ear.

'This is Jimmy Boullard,' introduced West. 'He owns that yellow speedboat Kiri worships. Jimmy was Royal Navy until they chucked him out, now he milks cows for a living.'

'True.' Boullard had a solemn, cultured voice. 'Fate has not been kind.'

'Jimmy was a rear admiral when he retired,' said Belle sweetly. 'He owns one of the best dairy herds on Jersey.' She sniffed. 'Other people retire to sit on their fat backsides and drink beer all day.'

'Beer?' West stiffened. 'I forgot. Everything else ready?'

'Naturally.' Boullard looked hurt.

'Anyone unusual been sniffing around?' persisted West.

Belle glanced at the black dog. 'Not according to Benny.'

'Good.' Purposefully, Jacob West hobbled off towards his shop. He returned with a small, clinking haversack over one shoulder, and winked at Laird. 'Supplies.'

The big black inflatable Laird had seen the previous day was at the quayside. Boullard boarded her, Benny close at his heels, and by the time Laird and the Wests followed them the outboard engine was muttering a thin haze of blue exhaust. As Boullard motored the inflatable out, Laird noticed that the retired admiral also had a Police Honorifique badge on the lapel of his jacket.

'Jacob.' Laird settled beside West and kept his voice low. 'How far do you trust Boullard?'

177

'Jimmy? He's all right,' said West easily. 'You mean the badge?'

Laird nodded.

'Remember I told you I'm a constable's officer? He's one step up, a vingtenier, my sergeant.'

The inflatable rocked and pitched a little as they cleared the harbour and met a light, choppy swell. Belle was seated for'ard, with Benny poised on the blunt bow like an eager, tail-wagging figurehead. West opened his haversack. Several tins of beer nestled inside; so did the blued steel of his Webley air pistol.

'For rats,' he said conversationally, taking out the Webley and hefting it in one hand. 'Belle doesn't like rats, and that damned dog is never around when you need him.'

Giving up, Laird leaned against the hard rubber hull as a pair of brightly billed puffins bobbed by in the swell. The Zodiac boat was making an unhurried way along the north side of the Merfleur reef, most of its weed-covered length exposed and dry as the tide was out. From their side he could see the way the reef shelved into deep water; he spent a moment watching a family of black cormorants standing in a row on a slab of rock, their large wings spread out like sails, drying themselves in the sun. On ahead, the low, green island with its lattice tower light

178

looked peaceful and pleasant.

Things were different on the south side of the reef. There the tide had left a long, unattractive stretch of shallows and shingle, isolated rocks and swirling eddies.

'We're not going far,' said West mildly. He squinted casually along the air pistol's sights, using one of the cormorants as a mock target. 'Relax, boy — enjoy it.'

'Whatever you want,' said Laird resignedly. Benny had decided to lie down at the bow, though his tail was still thrashing. Belle could have been sunbathing, sitting back with her eyes closed, one hand trailing in the water as the Zodiac muttered on. When he glanced round, Jimmy Boullard had one hand resting lightly on the outboard engine's controls and was eating an apple. He sighed. 'So I'll wait. But tell me more about Peter Frere.'

'You mean the way he used to be?' Jacob West paused, pulled the Webley's trigger, and there was a sound like a soft slap. Fifty feet away, a rusty tin can lying on the reef jumped into the air then clattered down again. 'Well, he's in his mid-forties. When he worked for Witchline in St Helier, he was their general dogsbody around the docks. He looked like a bank clerk, usually dressed like one too. He was harmless — maybe drank a shade too much sometimes, but never annoyed anyone.

He lived on his own — he had a wife who ran off with someone from the mainland.'

'So what happened?'

'The accident? No one ever knew everything about it for sure.' West laid the pistol on his lap. 'Like I told you, it was two or three days after the *Rosewitch* sailed that last time from Jersey. It was a hot summer. Some kids going for an early morning swim found Frere lying unconscious near the beach, at the foot of some steps. It looked as though he'd been there all night. He was hauled off to hospital in a coma, he was there for a long time — and when he did come out he was burned out mentally as well as physically, hardly even knew his own name.'

Laird stared at him. 'I thought you told me it was blood poisoning?'

'Let me finish,' growled West. 'The way he was before, Frere sometimes went hand-line fishing off the rocks. When they found him, he had lost one shoe, the other shoe was sodden with water, and his clothes were wet.' He shrugged. 'Frere's mind was a blank and stayed that way. But once the medics had done their tests they reckoned he had caught a weever fish, poor ignorant devil, then that he had handled it. You know about weever fish?'

'Yes.'

The thought was enough. Weever fish were small, but probably the most venomous fish of the temperate zone. Seldom more than a foot long, they were bottom fish which usually buried themselves in sand or shingle. They existed all the way down from Norway to the Mediterranean and off the African coast, yet were seldom caught. When they were, their deep black dorsal fin was a warning signal — they bristled with poison spines, the kind of poison that could mean paralysing agony, mind-shattering shock, sometimes death. He remembered a pathology lecture at medical school. There was no known antidote.

'I've only seen one once,' mused West. 'Nasty little devil. We threw it back fast.'

'Did they find his hand-line or the fish?' It had to be coincidence but coincidence with a total irony behind it.

'No chance, by the time they knew what to look for — ' West broke off and rose, staring ahead.

The Zodiac boat was level with the island now, keeping a cautious stone's throw out from the creaming edge of the shoreline. But Benny was on his feet at the bow and growling, his tail flat, in a hard line. There were no birds on the lattice tower, very few resting along the shore.

'Jimmy.' Cursing, West jerked round. 'Take her out, man. Fast!'

The outboard engine snarled, the Zodiac boat lurched in a tight turn — and a rifle barked twice from the island. One bullet slammed audibly into the Zodiac's side, the other sent the black dog tumbling and yelping into Belle's arms.

'Everybody down!' yelled Boullard, in a gale-topping roar from the stern.

They were still coming round, shipping water in the process. Belle had flattened herself protectively over Benny, the dog still yelping and wriggling to get free. Jacob West was cursing with a total, blasphemous monotony, his head down, his rear ridiculously in the air.

But there were no more shots, only a flock of the island's depleted seabird population circling and screaming. The buoyancy chamber punctured by the bullet was beginning to sag as it deflated, but it was only one cell of many, there was no danger there. The outboard engine's frantic clamour eased as Boullard slowed again, still steering in a circle.

Jacob West wriggled into a more dignified position and gazed anxiously at his wife. 'How's Benny?'

'Frightened.' She glared at him. 'Now ask about me.'

182

'Belle — ' West's mouth fell open in horror.

'Now you've asked, I'm fine.' Her face was pale, but she grinned at him.

Laird heard it first, the bellow of a powerful engine starting up. The growl increased, then a small speedboat hurtled into view from behind the island. Bumping through the swell, her bow coming up, she swung north with a white wake beginning to boil at her stern. There were three people in her cockpit area. One crouched over the controls, the second was trying to help a companion struggle out of the harness of a twin-cylinder aqualung. All three wore black scuba-diving suits.

The speedboat was a dull anonymous grey in colour. At that distance there was no chance of identifying her crew.

'Bastards,' said Jacob West pungently. Yet a faintly satisfied grin was breaking on his face as he watched the speedboat streaking away. 'Jimmy — what do you think?'

'Seek and you won't necessarily find,' said Boullard cryptically, with the same kind of grin. 'Not if you're looking in the wrong place.' Steering the Zodiac back towards the island, he nodded at the fast disappearing speedboat. 'Exciting. Can we do it again?'

'Over my dead body,' declared Belle fiercely.

'Why not, love?' murmured her husband. She was still nursing the dog, and West considered them affectionately, then straightened. 'But that boat heightens Frere's chances. Either they haven't got him, or they can't get much sense out of him.'

'Why?' Laird grabbed for support as the inflatable took a toss from a rogue sea. He glared at West. 'Do I get to share in this?'

'One of them was diving — you saw the aqualung. Another had to be on the boat, the third was standing sentry on this side, right?' West was confident. 'Diving means they know a little, or guess a little, but that's all.' The speedboat had vanished from sight. He nodded to Boullard. 'Take us straight in, Jimmy. No sense in letting our guest think we've gone mad.'

In another couple of minutes they were rounding the seaward side of the island. Laird blinked. He'd already realised the island was bigger than he'd first believed, now he saw its hidden surprise. This side was shaped like a lobster's half-open claw, with the swell rolling into a wide, deep gash which ran far back, a gash totally hidden from anyone looking out along the Merfleur reef.

Steering into the lobster-claw gap, Boullard throttled back. Hugging the south side, moving at a crawl, the Zodiac boat finally

184

nosed in towards a slab of rock. Jacob West tossed a grapnel line ashore as an anchor, then, as the rubber hull bumped, he hopped over to the rock on his good leg. Seconds later Benny was lifting his leg on a boulder and Boullard had switched off the outboard engine.

'Belle.' West turned to his wife as soon as they were all ashore. 'I don't expect that speedboat to hurry back, but we could use a lookout.'

She nodded and left, Benny barking at her heels.

'Got your bearings?' West glanced at Laird. 'We're on the south arm, those shots came from the north side.' He thumbed at the water in between. 'There's a fair depth out there, where they were diving. It just happens they were wasting their time. You're going to see why.'

He beckoned and limped off along the shore, deeper into the claw, with Laird following and Boullard ambling after them. In a moment they were crunching over smooth grey shingle which had a thick tideline of dark seaweed. Here and there Laird noticed an occasional speckle of white stone, a stone with the same narrow green veins as the one on Kiri Vass's desk. Then, walking on, he realised they were heading for a strange raised bank of shingle, like a low hill, where the white stones were scattered like confetti against the grey.

'Up you go,' invited West.

Laird scrambled up the small slope, reached the top, and suddenly understood several things.

He was looking down at a broad, shallow trench on the far side, a trench covered over by several lengths of home-made camouflage netting. But there were gaps in the netting. Down there, at the bottom, he could see the broken, skeletal stumps of what had been the ribs of an old wooden sailing ship. There were traces of the line of her keel. Here and there, protruding at drunken angles and like so many stovepipes, he could see the black barrels of cannon.

The cannon nearest him had been so worn by the action of time and the sea that the entire upper length of its long barrel had been worn away. Yet a cannonball still rested in the groove that remained.

'It's like I told you, eh?' Jacob West struggled up beside him, breathing heavily. 'Didn't I promise that you wouldn't get your feet wet?'

'You did,' said Laird softly.

The mix of shingle and bottom clay around the excavated ship held a few small pools of water. A fish lay dead where it had been stranded, damp ribbon strands of seaweed clung to some of the pathetic timbers. He could picture the way each tide would wash in then seep out again.

'This was Kiri's idea.' West poked at the netting with his stick. 'We get the occasional aircraft flying over, and we don't want to advertise.' He used the stick as a pointer back the way they'd come. 'There's nothing visible from the sea, small boats stay away because they're worried about rocks — so we've no troubles from idiots on yachts coming in for a picnic.'

Laird nodded. 'Does the island have a name?'

'Not on any chart I've ever seen.' West grinned. 'We'll think of one — how about Jacob's Bank?'

More feet crunched. Jimmy Boullard joined them, sending a small torrent of pebbles rolling down the excavated slope to the wreck below.

'Well, everything seems all right.' Boullard gave a pleased grunt as he looked down. 'I've a theory about what happened to her. When that storm hit her she was probably dismasted. Maybe she was abandoned.' He shrugged. 'You can imagine her hull being swept in, maybe bouncing off rocks going aground. Then she went down, settled — on a fairly even keel.'

'Our good luck,' murmured West.

'True.' Boullard rubbed a hand over his bald head, then tugged pensively at the patch of ginger hair behind one ear. 'The rest happens now and again. More storms, the sea on the move, great masses of shingle being washed in as she settled. She'd simply vanish. Who'd know about her?' He answered his own question. 'Nobody. Not even the Merfleur fishermen, though they maybe salvaged some wreckage washed in near the harbour.'

'But you won her back again.' Laird frowned at the long, raised bank on which they were standing, a bank littered with fragments of rotted wood and other debris. What he could see represented many long hours of hard work. 'How?'

'I said there were a few of us. But it's mostly due to Jimmy.' West clapped a hand on his friend's shoulder. 'Jimmy has a fancy Japanese farm tractor with a bulldozer blade and a bucket digger attachment.'

'I had to do some drainage work on the farm.' Boullard gave a deprecating smile. 'I discovered that I could bring the tractor out along the reef at low tide. I — ah — always bring a trailer. On the way back I've got the

188

trailer filled with seaweed. It's an excellent fertiliser.'

'But nice and ordinary looking as a load if anyone happens to see you,' agreed Laird.

'No one has — no one we know about.' Boullard looked slightly worried for a moment. 'I've got to say I'm not totally proud of what we've done to that wreck. I know some marine historians who would call it vandalism.'

'Vandalism with compensations,' murmured Jacob West. 'Jimmy, think positive. When we've finished you can buy yourself some new cows.'

Laird left them, easing in under the camouflage netting, sliding his way down into the trench in a rush of shingle. He landed near some twisted ironwork fittings, what remained of a sword hilt, and a flattened metal drinking cup. The man who had used them might have known John Paul Jones and his *Ranger*, had probably set off on that last voyage from France only worrying about being caught by a prowling British frigate.

He moved on under the camouflage netting until he came to the first of the broken hull ribs. Taking out his knife, he used a blade to test the wood. The point of the knife sank in a thumbnail's breadth then jarred against solid timber.

Waiting patiently above, West and Boullard allowed him to wander. He saw places where extra trenches had been dug, a couple with their sides shored up by new bracing timber but still partly waterlogged. Further along he stopped to examine one of the cannon, its muzzle choked by sand and pebbles. He kicked the edge of something metallic, stopped, and lifted a small crucifix. It had a broken thong, which disintegrated as he lifted it.

He replaced the crucifix where he'd found it. Somehow that seemed right — and he'd seen enough.

When he climbed back up the slope and emerged again, Boullard greeted him with a nod. But Jacob West was frowning at a patch of scrub not far along the shore. The black dog was there, growling, pawing at the ground, demanding attention.

'Jimmy?' West glanced at Boullard.

'We'll take a look,' said Boullard softly. He turned to Laird. 'That's our tool store.'

Laird followed them over. Benny lay down as they arrived, but kept growling.

A piece of dark green canvas hung like a door behind the scrub. Producing the Webley from his trouser waistband, West flicked back the makeshift curtain. It covered the mouth of a small cave. Inside were spades and a

190

pickaxe, lengths of timber and other stores. But Jacob West was sniffing as he looked around.

'Smell it?' he asked.

Laird nodded. The odour of stale tobacco smoke hung heavily in the air.

'Here.' Boullard stooped. When he rose again he held a small collection of cigarette stubs he'd picked up. Nearby, a length of rumpled canvas looked as if it had been used as a groundsheet. 'I'd say we had a lodger last night.'

'Frere uses cigarettes.' Jacob West's mouth tightened.

Laird raised an eyebrow. 'He knows about this place?'

'Yes.' West swore under his breath. 'My fault, like before. He's scared, he's on the run, he could have waded out last night — that's presuming he could thumb a lift out from St Helier.'

'But if he saw that speedboat come in, then he'd run again,' mused Boullard.

'Well, he's off the island now.' Jacob West made it a statement of fact. 'If he wasn't, Benny would have found him.'

Something glinted at the edge of the canvas. Laird bent and picked up a brass button with an anchor crest. It still had a broken thread attached.

'I gave him one of my old uniform jackets,' said West. 'It fitted where it touched, but he wears it a lot.' Stumping his way out of the cave, he glared around. 'Damn — damn everything!'

Laird laid a hand on his arm. 'Frere could still turn up.'

'I know that,' West snorted. 'But I think best with a beer in my hand. Belle went off with the accursed haversack!'

5

'I had a terrible dream a few nights ago,' confided Belle West. She was drinking beer, straight from the can, but with all the aplomb of a duchess taking tea. 'Jacob came home with all the *Vanneau*'s gold in the biggest shopping bag I'd ever seen. So I bought the largest solitaire diamond ring in the world. Except it had to stay in the bank, we couldn't afford the insurance premiums.' She sighed. 'If you had that kind of money, what would you do, Andrew?'

'Buy the bank,' he suggested. 'And a butcher's shop for Benny.'

She chuckled, her double chin wobbling. Half an hour had passed and they were sitting on a rock in the sunlight, watching the tide creep in. West and Boullard were a few feet away, patching the bullet hole in the Zodiac boat's hull. West had retrieved the beer, his wife had brought slab-like sandwiches filled with cold, thin-sliced steak and oozing with yellow butter. Benny had had his share of both and was asleep at her feet.

'How do you really feel about it, Belle?' said Laird.

'Now?' She glanced towards her husband. 'Worried, because I don't know what we do next.'

'Does Jacob?'

Wryly, she shook her head. Insects buzzed around them and a couple of tiny, fearless ringed plover were already scavenging for crumbs.

'Does Jacob what?' West had heard his name and came over. He helped himself to the last can of beer. 'Well?'

'Does Jacob know what happens next?' asked Laird bluntly.

'Some of it.' Jacob West opened the can and took a quick gulp from it as Boullard's thin shadow fell across the rock and the other man joined them. 'We talked, while we were fixing the boat.'

'You talked, I fixed,' said Boullard. He looked pointedly at the beer. 'Are you going to leave me some of that?'

'I suppose so.' West took another long gulp then handed his friend the can. 'We talked, boy. That speedboat could be only a start, things could get difficult. We'll have to arrange some kind of watch out here.'

'Mainly after dark,' mused Boullard. 'They'd be fools to try anything again in daylight.' He looked wisely at Laird. 'But you're thinking of Frere?'

194

'Frere,' agreed Laird.

'He'll turn up.' Jacob West frowned at a procession of tiny ants scurrying over the rock. 'I reckon it will be soon, probably on my doorstep at Merfleur.' He blocked the ants' path with a foot. Without hesitation they detoured round it but kept heading in the same direction. 'Still, it wouldn't take much to scare him off. A hint of police uniform would be enough.'

'There's another small problem.' Boullard bared his teeth in a humourless smile. 'Depending on what Frere knows about last night, some other people might like to get their hands on him. His best chance could be to come knocking at Jacob's door.'

'Then what would happen to him?' asked Laird.

Belle West gave a slow, frowning nod. 'I think I'd like to know that too.'

'Damn it, Belle, what do you think would happen?' Jacob West's face reddened. 'I want to talk with Frere before the paid police get their hands on him. So does Laird — maybe even more than I do.' He glared at Laird. 'I still say Frere didn't kill Newgrange. But he's wanted for questioning, right? Well, they'll get him, because that way he'll be a lot safer than he is right now.'

'Jacob isn't exactly doing himself justice,'

murmured Boullard. 'We know we can't keep the *Vanneau* a secret for ever — we've always known it. Whatever happens from now on, we take our chances.' He paused and rubbed a thumb across the Police Honorifique badge in his lapel. 'But at the end of the day, these badges don't fall out of cereal packets.' Another small smile crossed his face. 'Jacob's words, Laird — not mine.'

An embarrassed grunt came from West, but Belle gave a satisfied smile.

Later, when they left the island, the tide was coming in with surprising speed. An undersea clash of currents meant that the Zodiac boat lurched through a lumping patch of water as they cleared the hidden bay's lobster-claw entrance and turned for home. Part of the Merfleur reef was being washed by the light swell, part had already vanished. But Benny was back at his post at the bow and this time there was nothing to disturb the black dog.

West and Boullard were together at the Zodiac's stern, leaving Laird to sit with Belle. She was content again, humming to herself, ignoring the fine droplets of spray that came aboard. Laird stayed silent, having to accept what he'd seen and heard, uncertain where it all left him.

On the island, talking with Belle, adding

scraps he'd picked up from West and Boullard, he'd heard more about how the *Vanneau* had been uncovered. Initially the whole thing had been a light-hearted diversion. But that had changed. Within days they'd located traces of the French brig, then, immediately afterwards, the first of the gold coins.

They'd needed extra help. Belle West had ticked the names off on her small, podgy fingers, four people they knew they could trust and who had sworn the next best thing to an oath in blood that they'd stay silent. Jacob had brought in the local postman and a young veterinary surgeon from the next village, both scuba-diving enthusiasts. Boullard had appeared with his head cattleman and a garage mechanic who had been a Royal Marine sergeant.

Suddenly he thought of a question he hadn't asked.

'Belle.' He waited until she looked round. 'These four you told me about — any of them married?'

She nodded. 'All of them except the postman.' Her eyes twinkled. 'He has an understanding with a widow on his delivery round.'

'Do the wives know what's going on?'

'Of course. The wives — and the widow.'

She saw him wince and smiled. 'Suppose you were a woman. What would you think if your man kept disappearing at all hours? I'll tell you. You'd think he had another female hidden away.' She winked. 'When it matters, Andrew, a woman knows how to keep her mouth shut — knows how a lot better than any man born.'

Laird decided not to argue. The Zodiac boat was already steering for the silted entrance to Merfleur's tiny harbour.

Jacob and Belle West went ashore as soon as the inflatable was tied up, with Benny at their heels. Laird stayed to help Boullard, who had produced a metal fuel can and wanted to top up the Zodiac's tank. They had finished and were walking along the quay when West reappeared, hobbling rapidly towards them. He looked pleased as he arrived.

'Frere's around.' West used his stick to point back towards the cottage. 'We've had a visitor — in through the back door, and he only took some food. But I think he'll show again.' He glanced at them hopefully. 'I'd like to be here.'

'That means he wants me to drive you to the airport,' said Boullard dryly. 'All right. If you don't like the way I drive, close your eyes — most people do.'

Rear Admiral (retired) Jimmy Boullard drove a blue MG hardtop which had a compass mounted on the instrument panel and a 'Join the Navy' sticker on the rear window. Despite his threats he drove fast and he drove well. Twice he flashed his headlights as they passed a police traffic patrol car, twice the patrol car's occupants gave him the kind of wry acknowledgement which meant they knew his Police Honorifique status. At first, he talked with carefully disguised pride about his dairy cattle and their milk yields then, suddenly, he gave Laird a shrewd sideways glance.

'Suppose you don't get any help from Frere on your *Rosewitch* sinking?' he asked. 'What do you do next?'

'I wish I knew,' admitted Laird. 'Maybe keep prodding at the Mehrans.'

'I wouldn't try that with Diane Mehrans.' Boullard chuckled to himself. 'From what I hear, she'd blow you out of the water.' He gave Laird another sideways glance. 'For what it's worth, I've a small half-baked idea about Frere. Presuming he does have some fogged memory of what happened to that Witchline ship, he might even know that your firm paid out the insurance loss — agreed?'

'He might.' Laird was cautious.

'Jacob has spent a lot of money, more than he can afford to lose, on our funny French brig.' Boullard shrugged. 'Suppose — just suppose — that Frere had some vague idea of helping him by helping you and landing some kind of reward?'

'You're blaming the Mehrans?'

'They're available,' said Boullard dryly. 'One way or another — I've some banker friends on the island, the offshore investment kind, who say that Mehran Holdings are having big cash-flow problems again. People aren't exactly queuing up to give them money.'

Laird nodded. The ex-admiral's mention of money gave him the chance to ask a question of his own.

'Go back to the *Vanneau*. Whatever you find, how will you divide it out?'

'No problem there.' Boullard's eyes narrowed and he took the MG through a traffic gap which didn't seem to exist. He eased back on the accelerator. 'Agreed shares for all involved, on a sliding scale — prize-money style. It's down there — all we've got to do is find it.'

Boullard dropped his passenger off at the airport then took the MG away like a destroyer going for the kill. Laird glanced over at the terminal, thinking of Kiri Vass, but resisted temptation, collected the white Ford, and set it moving back towards St Helier.

The State Police headquarters block was situated on Rouge Bouillon, a street within shouting distance of the centre of town. Part of the headquarters building had once been an army barracks and looked it. The rest was modern glass and concrete. He left the Ford close to the public office and went in.

Two minutes later he was guided along a corridor to an office where a lean, dark-haired man greeted him with a handshake before dismissing the constable who had brought him. Detective Chief Inspector Tom Flambard was in his shirt sleeves, had a soft south of England burr to his voice and had the look of a man who had lost most of a night's sleep. The remains of a cheese and anchovy pizza lay in a cardboard box to one side of his desk.

'Sit down, Mr Laird.' He waved Laird into a chair and settled back in his own. 'This won't take long.' Flambard moved the pizza, searched through some papers lying underneath, and found the typewritten sheet he wanted. He looked up, his dark-brown eyes considering Laird with deliberate interest. 'We had this typed up, based on what you said this morning. But read before you sign it. People who don't sometimes have problems later.'

201

Laird took the sheet. 'Have Chris New-grange's parents been told?'

'Yes.' The brown eyes hardened at the thought. 'The American police broke the news first.' He scowled at the telephone in front of him. 'I spoke to his father half an hour ago — it's still breakfast time over there.' Flambard took a deep breath. 'I don't like to hear a man weeping over a 'phone line.'

'If they're flying over, Clanmore Alliance could pick up the tab.' Laird knew that even Osgood Morris would let it go through.

'They might appreciate that.' Detective Chief Inspector Tom Flambard barely nodded. 'I don't know when it will be. When Newgrange's mother heard, she collapsed. She has a heart condition, now she's in hospital.' He shrugged. 'Like to read that statement?'

Laird did, carefully. It was accurate, but still the right answers to the wrong questions. He took the pen Flambard offered and scribbled his signature.

'Any sign of your Peter Frere?' he asked.

'Your Peter Frere almost as much as mine,' said Flambard dryly. He shook his head. 'He could be off the island. Steal a boat, and even a child could get across to France. We've warned the French police. But you're sure you never met Frere?'

202

'I don't even know what he looks like,' said Laird truthfully.

'Yet he tried to contact you.' For a moment Flambard's eyes stayed steady on Laird. Then the detective went back to the pile of papers on his desk and slid a photograph across to Laird. 'That's how he was, three years ago.'

It was a grainy enlargement of what looked like a passport-size original. The man captured by the camera lens had thinning, curly hair, a narrow face, large ears, a weak mouth which was shaping a shy grin. It was the kind of boyish face that some men kept until late in life when they suddenly became old overnight.

'Still no?' asked Flambard.

'Sorry.' Laird shook his head.

'He doesn't look so good now. More like he went barefoot through hell and got thrown out at the other side.' Flambard retrieved the photograph. 'He had a bad time.' His expression didn't alter. 'You know about that?'

'I heard.' Laird saw no sense in denying it. 'Weever-fish poison.'

'It made him a local medical celebrity.' Flambard's voice stayed dispassionately factual. 'At least, till something better came along. It doesn't happen too often, anywhere. It also left him disabled — disabled, Mr Laird, not mentally ill. Call it the equivalent of coronary shock. He's brain-damaged, but not crazy or any other word you might use.' He paused. 'You still don't know why he wanted to meet you?'

'I wish I did.'

'I believe you.' The detective sat back and clasped his hands behind his head. 'But he kept on trying. We found a scribble on young Newgrange's desk pad. 'F. Emu — 9.30. L?' Except the 'L' had been scored out. I'd translate that as another 'phone call from Frere, that Newgrange arranged to meet him at the boat at nine-thirty, that Newgrange either tried to contact you and failed, or that he decided to go alone and win some credit.' He shook his head. 'I know, you didn't get any calls at the Leecom, you didn't get any messages. So we're back where we started.'

'Looking for Frere,' said Laird quietly. 'Do you think he's your killer?'

Flambard sucked his lips for a moment. 'Off the record? I doubt it. Our postmortem report says the stab wound that killed Newgrange achieved deep penetration — up under the ribs, into the heart. There was plenty of physical strength behind it. Maybe more than Frere could manage.' He tilted further back in his chair, his eyes still on his visitor. 'Any ideas, Mr Laird? I could use them.'

'You know where I was.' Laird turned aside the question.

Flambard nodded. 'We checked. You're fireproof, so is the man who reported finding him.' He saw Laird's raised eyebrow. 'One of our Police Honorifique, an old sailor who likes do-gooding. When it happened, he was visiting one of his pals, a retired rear admiral.' He shrugged his disgust. 'So what have we got? A boat that looks like it was hit by a hurricane inside, a dead body there, Frere gone, the murder weapon gone — '

'Fingerprints?'

'None that matter, so far.' Flambard sat upright and layed his hands on the desk. 'Still no ideas, Mr Laird?' Suddenly, without waiting for an answer, he rose. 'I'll see you out. It'll make a change from scowling at a wall.'

They left Flambard's office and walked back along the maze of corridors. Flambard's route led them out of a side door, into a yard cluttered with police vehicles. A constable wearing rubber boots and an apron was using a hose as he washed a patrol car. Still in his shirt sleeves, hands deep in his trouser pockets, Flambard screwed his eyes up against the bright sunlight. The constable with the hose was looking across at them. He gave Flambard a slow, deliberate nod then kept on with his task.

'Funny thing, being a cop,' said Flambard, the south-coast burr in his voice more amiable than ever. 'You never know when you're going to trip over something that matters. Know much about cops, Mr Laird?'

'I've met a few.' Laird saw Flambard was smiling. 'I've got that kind of job.'

'It seems that way.' Flambard thumbed towards the constable. 'I've had Dave stuck here all afternoon, washing one damned car after another. Waiting on you. Shall I tell you why? Dave was at the airport late this morning, making sure a certain — uh — lady we'd invited to leave got on her flight. He saw Jacob West. There was someone with West, someone Dave thought he recognised from a newspaper photograph. I heard, I wondered — '

'Then you checked?' suggested Laird resignedly.

'Good question.' Flambard's smile had hardened, the burr in his voice had become a growl. 'A strange thing about cops is the way we hang together — none of us wants to hang separately. How's it in your job?'

'The same.' Laird cursed the newspaper photograph, braced himself for what might come next.

'Happened I remembered something odd,'

said Flambard. 'How, over the weekend, some cop in Southampton telexed to ask if we knew anything about a piece of his local dockland slime who drowned after being in Jersey for a dirty weekend. The telex hinted there was a shipping fraud angle. So — '

Laird nodded. 'You wondered?'

'You're damned right. I called the Southampton cop. Then I called a Fraud Squad pal of mine in London. He knew you too. For what it's worth, they both send their regards.' Flambard's mouth tightened. 'That little two-way charade in my office was to see which of us was the more devious bastard — I'd say you won. You work for Clanmore Alliance, yes. But you're not a publicity clown, you're on their sharp-end fraud team. Agreed?'

'The job is marine claims assessor,' said Laird dryly. He shrugged. 'I'm sorry.'

'That's a start.' Flambard glared across at the waiting constable and thumbed him on his way. Switching off the hose, leaving it dripping, the man ambled off. Flambard turned again to Laird. 'Now, exactly what the hell are you doing on Jersey?'

'Working. Chasing a shipping fraud that cost us several millions.' Laird shrugged. 'It happened a long way outside British jurisdiction, in international waters. But there's a

Jersey connection.'

'That's all I need.' Flambard swore under his breath. 'Was young Newgrange working for you?'

'No. He knew nothing. He was just putting out the welcome mat for a visitor.'

'So it was a nuisance when he got himself murdered?' suggested Flambard acidly. 'You expect me to believe that line?'

'Believe what you want,' said Laird. 'I can't stop you.'

'Could you blame me? I'm not in a happy mood.' Flambard scowled and scratched the back of his neck. Then he sighed and his manner thawed a little. 'Let's start again. You're saying you honestly don't know why he was killed?'

'Why — or how.' Laird shook his head.

'All right.' Flambard sucked his lips. 'You're a problem, Laird. Several problems — like, for instance, do I let you stay here or do I throw you off the island?'

'You do your job, and I'll do mine.' Laird watched a police van murmur into the yard and stop. 'I don't need to be loved.'

'You're in no danger of that.' Two policewomen had emerged from the van. They dragged out a massive, handcuffed prisoner and hustled him into the building. Watching, Flambard gave the faintest twitch of a smile. 'There's an old story I like. It's about the Arab sheik who surprises his neighbours when he hires the local desert bad-hat as a bodyguard. When the neighbours ask why, he says he'd rather have the bad-hat inside his tent looking out than outside his tent looking in.'

'That's the cleaned-up version,' mused Laird.

'Happen I'd take help from the devil himself if it made sense,' said Flambard. 'Though say that to my sergeant and I'll call you a liar.' He frowned at his feet for a moment. 'A straight question, off the record?'

'Off the record.' Laird had to back his own judgement of Detective Chief Inspector Tom Flambard.

'Does your target on Jersey have a name?'

'Yes.' It was the question he'd expected. 'Do you remember a ship called the *Rosewitch*?'

'I do.' Flambard stiffened for a moment then moistened his lips. 'You mean Witchline Shipping — Mehran Holdings? For real?'

'For real,' agreed Laird. 'Surprised?'

'I'm not allowed to be surprised. It's against Force Standing Orders.' The soft dry burr was back in Flambard's voice and he grimaced. 'This is Jersey — we got a better class of crime here. But Mehran Holdings?'

He whistled through his teeth. 'How much evidence?'

'Enough that we won't let go.'

'Yet you were with them last night.' Flambard's face was a mixture of emotions. 'You play dirty, don't you?'

'I don't have to like it.' He saw Flambard wanted more. In a few sentences Laird gave him the basic background to the *Rosewitch* sinking — and why he'd gone to Southampton. But he stopped it there; he left out all mention of what had happened to him on Jersey — particularly when it involved Jacob West.

'There's more.' Flambard wasn't totally satisfied. But then he seemed to change his mind. 'All right, I won't ask — for now. But a man was lost when the *Rosewitch* went down, a man died at Southampton. Newgrange could well be number three.' He scowled to himself. 'Except there's the Frere situation. I was dropped a heavy hint from on high — the attorney-general's office. I was to keep my options open.'

'That sounds reasonable,' murmured Laird.

'But if Frere gets in touch with you, or tries to get in touch, I want to know.'

'You will. There's a chance it could happen.'

'That's what I thought — and I'm trying

very hard to be patient.' Flambard eyed him suspiciously. 'Now tell me how you know that old pirate, Jacob West.'

'I used to be Merchant Navy, we've a mutual friend,' said Laird.

'And all of you sailed under the skull and crossbones, I suppose?' Flambard was cynical. 'Laird, maybe I'm going to regret this. But I'm fool enough to presume that basically we're on the same side. I'm going to give you some rope. But the moment I feel different, I'll haul you back in again.'

Laird nodded. 'No argument from me.'

'Good. Talk to me or my sergeant, Sam Moisan. No one else. Suppose I want to contact you?'

'Try Jacob West or his wife.'

'Not your hotel? I won't ask why.' Flambard gave a brief, lopsided grin. 'One piece of advice. We've never nailed a Mehran for anything bigger than a speeding ticket. They're on first-name terms with what's supposed to be our social elite. But we've heard stories — only stories, no proof, no willing witnesses.' Suddenly, he was very serious. 'Watch them. I'd hate to come looking for you somewhere at the bottom of Witchlove Haven — we couldn't afford the overtime.'

Though he hadn't wanted it to happen that way, Andrew Laird felt a degree of relief as he drove away from police headquarters. Sooner or later something like that had had to happen and he reckoned he'd been lucky in the man he'd come up against. Detective Chief Inspector Tom Flambard was a kind of cop he'd met before. Laird felt he could trust the lean, dark-haired man, that Flambard didn't particularly police by the rule book — but there was a counter-balance. Part of it might be the wreck of the *Vanneau* and its secrets. If Flambard discovered he was being used in a way he didn't like, then Laird had no illusions. Flambard would 'haul him back in' on that rope. That seat on the next flight out would be waiting.

Yet Flambard's flat warning about the Mehrans, the way he had accepted the *Rosewitch* situation, underlined the kind of tightrope-walking act that was still waiting, and emphasized its grim reality. The stakes were high; so were the risks.

Laird's mind was still busy as he steered the Ford through the centre of St Helier. He took a short route of one-way streets and junctions, emerged at the harbour area, and slowed as he reached the basin where the

Emu was berthed. But there was still a police guard on the quay and he drove on.

A little later he parked the Ford outside the Newgrange Agencies office. When he went over, the door was locked and had a 'Closed' sign, but he saw a figure moving inside. When he knocked, a young, sad face looked out, then Liz Hatton opened the door and allowed him in.

'I'm just tidying up, Mr Laird.' Newgrange's teenage assistant still wore her black sweater and white skirt. She had tied a black ribbon round her henna-coloured hair. But if she had decided to dress the part, the rest was genuine. Her eyes were red, and she looked ready for more tears as she locked the door again. 'The police said I could be here. Then — well I don't know what to do after this. Can you tell me?'

'Go home, Liz,' said Laird sympathetically. 'Give things time to settle.'

'But there's mail, there will be 'phone calls.'

'Forget them.' Laird guided her over to her desk and made her sit down. 'How did things go with the police?'

'All right. They've finished here.' Her lower lip trembled a little. 'It was a Sergeant Moisan and a woman. She was decent enough, but I could do without him.' The henna-coloured hair shook unhappily. 'It's bad enough trying to believe Chris is dead.'

'You seemed to get on together,' encouraged Laird.

'He was good for laughs. I liked him a lot.' Liz grabbed a handful of paper tissues from a box, wiped her eyes, and blew her nose. 'It shouldn't have happened, Mr Laird — it shouldn't. Who'd want to kill a nice big — big idiot like Chris?'

'Did he have a steady girl friend?' asked Laird.

'You mean a relationship?' She stopped the tears long enough to eye him coldly. 'No. At least, not one in particular. Why?'

Laird shrugged. 'I'm trying to make sense out of it, Liz. The same way the police are.' He saw the tears starting to trickle again, gave her a fresh handful of paper tissues, and let her mop up. 'Was he still here when you left last night?'

She nodded. 'He said he'd be working late. He wanted to have our books up to date, in case you were interested in them.'

'I see.' The thought made him wince. 'You know the police found a note on his scratch-pad, as if another telephone call from Peter Frere had come in?'

'It must have been when he was here on his own.' The girl was certain. 'Frere didn't call

214

again before I left.'

'What about visitors, people who just walked in?'

'We had a few clients — the usual kind of thing, people wanting claim forms.' She was puzzled.

'Not them. But anyone else out of the ordinary from — well, after I left.'

'I'd have told the police if we'd had any strangers look in.' She frowned at him.

'It could have been someone you knew,' encouraged Laird.

'After you left?' Having to think, she wasn't crying. 'Well, there was Ray Garris — '

'The Mehran director?' Laird tensed.

'Yes. It was his second visit. He'd been earlier in the morning, I heard him talking to Chris. He knew you were coming, he was asking Chris what he knew about you.' She managed a weak smile. 'I think that's why he came back, to find out more. He talked with Chris in the back office.'

When she had left work, she had gone home. She'd then gone out for the evening with a girl friend, they'd split when they picked up two Irish boys at a disco out along Five Mile Road. She'd arrived home late, to find a police car parked outside her door. She knew nothing more.

'Much more to do here?' asked Laird.

'No.' She looked round. 'I'm nearly finished.'

'I want to use the 'phone in Chris's room, then I'll help you lock up.'

Laird left her and went into the private office, closing the door. The room was covered in smudges of grey fingerprint powder; he could see the way in which drawers and cupboards had been searched. Even the camp bed had been unfolded. Sitting in the big chair which Newgrange had prized so much, he used the red 'direct line' 'phone, dialled the Clanmore Alliance number in London, and got through to Osgood Morris.

'You took your time,' complained Morris. 'I've been waiting. I even missed lunch — '

'Your next stop is an executive ulcer,' said Laird sarcastically. 'I've just been chewed by the State Police. They know why I'm on Jersey.'

'Damn,' said Morris unhappily. 'What happened?'

Laird told him briefly, then added a tight update on the rest of the story. He included a factual mention of Jacob West and his *Vanneau*, but, as he'd expected, Morris almost brushed that aside.

'I'm not interested in beachcombing treasure hunters and their stupid little games,' said Morris impatiently. What's important is that you've kept the peace with this Chief Inspector Flambard. But am I right about the rest, that you're no further forward with the *Rosewitch* sinking or the Mehran family?'

'I'm counting on getting to Peter Frere,' said Laird patiently. 'I told you — '

'And I heard,' snapped Morris. 'You say Frere is on the fringe of this treasure-hunt nonsense, and that some other helpful comedian has a rifle. Remember the chairman's policy, of course — don't take unnecessary risks. But you'll need to push harder.'

'I'm trying.' Laird scowled at the telephone mouthpiece. 'Does Tony Dello know about Newgrange yet?'

'I — ah — broke the sad news.' Sanctimoniously, Morris altered his voice. 'Naturally, he was distressed. I told him to take the rest of the day off, visit the former Mrs Dello, and break the news. I gather he did.' He pushed that aside. 'You're sure this 'phone line is secure?'

'Yes.'

'Then I can give you some practical help. You were puzzled about the way the new Mehran marina development was being financed. The answer is they're in trouble. On the one hand, they're trying desperately to raise additional investment capital, on the other they're having to struggle to keep their existing loans serviced. The most recent try involved a West German investment trust, but that's something else that has fallen through. They're in a mess, every way there is, whatever kind of smiling face you're getting.' Morris paused, a puzzled note entering his voice. 'Though that is the odd thing about it. Any dealing that's going on, they still seem so damned confident. Like tomorrow won't happen — or they've something up their sleeves.'

'It's possible.' Laird felt a warning tingle in his mind, without being totally certain why. Then he remembered the way Paul Mehran had promised his sons the chance of that new power boat. 'I'll watch for it.'

'Do that.' Morris gave a peevish sniff. He disliked it when he forecast one thing yet another still kept happening. 'There's another small aspect you might want to know about — if you're still interested in your Crab person when he visited Jersey, from Southampton.'

Laird frowned at the red telephone. 'Go on.'

'Credit card bills. Our computer spoke to some other computers in a friendly way. Peter Varrick's credit card records are still held.' It

218

was a casual understatement of several rules being broken. 'Varrick paid his hotel bill and made a few purchases. The — ah — lady he was with was awarded a gold watch. The only unusual item is that he paid for a day-return trip by hydrofoil from St Helier across to St Malo in France.'

'Alone?' asked Laird sharply.

'Yes. So it seems. A business trip?' Morris's voice was dry.

'Maybe putting some pieces together. Roder, the other Mehran director, is over in St Malo.'

'A dangerous place, France' mused Morris. 'So many French live there.' The joke amused him. 'Inevitable, I suppose.'

Laird managed to say goodbye and hung up.

When he went back through to the front office he found Liz Hatton was ready to leave. She had a few personal items in a shopping bag and was holding a framed photograph in one hand.

'I thought I'd take this. Do you think anyone would mind?' Shyly, she showed it to him. 'He had this taken the day we opened here. I — well, nobody knows what will happen, do they?'

Laird looked at the photograph. It had been taken outside the little insurance office.

Chris Newgrange and Liz were posed under the Newgrange Agencies sign. Both were smiling, Newgrange had his arm around her shoulders.

'I think he'd want you to have it,' said Laird gently.

She tried to smile, couldn't, and put the photograph in her bag.

*   *   *

Diane Mehran was next on his list. Visiting Mehran Holdings, particularly now, wasn't a happy thought. But it had to be done, he couldn't afford to make waves.

He drove the Ford back towards the town centre, saw the electronic boards showed every car park full, and crawled with the other traffic as near as he could to King Street. Then he managed to squeeze the little car into the only space in a line of illegally parked vehicles in a quiet, narrow side street just around the corner from the Mehran building. When Laird went into the high-rise block the uniformed doorman used an internal telephone to check, then indicated the lift.

'Third floor, Mr Laird.' The man was bored; he had an open book on his desk.

Laird went over, past the lobby garden, and saw one of the lifts was coming down. It stopped, the door slid open, and the man who stepped out stared at him, reddening.

'Hello, Jody,' said Laird mildly. 'Keeping busy?'

The Witchlove Haven explosives man formed what might have been meant to be a smile. He had a cut on his forehead and a bruise above one eye, the kind of injury which might have been caused by contact with a car windshield.

'You've hurt your head.' Laird made a concerned noise. 'Did you have an accident?'

The man gave a vague grunt, scowled, and strode past him heading out.

It made Laird feel better. When he took the lift up to the third floor and went into the Mehran Holdings office, an eager, smartly dressed counter clerk pounced on him.

'Miss Diane is in a meeting, Mr Laird,' said the youngster earnestly. 'She'll be clear in a minute or so. She says can you please wait?'

Laird nodded. There were about half a dozen staff working in the outer office and he was led past them, into a carpeted corridor. There were anonymous doors leading off it and his guide opened one and ushered him through.

'Miss Diane will be along directly. This is her office.' The youngster indicated a two-seater couch beside a low, glass table.

'Make yourself comfortable, Mr Laird. Can I get you coffee or anything?'

Laird shook his head, settled on the couch and the counter clerk vanished, leaving the door ajar. It was a large room, with an executive desk. A progress chart was on one wall, a between-the-wars watercolour painting of a steamship beside it. A three-quarter length cased clock ticked gently in a corner next to a steel filing cabinet. But he noticed a vase of flowers on the desk and a pair of woman's comfortable slip-on shoes waiting on the floor beside the clock.

'So you found us,' said a voice.

He looked round. Simon Mehran was leaning in the doorway, a cool smile on his tanned, hawk-like face. He was wearing an open-necked white sports shirt with tailored blue yachting trousers and blue canvas shoes. A fringe of dark, curly hair showed on his chest and he had a gold ID bracelet on his left wrist.

'On leave from Witchlove Haven?' asked Laird mildly.

'Hauled in for a talking session.' Simon Mehran thumbed at the corridor. 'They talk, I listen.'

'They?'

'The grown-ups.' Mehran was sarcastic. 'Directors' meeting.' He changed the subject, and was surprisingly amiable. 'How do you like St Helier?'

'All right, what I've seen of it,' said Laird. 'Busy.'

'Parking a car can be hellish in the tourist season,' sighed Mehran. 'Where did you leave your wheels?'

'My borrowed wheels,' corrected Laird. 'That side street round the corner.'

'Traffic warden alley. You'll get a ticket.' Mehran grinned, raised a hand, and went away leaving the door half open.

Another few minutes passed, an occasional figure scurried outside in the corridor. The chart on the wall related to nothing more significant than hire-car movements and staff work schedules. At last, Laird heard a door open outside, then voices. He looked round to see Paul Mehran and another man, a thin, straw-haired stranger, stride past outside. A moment later Diane Mehran came into her office. She seemed flushed and angry. Following her, by comparison calm and unperturbed, came Ray Garris. The small, thickset man greeted Laird with a nod, his hands in his jacket pockets. Whatever had been going on, the Mehran associate director didn't seem upset.

'I'm sorry, Andrew.' Diane Mehran almost threw a pile of papers on her desk. 'We had to have a meeting. It went on and on — '

'And on again,' said Garris laconically. His pug-nosed face shaped a grimace. 'Just a few small problems.'

'Not for the first time.' Diane Mehran's voice was acid. 'Always things I didn't know about.'

'That way, life stays interesting.' Garris grinned, showing his gold-filled teeth. He turned to Laird. 'I thought I'd say hello again. You haven't had much of a welcome to the island, Laird — I mean that business last night, Newgrange being killed. I knew him, I even looked in on him for a couple of minutes yesterday.'

'I heard,' said Laird vaguely. 'Business?'

'Some personal business I wanted to ask about. Nothing important.' Garris glanced at Diane Mehran again. 'I'll get out to the Haven and knock some heads together. All right?'

She nodded, and Garris left them. Sighing, Diane Mehran grimly closed the door, came over, and sank into the couch beside Laird. She was still wearing the blue suit he'd seen that morning.

'A tough meeting?' asked Laird sympathetically.

'Yes. We have a few like that.' She turned to face him, her green eyes still angry. 'Always

224

for the same reason, helped on by my cousin Paul.'

'What's the problem?' murmured Laird.

'He thinks that because I'm female I can be kept in the dark about some of what's going on.' Saying it seemed to help and her mood thawed. 'So we had our usual small war. What about you? Have you been to the police?'

Laird nodded. 'I talked with a Chief Inspector Flambard, then signed that statement they wanted.'

'Have they traced Peter Frere?'

'Not yet.' He shook his head. 'They don't seem to have made much progress in any direction.'

Diane Mehran shrugged and seemed to lose interest. 'Paul is going to try to look in before you go. Don't count on it.'

Laird smiled. 'I saw him go past in the corridor with someone.'

'Erick Roder, over from France,' she told him. 'Paul wanted a full board meeting.'

'Plus Simon?'

'Simon — who arrived late as usual.' Diane Mehran had shifted on the couch and there was no real gap between them. She moved again, and her shoulder brushed his. 'Did your London office agree you could stay on?'

'Yes, if I keep a low profile,' said Laird. 'When do you expect Simon's brother back from Hong Kong? I'd like to talk to them together.'

'About those race details?' She shrugged. 'Matt should be here by the weekend — Saturday or Sunday. What will you do till then?' The question came casually, but her hand touched his arm. 'I don't mind showing you some of the island — and we promised you another chance to see over the marina.'

'I haven't forgotten.' Laird looked at her again. The auburn-haired Amazon still had some of her defences up but seemed oddly vulnerable. He caught himself wondering how much she really knew about what was going on. 'But maybe we'd better leave any arrangement until things get sorted out.'

'Yes, of course.' She misunderstood, the way he'd hoped. Suddenly she sat upright. 'Could you use a drink? I've a medicinal bottle hidden in the filing cabinet.'

'Another time.' Laird shook his head. 'Anyway, it's time I left. You've things of your own to do. What's the biggest problem from your meeting?'

'For me? I'm like Ray Garris — I've some heads to bang together in the cause of efficiency.' Something in her voice told him she was lying. Then she looked away. 'Well, I suppose I can always work late at it tonight, I've nothing better to do.'

'You think of me, I'll think of you.' He avoided the obvious invitation. 'I've a report to write for London, they want it telexed first thing tomorrow.'

'Say good things about us, Andrew. We want that sponsorship.' Diane Mehran's brittle business manner slipped back in place as he rose. 'We need it — and you and Clanmore Alliance wouldn't regret it. That's a promise.'

She walked with him along the corridor and through the main office, then stayed until he got into the lift. She was still smiling that bright, brittle smile as the lift door closed. Laird drew a deep breath as he started down. Diane Mehran was a puzzle, an enigma in several ways. But the tall, heavily built woman was also a lonely woman — even if she would probably have laughed at the idea.

* * *

It was bright and warm outside. The tourists thronging the town centre were mostly on the shaded side of the streets. They were noisy, they were sweaty. Some were cheerful, some looked limp. But they were spending money fast enough to keep any shopkeeper happy.

Laird got through into the side street where he'd left the Ford. Arriving at the car, he reached for his keys. Then he forgot them. Two figures were reflected in the car window, coming out of a doorway, rushing on him from behind. He spun round, registering the raised cosh in one man's hand and the way the other man was hauling out a length of chain from under his jacket.

That glimpsed reflection gave him maybe two seconds of warning. Instinct took over, instinct and dirty-fighting reflexes honed in years when all that mattered had been that he made it back to his ship in one piece. Neither of his attackers spoke, he was only conscious of two brutish, leering faces.

Get in first — that was the golden rule. Laird threw his hands out and back against the Ford's metal for support, kicked, and the heel of his right foot pistoned against the first man's crotch with a thud like a slack drumbeat. He heard the man's high-pitched scream, saw him fold and start to go down, then had to throw himself sideways as the second man came in with the chain.

Swinging, the chain crashed against the Ford's roof and with a snarl the thug behind it brought his arm back for another scything blow. Then his eyes widened as, instead of retreating, Laird sprang at him.

It was one of the oldest, most effective street-fighting moves in the western world.

Laird's hands grabbed the man's jacket lapels, pulling him close. Then, as he smelled the man's foul breath, Laird butted his head hard and fast into that face, hard enough to smash the man's nose and hear a crunch as his teeth broke.

The chain dragged weakly across Laird's back as the dazed, confused attacker made a feeble attempt to struggle. In the background, the first man was staggering to his feet again. It was time to finish things. Releasing his grip on the jacket, Laird seized his opponent's right wrist in a two-handed lock, twisted him round in a vice-like grip, then used all his strength in a pump-handle jerk.

The snap of a breaking arm bone was followed by a howl of pain. The chain clattered on the street. Laird let him go and two injured, frightened figures stumbled away, only wanting to escape.

'Nicely done, son,' said an approving voice. Laird swung round, then relaxed. A small, grey-haired woman was standing a few feet away. She was elderly, beaming, and carrying a shopping bag. She winked at him. 'I like to see a man who can cope like that. Do you want the police or me as a witness?'

'No thanks, ma.'

His two would-be attackers had already vanished down a lane; there was no one else in sight. Laird wiped a hand across his face and found a small trickle of blood. It came from a gash on his forehead, his price for the head-butt. 'Why look for trouble? But I'm glad you stayed.'

'So am I, son.' The woman chuckled. 'That was the best excitement I've had in years.'

Still beaming, she left. Taking a deep breath, Laird kicked the abandoned cosh and the length of chain into the gutter. He was under no illusions. The attack had been no casual meeting. But how had it happened? Why had it happened?'

As the pieces fell into place, his mouth tightened. First, there was the way he had met Jody as the Witchlove construction man was leaving the Mehran offices. Then there had been Simon Mehran, who so casually asked where the Ford was parked. Jody had his own score to settle for the way his car had been sandwiched that morning. If some people in the Mehran organisation felt it might be convenient to have Andrew Laird out of circulation for a day or two, if Simon Mehran had known a quick way to contact Jody — yes, there had been time to organise a couple of harbour rats, tell them where to go, and tell them the car to watch.

But why? It strengthened a tendril of suspicion that had been growing in his mind.

Something was due to happen soon, something vital to the Mehrans' financial future, perhaps their financial existence. Whatever it was, whether it involved the uncovered wreck of the *Vanneau* or not, whether Witchlove Haven played a role or whether there was another, totally different factor, the missing Peter Frere might still hold the key.

Things had come a long way since a Spanish woman had complained about her washing machine. But the trail of death and violence couldn't go on for ever.

Laird straightened and turned again towards the car. This time he saw a slip of paper in a small plastic envelope which had been stuck to the windscreen glass. Swearing softly, he ripped it free and stuck it in his pocket.

He'd got himself a parking ticket.

$$\star \quad \star \quad \star$$

First, he had to tuck the Ford out of sight. Laird drove it round to the Green Street car park and was in luck. There were spaces, one of them well back among the lines of vehicles. From there he walked to the first hotel he saw, where he washed the blood from his face in the men's room. The cut had stopped bleeding and he went back into the hotel's

231

busy lobby and found a pay 'phone.

He had two calls to make.

Kiri Vass came first. He called the airport number, asked for her, and was put through. She sounded surprised then relieved to hear his voice.

'I need a favour,' Laird told her. 'Paul Mehran flies his own private aircraft. I need to know if he flew it today, if he filed any flight plan, and if he carried passengers either way. Can you do it?'

'Easily.' She was confident.

'I'd like anything else you can get on that plane. How often Mehran uses it, destinations, if he ever clears cargo through customs.'

'I can try.' She was puzzled. 'But why?'

'There's something happening with them. I'm not sure what, but I want to fill some gaps.'

'If the right people are on duty, there shouldn't be too much of a problem.' Her manner changed. 'I want to talk to you anyway — not at Merfleur and somewhere away from the airport. I'll be clear of here in another hour or so.'

'All right.' It was his turn to be puzzled. 'Where?'

'Make it Mont Orgueil Castle, near the Queen Elizabeth Gate. In about an hour and a half?'

'I'll be there,' he promised.

He said goodbye, broke the connection, then checked the directory, fed the pay 'phone more money, and dialled police headquarters. He asked for Chief Inspector Flambard but it was a suspicious Sergeant Moisan who came on the line.

'He's out,' said Moisan curtly. 'But he told me about you, Laird — and thanks for this morning. You left me looking a prize idiot, didn't you?'

'I've been making my own mistakes,' said Laird wryly. 'Suppose we agree I owe you a drink?'

'A damned big one.' Moisan thawed a little. 'The boss has gone out to Merfleur. He said that if you called I was to tell you he won't frighten the natives, just remind them we exist. Where are you?'

'At a pay 'phone in town. Keeping in touch the way I promised.' Laird looked round, but there was no one showing even the slightest interest in him. In a few short words he told Moisan what had happened in the side street.

'Are you making a complaint?' Moisan was suspicious.

'No. But if a couple of casualties turn up somewhere, looking for treatment — '

'We'll hear about it. Then we'll keep an eye on them — not the kind they'll know about.'

This time Moisan chuckled. 'If we get anything interesting, we'll let you know.' He paused. 'Tom Flambard told me not to call your hotel. But suppose it matters and we've no option?'

'Then, whether you get through to me or leave a message, say you've got to see me again,' suggested Laird. 'Make out there's something you want added to my statement.'

'There's nothing like the truth,' said Moisan sarcastically.

Laird ended the call, hung up, and left the hotel. He had one more item on his mental list, a nagging gap in his memory that made him wish he'd paid more attention to a now half-forgotten medical-school lecture.

A hospital library would have given him the answer, but that would have involved too many explanations. Not many public libraries or bookshops were likely to stock what he needed. But he knew another way, a certain way.

He set off through St Helier's crowded, noisy streets, heading for the harbour. On the way he was offered 'first drink free' vouchers for nightclubs, jewellery store leaflets, and the inevitable chance to take a stake in the Jersey state lottery. Flower sellers were pushing for late-afternoon trade, cafés and restaurants were getting ready for the evening. He could have purchased a 'Jersey special' cabbage-stalk walking stick, any shape of red island pottery, or a seat of his choice on a late-night bus outing.

All that had faded by the time he reached the working area of the harbour. Offshore, a flotilla of sailboards were having some kind of race round a buoyed course, being tossed by the wake of a big passenger hydrofoil on its way in from France. A couple of work-scarred fishing boats were heading out for a night's work, their crews exchanging shouted, friendly insults. The dockside smells, the coiled ropes and rusted cables, the thud of someone's idling diesel engine made him feel more at home.

Laird found what he wanted near the ferry terminal. It was a marine stores warehouse, a long, low-roofed cavern of a building. When he went in, every rack and shelf seemed to groan under the weight of spares and stock.

An assistant came across the plain wood flooring, a wizened little man in overalls with a face like a dried-up apple. He looked at Laird with initial suspicion, then seemed to accept what he saw.

'Looking or buying, mister?' he asked bluntly.

'Looking,' said Laird.

'Go ahead.' The little man gestured an

all-embracing invitation. 'If you get lost, shout — not that anyone will hear you.'

The sea has its own technical literature, with a complexity and diversity that would startle any landsman. The warehouse's book section was a long gallery of shelves filled with manuals and instruction volumes, bound editions of notices to mariners, star charts and ephemeris tables, the exotics of flags and flag etiquette, the sober ledger guides to shipmasters' business, and a hundred other basic subjects.

The books Laird needed were sharing a shelf with gazetteers of sea-traffic separation routes and the latest editions on tides and tidal streams. Any ship on passage was a largely self-contained unit and had to carry some basic medical textbooks. They were mainly written for crews who might have to treat injury or illness with what they had available, doing their best to sustain their patient until skilled help could be reached. But some, specialised in their own right, dealing with the sea and its perils and written by experts in their particular field, had a honed, economical accuracy and a total clarity. His luck was in. He found the one he wanted, a slim book bound in red and devoted to dangerous sea life. Laird took it over to where a packing case offered a handy reading table and began turning the pages.

Any innocent who paddled barefoot along the water's edge or who went swimming further out would have been horrified within a few pages by its clinical text and stark illustration. Every ocean in the world had its perils, every sea coast hid its lurking dangers. Some were rare, some were relatively commonplace in an underwater jungle where the basic rule was survival.

There were the destructive biters, from the white shark and great barracuda to the pugnacious killer whale. There were grippers, like the tridacna clams of the Pacific and Europe's moray eels. There were the stingrays and whiprays of sub-tropical coastal waters, some able to drive their barbed 'whip' tails straight through flesh and deep into bone. The Australian sea-wasp jellyfish stung in a way that could bring death in eight minutes. A variety of Indian Ocean sea urchin was a potential killer. Then there were sea snakes and stonefish — the stonefish rated as deadly as a cobra.

Laird stopped there, checked the index, found the entry for weever fish, then read carefully.

It was like an echo of that lecture years ago, the writer acknowledging he was drawing on data from the US Navy Hydrographic Office.

Weever were 'very venomous fish of the temperate zone', which usually buried themselves in sand or mud with only their heads exposed. When a target of any kind came near, they struck — the kind of anti-social attitude that meant it was just as well their numbers were low. For a weapons system, the weever fish could stab with a row of needle-sharp spines loaded with a poison similar to snake venom. It was a poison which was both a neurotoxin and a haemotoxin, attacking both the nervous system and the blood. Within minutes the result could be excruciating, screaming agony, convulsions, then loss of consciousness. Basic treatment was similar to that for a snake bite. If the victim lived, even partial recovery could take months.

Footsteps sounded on the wooden flooring. He looked up as the wizened little warehouse assistant ambled past.

'If it's really necessary, we sometimes sell a book,' said the assistant acidly. 'We're not proud.'

Laird smiled and went back to the small print. There was the basic treatment to be given by whatever unfortunate ship's officer was in charge of the first-aid chest, then the complications that might ensue.

But three warnings were in heavy print.

'EVEN SOME TIME AFTER ITS DEATH A WEEVER MUST NOT BE HANDLED CARELESSLY.' 'A PATIENT'S NATURAL RESISTANCE IS CONSIDERABLY LOWERED IF HE HAS BEEN A HEAVY USER OF ALCOHOL.' 'IMMEDIATE TREATMENT IS VITAL TO REDUCE THE RISK OF DEATH OR PERMANENT DAMAGE TO THE NERVOUS SYSTEM.'

Peter Frere could have been a simple three-time loser. Frowning, thinking hard, Laird closed the book and returned it to its shelf. There were still things which didn't make sense. A hospital, presented with Frere's kind of emergency admission, should have spotted something like the wound left by a weever spine — or maybe even found part of a broken spine embedded in the flesh.

If either had been there in the first place.

If it had been an accident while Frere was fishing.

If it hadn't been something else.

One small portion of that medical-school lecture had come drifting back into his mind. The professor concerned had believed that one case example was worth hours of theory. He had wanted his students to remember that a poison could be old, could be dried up, could be forgotten — and could still kill.

The example had been local enough. An Edinburgh housemaid had been dusting her way around her employer's study. There were trophies on the walls from years earlier when her employer had made his money in South America. The housemaid had scratched her hand on the tip of an old poisoned arrow, ignored the tiny wound — and collapsed a few minutes later.

Two hours of artificial respiration, then hospital treatment saved her life. For several days she kept lapsing into sudden drowsiness.

Old poisons, old venoms could kill.

Suppose it had been meant to be like that with Peter Frere, that he had been an intended murder victim? Laird could think of a dozen ways in which the weever poison could have been used.

Peter Frere had lived, despite the odds. But the strange, burnt-out wreck which had survived might have been regarded as no longer a danger.

Andrew Laird made his grim way out of the warehouse and into the bright, early evening sunlight. If he was right, then Peter Frere had been left to the next best thing to a living death.

The *Rosewitch* score was still mounting.

6

A Union Jack flag flew high over Mont Orgueil Castle, whipped by a wind from the sea. Towering over the busy, bustling village of Gorey and its yacht harbour, the castle was a huge fairy-tale fantasy of a structure, a medieval fantasy with a history which went back to the twelfth century.

The name meant Mount Pride. Enlarged and strengthened by succeeding generations, the first stone walls with arrow-slits for archers had gradually acquired more and more ramparts and bastions. The early defensive *mâchicoulis* — neat holes lovingly placed through which to pour down boiling pitch on unwelcome visitors — had given way to squat embrasures for cannon. Located on its freak plug of rock, strategically placed between England and the rest of Europe, war had washed around the castle over those centuries. Sieges and sorties, the occasional beheading of important prisoners had all featured in its history.

Even in World War Two, German occupation troops had added machine-gun posts and observation posts facing the sea. But now the castle was only a monument, a tourist attraction. Its military figures were costume dummies in a museum where there were taped multilingual commentaries with sound effects.

Leaving his car on a grass field car park, Andrew Laird went in across the bridge spanning the dry moat. Posters advertised an open-air floodlit performance of a Shakespeare play for the weekend. Some late visitors were buying souvenirs at a kiosk. He went on, past old guardhouses and iron gates, climbing seemingly endless flights of worn, stone steps. At last, short of breath, he reached the great arch of the Queen Elizabeth Gate.

Kiri Vass was not far away, easy to spot with her raven-black hair and dark grey airline uniform with its flash of white blouse. She was standing beside a low battlement wall, looking down at the view below, but she heard his footsteps as he came over. Glancing round, a gust of wind tousling her hair as she stepped away from the shelter of the wall, she greeted him with a wry smile.

'I watched you coming up,' she said. 'Sorry about the climb.'

'I needed the exercise.' Laird looked over the battlement wall, seeing part of the way he'd come up. 'Why here?'

'I could make sure you weren't followed.'

Kiri moved, using him as a windbreak, and brushed the hair back from her face. She gave a sudden frown. 'What happened to your head?'

'I got into an argument, that's all.' Laird had almost forgotten the cut on his forehead. 'I'll tell you later. How did you get on?'

'Paul Mehran and his plane?' Kiri Vass shrugged, as if she had something else on her mind. She considered the cut for a moment longer. 'Everything seems normal enough. It's a four-seater Piper Comanche, he bought it about three months ago — not long after he got his private pilot's licence.'

Laird nodded. Overhead, he could hear the growing crackle of the flag and the slap of halliards against its pole. 'What about today?'

'He filed a flight plan for St Malo, left Jersey about 8 a.m., landed back here at about 10 a.m.' She kept it tightly factual, obviously still puzzled. 'He brought a passenger named Roder back with him from France. As far as I know, Roder is still on the island. Roder had a briefcase, no luggage.'

'And the general picture?'

'Pretty much what you'd expect.' Kiri Vass huddled closer as a new gust of wind whistled around the old stonework. 'Any pilot flying out beyond the island is supposed to file a flight plan. If he's landing in France or the

243

UK mainland he goes through customs and immigration there, and on his return here, though it's usually a formality. Most of Paul Mehran's flying has been purely local or an occasional hop across to France. No fixed pattern.'

'What about passengers, cargo?' persisted Laird.

She shook her head. 'Nothing more than you'd expect. He doesn't run a taxi service, but he may bring in an occasional crate of wine from France. You're talking smuggling?'

'I wish I knew,' he said grimly. 'Does Simon Mehran have a pilot's licence?'

'No.'

'You know the airport. Could Mehran land, then maybe drop off a passenger before he checked in?'

'It's possible, I suppose.' She shrugged. 'Possible but risky. Or he could touch down in a field somewhere — except this is a small island, people would ask questions.'

'What about after dark?' He was beginning to feel he was wasting time. But Paul Mehran and his aircraft were an aspect too obvious to ignore.

'Forget that.' She gave a sympathetic smile. 'There's an almost total night-flying ban over Jersey. It's strictly enforced. Mustn't disturb the tourists in their little beds.'

Laird swore under his breath, turned away for a moment, and looked down. Far below, at the foot of the castle rock, Gorey village and its yacht harbour looked like toy-town creations. The tide was in. A big French hydrofoil was moving away from the main quay, a scattering of small yachts and other pleasure craft dotted the rest of the water. An hour or so would probably see the French passengers back on their own soil.

'Andrew — '

He turned at her voice. Kiri had turned up the collar of her jacket against the wind and he saw she was shivering.

'I'm sorry.' Suddenly he realised how chilly it had become where they were. 'You had your own problem, one you wanted to talk about.'

'Yes.' She hesitated, then looked at him in a strange, almost doubtful way.

'Still worried about Jacob and Belle?'

'They're part of it,' she said cautiously. 'I wish — yes, I wish we'd never got into any of this. But we are — and there's something else now, something I don't want them to know about. Will you give me your word?'

'Everybody's getting my word on something,' said Laird grimly. 'But for whatever it's worth, you've got it.'

'I've heard from Peter Frere.' She looked

away. 'I know where he is.'

Laird swallowed. 'You mean it?'

'He telephoned me at the airport — I know his voice, it wasn't anyone else.' She faced him again, earnestly. 'He still wants to see you — but no one else. The way things are he's even frightened of seeing Jacob because he knows Jacob is a constable's officer.'

'That didn't stop him raiding the cottage today,' said Laird sarcastically. 'Did he tell you that?'

'He made the call from there.' She nodded calmly. 'Andrew, it wasn't easy to make sense out of him, but he swears he didn't kill Chris Newgrange, that he hasn't hurt anyone. He — well, he sounded desperate.'

'Where is he?'

Kiri eyed him shrewdly, carefully. 'Will you tell the police?'

'No.'

Satisfied, she relaxed. 'He's hiding near Merfleur. We've to meet him tonight, late on. I promised there would only be you and I.'

He nodded. 'What time?'

'About ten o'clock. We'll need a boat — I phoned Jimmy Boullard and we can borrow his.' She gave a soft chuckle. 'I couldn't tell him why, I can't help it if he has the wrong idea — and a surprisingly dirty mind.'

'As long as he enjoys it,' said Laird wryly.

Peter Frere — it was a totally unexpected gift, one that could make all the difference, as long as his luck held. A fresh gust of wind moaned around the castle and brought him back to the present. 'When are you due back at the Wests?'

'When they see me.' She was puzzled. 'Why?'

'We're going down to Gorey.' Laird took her arm. 'We'll find a drink and something to eat. We've both earned it.'

★ ★ ★

Kiri Vass's car was parked not far from his own. They drove both vehicles down the steep, narrow road which led to the village, left them at the little harbour, and walked from there. The French hydrofoil had gone, most of the people around seemed to have come ashore from yachts moored for the night, and it was several degrees warmer than it had been up at the castle. Even the wind seemed to have died away.

They found a restaurant bar which had a balcony with a view. The bar was crammed with more of Gorey's yachting fans, large, noisy men with heavy sweaters and suntans, their women equally noisy and wearing suntops and tight shorts, but the balcony was

247

quieter. A plump, cheerful girl with a French accent gave Laird and Kiri a corner table and took their orders.

It was a simple menu. They each settled for a steak and shared a bottle of wine, and while they ate they talked, the noise from the bar drowning any risk they'd be overheard. Quietly, factually, Laird told her what he knew, what had happened, and what he suspected, and saw Kiri Vass's dark eyes gradually widen with a mixture of horror and near disbelief.

'It's a total mess,' she said suddenly and bitterly. She pushed aside some of the steak, her appetite gone, and rubbed a finger round the rim of her glass. 'Suppose you're right — particularly about what happened to that poor devil Peter Frere? What kind of people are they?'

'The Mehrans and their friends?' Laird shrugged. 'Right now, fairly desperate.'

'And now Merfleur is part of it.' A late yacht was coming into harbour, sails lowered, using an outboard engine as it crept towards a mooring. Her eyes followed it for no particular reason. 'I'm getting to wish I'd never found those damned pebbles — '

'But it happened,' said Laird dryly. 'It's not your fault that Jacob is such a stubborn old devil.' He smiled at her across the table.

'Keep him out of trouble, and give the rest a little time. It'll work out.'

She nodded doubtfully. 'I'll talk to Belle. That's the best way to handle him.'

'Not too many people find a personal treasure ship,' mused Laird.

'One found, one to go,' she said grimly. 'That's what my father was going on about in his last letter — that there were two French ships, that I should keep an eye open for the other one.'

Laird chuckled. 'I'm surprised he isn't here.'

'You don't know him.' She wrinkled her nose in mock despair. 'He stopped being interested when he knew where those stones originated. The rest isn't important to him. He says he'll maybe come over when he can find the time.' She frowned. 'I'm thinking of taking some time off work. I've a few days due. It might help Jacob and Belle if I was around.'

'To keep an eye on them.' Laird nodded a slow agreement.

A burst of noisy laughter reached them from the bar. Kiri glanced round, smiled a little, then faced him again.

'Tell me about Diane Mehran,' she said unexpectedly. 'What do you make of her?'

'That's difficult,' he admitted.

'So I've heard.' A glint of frosty amusement showed in her eyes. 'She's close enough to it all. But even if she isn't involved, I've heard stories about one or two men who left skid-marks trying to get away from her.'

He grinned, finished the wine in his glass, then pushed back his chair.

★ ★ ★

They drove to Merfleur through the late summer sunlight, Kiri leading the way in her Volvo, Laird close behind with the Ford. Most of the traffic on the way was obviously tourist cars out for an evening drive. They left them behind when they turned off at the Norman church and travelled the last narrow stretch of road down to Merfleur Point.

Belle West was working in her cottage garden. She looked up then waved as the two cars drew in. Another vehicle, Jimmy Boullard's MG, was already parked near the old harbour, but for once there was no sign of Benny, the dog.

'Jacob took him for a walk along the shore,' explained Belle when they reached her. 'He's got that damned air pistol with him, but he shouldn't be too long.'

'And Jimmy?' Laird indicated the car.

'He's doing his night guard at the island.'

Belle shook her head in total disapproval. 'Jacob took him out earlier — nobody else could get here at short notice. They're a pair of old fools.' Then a twinkle showed in her eyes and she considered Laird for a moment before turning to Kiri. 'The speedboat is in the water, like you wanted. Do I ask what you both think you'll be doing out there?'

'Are you sure you'd want to know?' asked Kiri blandly.

'At my age?' Belle West's plump, round face shaped a grin. 'Yes. Are you going to change out of that uniform first?'

'If I get the chance,' said Kiri.

She went into the cottage. Still grinning, Belle West followed her through the door.

Left alone, Andrew Laird made his way down to the harbour. The yellow speedboat was moored beside the black Zodiac boat, waiting, tugging lightly at her mooring line as the gentle swell rippled in. Small, chunky, she had a two-seater cockpit and a powerful-looking inboard engine. Her name, *Cloth-cap*, was painted at the stern. He smiled a little. The one-time admiral had a down-to-earth sense of humour.

Turning away, he started off again, in the direction of the old Martello tower. Close up, it was still impressive. The stonemasons who had built it would have been proud of the way

251

their work had survived. It was about forty feet high, with what had probably been a gun platform on top, and the round tower had been intended as a year-round home for its tiny garrison. He could see the original door, about halfway up the stonework, which would have been reached by a ladder the garrison could draw in after them. But a later door had been cut and fitted at ground level.

He heard barking, then saw a black shape charging towards him. In another moment Benny was greeting him enthusiastically while a cursing, grumbling Jacob West limped rapidly to catch up.

'Get down and stay down, you great stupid brute,' thundered West as he arrived. The dog broke off and circled them, tail wagging, and West scowled his despair. 'One day that beast will understand who happens to be boss — but don't ask me when.'

'Enjoy your walk?' asked Laird mildly.

'Not bad.' West winked. He had his haversack over one shoulder, the butt of his air pistol clearly visible. 'Nothing like plinking a few empty bottles for soothing the nerves, boy. Did Belle tell you we've got Jimmy out at the *Vanneau*?'

'Doing his night watchman.' Laird nodded.

'He's a night watchman with a pump-action shotgun,' said West with cheerful satisfaction. 'He's no great shot, but with a gun like that, who has to be?' He paused. 'Did you know we had the paid police over this afternoon, asking the same damn-fool questions again?'

'I heard,' said Laird soberly. 'I had my own session with them. They know the real reason I'm here.'

'Damnation.' Jacob West's smile faded. 'What did you tell them about us?'

'Nothing that matters.' Benny had settled beside Laird. Stooping a little, he scratched the dog behind one ear. 'They're not the people you should worry about.'

'I know — and I've Belle to consider.' West's mood was suddenly serious. 'I told her she should move out for a day or two. She told me to go to hell.' His confidence blossomed again. 'I'm still a constable's officer. They'd be fools to try anything here.'

'A constable's officer might not worry them too much,' said Laird stonily. 'Be careful. How about Peter Frere? Any more traces of him being around?'

'No.' West shook his head. 'Except I thought he'd only taken food when he broke in, but he also damn well went off with a pair of binoculars of mine.' He pursed his lips. 'They cost good money, I want them back.'

'He'll turn up, they'll turn up,' soothed

Laird. 'You still think he'll come back again, don't you?'

Gloomily, Jacob West nodded. Together, the dog at their heels, they started back towards the cottage.

'Funny things, shipwrecks,' said West suddenly. He used his stick to point towards his wife's garden. 'See those lilies?'

Laird looked and nodded. One corner of the garden was filled with the plants, all in flower, a full-blossomed splash of colour.

'Guernsey lilies, that's why Belle likes them so much.' West sucked his lips noisily. 'Guernsey be damned, that was a shipwreck even earlier than our *Vanneau* — seventeenth century. A merchantman on her way back from Africa piled up on the rocks off Guernsey. A few bulbs she had aboard were washed ashore, some rooted, then flowered, and the locals had never seen anything like them before. So now you get Guernsey lilies growing all over the Channel Islands.' He grunted derisively. 'They're ruddy African lilies, they shouldn't be here — but who admits it?'

'It happens,' said Laird mildly. 'Even with people.'

'Yes.' Jacob West gave a surprising growl of a laugh. 'Boy, ever thought what it would be like if everybody was told 'Go back

254

where you belong', eh?'

Laird shook his head. 'Would that include Belle?'

'I hadn't thought of that,' admitted West. He grinned. 'But at least you'd be able to find a place to park a car in St Helier.'

Kiri Vass came out of the cottage as they arrived. She was wearing denim trousers, a black sweater and a water-proof jacket, and lace-up canvas sailing shoes with rubber soles. For a moment West considered her with a frown.

'Remember your tides and currents out there,' he warned. 'And don't stray too far — that toy of Jimmy's is no sea boat.' He glanced at Laird. 'The weather forecast is all right, though there could be some fog later. When will you be back from this damn-fool jaunt?'

'Late,' said Kiri easily. 'Stop twittering, Jacob — go and annoy Belle.'

Muttering to himself, West nodded and went into the cottage.

'What about Belle?' asked Laird. 'Did you tell her anything?'

'She guessed. She was disappointed,' said Kiri. 'But she won't say anything to Jacob.'

★ ★ ★

Relegated to the passenger side of the *Cloth-cap*'s cockpit, Laird had nothing to do but watch as Kiri Vass took the yellow speedboat out past the Merfleur reef. She kept the engine note at a quiet murmur, one hand resting lightly on the small steering wheel, and he saw her glance more than once towards the island where Jimmy Boullard was on guard over the *Vanneau*. But there was no sign of the retired admiral and only the usual vast horde of white seabirds perched on the latticework light tower.

'All right?' she asked as they left the reef astern. Her face came to life when he nodded and her free hand reached for the throttle lever. 'Hold on then.'

The speedboat's engine rasped, their wake became a churning foam, and her bow rose. In a few seconds they were racing over the light swell, an occasional fine curtain of spray drenching aboard, the little hull thudding and bumping as it met the occasional larger wave. Kiri Vass's eyes sparkled, her mouth parted in a white-toothed grin of delight, and she gave Laird another sideways glance.

'More?' She had to shout above the engine noise.

'Why not?' Laird met her grin and nodded.

'Here we go then.' Eyes sparkling, she opened the throttle wide and the little yellow

256

speedboat exploded to full life.

Kiri Vass knew how to handle her charge. As the bow angle increased, the *Cloth-cap* bumped and bored on, carving an even broader white wake. Salt spray stung at Laird's face and the engine note became a howl of power as they curved and snaked through the open water. Then, as suddenly as it had begun, it ended. Easing back the throttle, letting the engine die down to a soft, steady murmur, Kiri brought the speedboat round in a wide, sedate turn which pointed them back towards the shoreline. They'd come further out than Laird had realised. The sun was setting, the light beginning to fade.

'Well?' she asked happily. 'Pretty good?'

'Not bad,' said Laird, then chuckled at her disappointment. 'Yes, better than good. You know how to handle her.'

'You mean, I like showing off.' She grinned, then turned in her seat and nodded astern. 'That's the Ruau Channel. You see the lighthouse and those two groups of rocks?'

He nodded. They were a few miles out, the lighthouse nearest, the two groups of rocks — some of them big enough to be called island — beyond it to the northeast.

'That's the Ecrevière light; any you see further out are on the French coast. The rocks are Les Ecremouand and Les Dirouilles, good places to stay away from unless you know what you're doing.'

'So where are we heading now?' The speedboat seemed to be making a leisurely way parallel with the shore. Merfleur Point was somewhere to the south, there were no landmarks he recognised and the light was still greying in.

'We've gone past where we're going, in case anyone noticed us. We'll double back shortly.' She frowned at him. 'Or is that being too careful?'

'No, do it.' Laird moistened his lips and felt the taste of salt. 'What about Frere? Will he expect a signal?'

She shook her head. 'He knows where we'll be.'

They idled on for another spell, with no other craft in sight and dusk gradually blurring the coast. Then at last they turned and began to backtrack again, gradually easing in. Laird could see the white glint of surf on rocks, then the moving lights of a car on an inland road. The dark shape of a large bird flapped low overhead, then vanished, and the first faint hint of a light mist began to drift around them.

Kiri's face had become a silhouette. He could sense her tension as she kept the little *Cloth-cap* muttering along, heard her soft sigh of relief as the moon broke through some cloud. Suddenly she was satisfied. The speedboat's bow swung round and they were creeping towards a low, black headland of rock, then rounding it into a tiny bay. Easing the wheel, the engine barely ticking over, Kiri brought them towards the remains of a tiny derelict landing stage. They bumped gently, and Laird scrambled on to a rotted gangway and secured a mooring line. The *Cloth-cap*'s engine died, and they made their way ashore.

'We're only about a mile and a half north of Merfleur, but nowhere near a road,' explained Kiri. 'Now — ' She nodded at a sharp rise of ground ahead ' — we go straight up. It's not far.'

It was a short climb, but harder than it looked. There was a narrow hint of a path, but it was partly overgrown with thorny scrub and littered with loose stones and damp, slime-covered rock. At the top, Laird found they were standing beside the collapsed remains of another old Martello tower. Whatever had happened to it, what was left was like a broken stump.

'Here?' he asked.

'This is where he said. Now we just wait.' Kiri glanced inland at a dark tangle of low trees and scrub and sighed. 'He probably knows we're here already. But if he wants to make sure we're on our own, he could take his time.'

Hunted animals acted that way. For Peter Frere, maybe there wasn't much difference. Laird gave a resigned nod then stiffened. The faint beat of an engine was coming in from the sea, gradually growing in strength. He walked a few paces to where he had a clearer view, strained his eyes against the night while the sound grew louder, then another break of moonlight and a shift in the light mist gave him a glimpse of the cause. Moving fast, showing no lights, another speedboat was heading up the Ruau Channel.

It passed them, heading northeast and not far out. He swore softly. The unlit craft, like a scuttling beetle, looked remarkably like the speedboat he'd seen escape from Merfleur Point only twelve or so hours earlier.

Kiri was beside him. He heard her sharp intake of breath and knew she'd also seen the stranger. But it went on, the engine noise gradually fading, heading arrow-straight in the same direction.

'What do you think?' he asked.

'Heading for France — Cherbourg's up that way.' She touched his arm. 'Looking for us?'

Laird shook his head. The way it had passed, the mystery speedboat had business of its own to attend to, the kind the people aboard didn't want to advertise. But it had been there — that was well worth remembering.

A full half hour passed in the darkness beside the broken Martello tower. Laird sat on a block of fallen stonework, resigned to waiting, getting a small amusement from the impatient way Kiri prowled around.

'How well do you know Frere?' he asked.

She shook her head. 'I've only spoken to him a few times. It's hard to say — I suppose I've just tried to be kind to him.'

'But he knew that you could find this place?'

'Belle and I brought him here once, on an outing.' Kiri shrugged, her face lost in the shadows. 'It was like taking a child on a picnic. He seemed to enjoy it.'

The waiting went on. Occasional night rustles reached them from the scrub. Once there was a sudden, high, chilling scream as an unseen predator struck and killed. Then, exactly as Laird was ready to suggest giving up, there was a louder rustle. A figure rose from the scrub and came cautiously towards them, glancing anxiously from side to side.

'Hello, Peter,' said Kiri. She beckoned. 'It's all right — just the two of us, the way I promised.'

261

The man came nearer, out into the fitful moonlight. Peter Frere was taller than Andrew Laird had anticipated, fragile in appearance. The old uniform jacket he'd been given by Jacob West hung like a sack across his narrow shoulders. His hair was thin and unkempt and he had aged almost beyond belief from the police photograph Laird had been shown.

'This is Andrew Laird,' said Kiri in the same soothing voice. 'You wanted to see him, didn't you, Peter?'

'Yes.' Frere gave him a nervous smile, looking at him with eyes that could have belonged to a frightened rabbit.

'Hello, Peter.' Laird gave him a deliberate, friendly smile. 'I'm glad to meet you. Come and sit down.'

Cautiously, Frere came nearer, then sat on one of the fallen blocks of stonework. He was unshaven and kept licking his lips.

'I've brought you a few things.' Kiri reached into her jacket. 'Cigarettes, matches, and a chocolate bar.'

Frere gave a pleased, throaty noise, and grabbed them from her hands. The chocolate bar went into a jacket pocket; he opened the cigarettes and lit one. He drew deeply on the smoke, then sighed. His hand holding the cigarette was shaking.

262

'Peter, you've been trying to see me,' said Laird. 'Why?'

'I want to tell you about something, Mr Laird.' Frere spoke in a halting voice, as if each word was being forced out. 'Kiri says I can trust you.' He moistened his lips. 'Mr Laird, I haven't done any wrong things.'

'Then you've nothing to worry about.' A soft murmur of wind rustled the trees in the darkness and Laird waited until it passed. 'But you've seen things, haven't you, Peter? Things that made you run away?'

Frere bowed his head. The cigarette glowed red as he drew on it again, but he didn't answer.

'Let's talk about why you wanted to see me.' Laird chose his words as if speaking to a child. 'Is it about a ship called the *Rosewitch*?'

Frere jerked, and glanced at Kiri. She gave a slow, definite nod of encouragement.

'I've been ill, Mr Laird.' Frere's voice stumbled, then took on a proud note. 'But I'm getting better. I can remember more things now. I keep trying, it keeps happening.'

'That's good,' encouraged Laird. 'Can you remember why you were ill, what happened?'

'No.' Frere's shoulders slumped. 'I have dreams, bad dreams — that's all. When I wake up I feel sick — but I can't remember why.'

263

'But the *Rosewitch* is different, isn't it?' coaxed Laird. 'You can tell me important things about it, can't you?'

'If I did, your insurance company would pay a big reward, wouldn't they?' Frere was eager. 'I've a friend who needs money, Mr Laird. You could pay him instead of me, couldn't you?'

'We could,' agreed Laird. 'Do you mean Captain West?'

'Yes. That's right.' Frere beamed and nodded.

'So you can tell me now, can't you?' Laird saw Kiri was waiting to intervene, but silenced her with a fractional shake of his head. 'Let me guess, Peter. You saw something strange about the *Rosewitch*, didn't you? That last time, when she sailed from Jersey?'

'I liked working for Witchline Shipping.' Frere frowned at his feet. 'I had a little office in one of the dock sheds — it was nice. There was a reason why I had to work very late that night.' Suddenly there was a childish indignation in his voice. 'Maybe I had been drinking. But not a lot, and I don't tell lies, Mr Laird. It's bad to tell lies — and I did see them. I really did.'

'Who did you see?' It was Laird's turn to feel bewildered.

'Those men. Those other men who got on the ship,' said Frere earnestly. He took a quick draw on his cigarette, then scowled at the smoke. 'They didn't think anyone saw them. But Peter Frere did. For a long time, after I was ill, I thought it was just one of those dreams I have. Now it's clearer, Mr Laird — it was real.'

'These other men,' said Laird softly. 'How many were there?'

'Maybe a dozen. Maybe — yes, maybe more.' Frere brightened. 'They came in a little bus — a minibus.'

'You're sure?'

Frere nodded. A sudden, wild possibility forced its way into Laird's mind, leaving him speechless for a moment.

Kiri frowned. 'Peter, couldn't they have been the *Rosewitch* crew just coming back from a night out?'

'No.' Frere shook his head with total conviction. 'I saw them too. They were on the ship when the other men went aboard.'

'So what did you do?' asked Laird, recovering. 'Did you tell anyone?'

'In the morning.' Frere rubbed a hand down one side of his unshaven face, his voice uncertain. 'I — yes, I think it was the morning. It was Mr Garris I told.' His indignation surfaced again. 'He laughed at me. He said I must have been drunk. He told me to go away.'

'So did you tell anyone else about it?'

'I can't remember.' Frere gave a hopeless shrug. 'I was ill after that, Mr Laird. The doctors said I could have died. I — no, I don't think so. Mr Garris laughed, but he was angry too.' The man brightened. 'But maybe it's important, isn't it? What happened to those other men, Mr Laird? Do you know?'

Laird shook his head. Then, slowly and carefully, he coaxed Frere through it again. He had known worse witnesses — Peter Frere was hazy on detail, but when the man's damaged brain met a blank then he said so. He'd been working late because he'd fallen behind on some paperwork. Nobody had known he was in his little office — it was more of a cubicle. He'd finished and had been leaving when he'd seen the strangers arrive. Why hadn't he challenged them? Frere could only shrug. But how many people would have looked for trouble that way?

Then, at noon the next day, the *Rosewitch* had sailed. Before the end of that week her crew — her official crew — had taken to the lifeboats. And the other men? There was an answer which almost screamed at Laird, which could explain so many things.

'You've done well, Peter.' He saw the man's

near exhaustion at the amount of mental effort involved. 'Take a rest for a couple of minutes.'

'Will it be a big reward?' asked Frere hopefully. 'Captain West is a good man. I want to help him.'

'You won't be disappointed,' promised Laird.

He left the man and walked the few steps to the edge of the slope overlooking the beach. Out across a blackness of water the Ecrivière light was flashing steadily. Further out, little more than bright pinpricks, two other lights on the French coast winked in a different rhythm. He heard footsteps, then Kiri Vass was at his side.

'You were warned how he is, Andrew.' Her voice was doubtful. 'He may believe what he's saying, but you can't really trust him.' She kept her voice low. 'All right, I've never heard him speak so much before. But how much of it makes sense?'

'A lot, a hell of a lot,' said Laird grimly.

Somewhere in the depths of Peter Frere's husk of a scarred mind, he had to know it too — even if he couldn't understand why. It was enough of a motive for the first attempt to kill him. Maybe he'd been allowed to live because of the way he'd been left, but the same people might now be eager to finish the job if they thought there was a risk of memories returning.

Kiri sighed. 'Does it stay a secret, or can I join in?'

'Put it together,' invited Laird. 'I was sent here because we believed the *Rosewitch* landed some of her cargo then was deliberately scuttled for the insurance money.' He glanced back towards Frere, a dark silhouette in the night. 'Believe his story, and we were wrong — it wasn't so simple. The *Rosewitch* sailed with two crews aboard, the official crew to abandon ship and row ashore so they could tell the tale, and the second crew to stay aboard.'

'She didn't sink?' Kiri's attitude stopped just short of incredulous disbelief.

'She didn't sink,' agreed Laird bitterly. 'She probably changed her name and her appearance, that's all.'

'But a man was drowned — '

'So everybody was told.' It was the kind of authentic touch Laird could almost admire. 'He probably just stayed aboard. Then Witchline get a full payout on their ship and cargo, then double that up by selling their 'lost' ship to someone else.'

'You really mean that?' Kiri was still bewildered.

'It happens,' said Laird flatly.

A ship vanished, another ship turned up later in distant waters. The name could have changed, the superstructure could have been radically altered, the ship would operate far away from her previous haunts. Now and again there would be whispers, then facts to back them — and the rogue vessel would vanish again, ducking off the main shipping lanes, her new owners impossible to trace.

Marine insurance firms knew it happened, sometimes could prove it happened. But the cumbersome process of law seldom caught up in time. One ship had been identified in the Baltic, believed to be using her third change of name and yet another flag. Two others, strongly suspect, had been operating among the Pacific islands and off the coast of East Africa respectively — then had vanished again. Insurance firms dreaded the possibility they'd paid out total-loss claims twice on the same ship.

But this time, for what his evidence might be worth in a court, they had Peter Frere — and Laird had other questions to ask him.

He walked back to the ruins of the Martello tower. Frere was exactly where they'd left him. The only change was he had stubbed out his cigarette and was munching happily on the chocolate bar.

'How much will the reward be?' he wanted

to know. 'Will it be a lot of money?'

'It could be, Peter.' Laird stood over him. 'As long as we're sure you had nothing to do with Chris Newgrange's death.'

'Me, Mr Laird?' Frere's mouth fell open, a look of horror showed on his face. 'I told you — '

'Did you know him?'

'No.' Frere's fingers convulsively mashed what was left of the chocolate bar. 'I swear I didn't hurt him. I didn't hurt anyone.'

'If you didn't know him, why did you telephone him?'

'I saw the newspaper photograph, the one with you together.' Frere began to shake, his fear coming back. 'The newspaper said who you were. Then my head felt sore, but I knew Clanmore had insured the *Rosewitch*.'

'Chris Newgrange said he gave you my hotel number,' persisted Laird. He hated pressuring Frere but there was no other way. 'Why didn't you try to get me there?'

Frere bit his lip. 'Frightened — '

'You were frightened. Why?'

'You know who owns that hotel, don't you, Peter?' suggested Kiri Vass quietly.

Frere gave a quick, hunted nod, looking away.

'There's something else I don't understand about you, Peter.' Laird felt Kiri's growing hostility to what he was doing, but kept on. 'Captain West is your friend, yet you stole from him. You stole coins from his wreck, then sold them, didn't you? Just so you could buy booze.'

'Yes.' It came in an ashamed whisper. 'Those coins. They were very old — I was very bad.' Suddenly Frere buried his head in his hands and began to weep.

The sound made Laird feel guilty. He laid a hand on Frere's shoulder and felt the fragile figure react as if stung.

'It's all right,' he soothed quickly. 'Nobody is going to harm you.'

Frere looked sideways at him, still cringing. Gradually the sobs died.

'Mr Laird has to know things, Peter. Otherwise he can't help,' murmured Kiri. She almost pushed Laird aside, knelt beside Frere, and took his hands in her own. She looked round at Laird, her fine-boned face furious. 'I'll ask him anything more you need. You want to know about the coins, and what else?'

'The *Emu*, and the way young Chris was killed,' said Laird warily. 'Good luck with it — I've had enough.'

It took another quarter of an hour of slow, exhausting work, Laird listening in the background, Kiri Vass asking the questions,

271

sometimes having to go back on an answer to make sure.

It was worth every minute.

The coins were reasonably simple to explain. Peter Frere had helped himself to three gold coins he'd found in the excavated mud and shingle during his only visit to the *Vanneau*. He had kept them in a pocket for weeks, his special secret. But then had come a day when he had no money and the temptation was too much.

He had produced the coins in a harbour-side bar, he had sold them to the bar manager for exactly £50 — which gave the bar manager a profit of a few hundred per cent. He'd told the bar manager he had found them while beach-combing; he had been cunning enough to say he couldn't remember where.

And the bar manager, knowing him, had accepted the story. Things like that did happen along the Jersey coast from time to time. Since then a few men had asked Frere about the coins. He didn't know the names of the men, but he'd stuck to his original story.

As far as Frere could be coaxed to tell them, it ended there. Sitting back on her heels, drawing a deep breath, Kiri moved on to the night Chris Newgrange had been killed.

Peter Frere began weeping again and wanted to leave. They soothed him, they talked to him, Kiri held his hands again.

At last, he told them.

First, he had made yet another telephone call to Chris Newgrange's office, saying he wanted to meet Andrew Laird. Newgrange had set up the 9.30 p.m. meeting, had wanted to know where Frere lived, and when he heard about the *Emu*, he had said they'd meet on the motor cruiser.

'So then you felt you needed some extra courage,' suggested Laird. 'So you had a couple of drinks, because you still had enough money left to pay for them?'

Frere gave a shamefaced nod. The night was becoming cold and they saw him shiver. But that was for another reason.

He had walked back towards the *Emu* and had reached the harbour basin about ten minutes or so before his visitor was due. But, whatever else he'd lost, Peter Frere still retained an animal instinct for survival.

As he'd walked through the swirls of fog and along the black shadows of the quayside he had known something was wrong. Then he saw the *Emu*'s cabin door was open and that there was light inside. Frightened but curious, he had climbed down to the next moored boat, which he knew to be empty, then hidden behind its deckhouse and listened. He heard an occasional noise, an occasional murmured voice, but that same animal instinct told him not to move, not to do anything, even when the noises and the voices stopped and the cabin lights went out.

Minutes later, Chris Newgrange had walked along the quay, had stopped at the *Emu* and had climbed down the iron ladder to her deck.

'You saw him?' There was horror in Kiri Vass's voice. She stared at Frere. 'Peter, why didn't you stop him, warn him?'

'Leave it, Kiri,' said Laird quietly. He thought what he himself had seen that night; he knew it would have been like expecting a rabbit to jump out and tackle a fox. 'Just tell it, Peter. We understand.'

Frere gave him a look of gratitude and nodded quickly.

He had seen Chris Newgrange knock on the cabin door, wait, then go down into the darkness. He had heard the quick sounds of a scuffle, then a cry which had left him quivering in terror. The lights had come on in the cabin. Then two men had emerged, scrambling back up to the quayside, running off into the dark and the fog. He hadn't recognised them, he didn't think he would know them again.

'Did you go into the cabin?' asked Laird.

Frere nodded, his eyes closed.

'Then you ran,' persisted Laird. 'Why?'

'I didn't want to be blamed, Mr Laird. It all gave me a headache, a terrible headache.' Frere swallowed. 'I don't know what to do when I get a headache.'

So he had run, he had walked, he had stolen a bicycle and pedalled, until he reached Merfleur Point — somewhere he felt safe. He had hidden the bicycle in some bushes.

'You're going to have to tell the police,' said Laird carefully. 'You'll have to go back, Peter. Plenty of people will help you — people like Captain West.' He saw the doubt on the man's thin, stubble-fringed face. 'He knows about the coins, he's not angry.'

'I can't — ' Agitated, panic in his eyes, Frere jumped to his feet.

'You'll be safe, Peter,' said Kiri quickly.

'It's late, I'm tired.' Frere backed away. 'Tomorrow — yes, tomorrow.' Like a cornered animal, he watched them both. 'That's what I'll do. I'll come to Merfleur Cottage.'

'When?' demanded Laird.

'In the morning. Some time in the morning.'

Then, too quickly to be stopped, he bolted

275

for the scrub. Before Laird could follow, Kiri had grabbed his arm.

'Let him go.' She stared at the spot where Frere had disappeared into the shadows. 'Catch him, and you'll make things worse.'

'All right.' Laird gave a reluctant nod. At least he had heard the man's story. He had gained what had to be the real truth about the *Rosewitch*, and he now knew how Chris Newgrange had died. But the scrub and the trees seemed to mock him. 'Tomorrow. Do you think he'll show?'

'What else can he do?' she asked.

Leaving the ruined tower, they started back down the slope towards the beach and the boat. Then Laird frowned, raised a hand, and stopped. The sound he had heard grew louder, the steady thud of diesel engines, and he saw the cause coming down the Ruau Channel. Navigation, deck and cabin lights all on, one of the big passenger ferries was making a leisurely way south from the French mainland. He glanced at Kiri.

'They're positioning her for the morning — it's usual,' she explained. 'She'll be heading for St Helier or Gorey, no passengers. It's what some of the fishermen call the Ghost Run.'

Laird nodded. Repositioning ships and aircraft was common enough. He watched as the brightly lit ferry passed the entrance to their little bay, the beam of the Ecrevière lighthouse stabbing the night as a background. But there was something else out there.

'Hold on.' He pointed astern of the ferry boat. 'Do you see it?'

'Where?' Kiri Vass caught the urgency in his voice and stared hard in the direction he indicated. 'There's not enough moonlight. I — ' She stopped short as the lighthouse flashed again, then gave a quick gasp of agreement. 'Yes, I've got it.'

It was the same speedboat they'd seen earlier, when it had been heading up the channel. Still running without lights, keeping at the same speed as the ferryboat, keeping in station about 500 yards behind its brightly lit silhouette, it was more or less crawling along. Laird kept watching, lips pursed. Out there, the ferryboat's crew would have no idea they were being followed. The noise of their diesels would totally drown the sound of the speedboat's throttled-back engine.

Yet what was going on? He gave a soft grunt of understanding. It was sheer luck he had spotted the smaller craft behind that blaze of lights. But the same thing would apply to any casual radar scan. The ferry would show prominently; the small, low profile of the shadowing speedboat would either be lost in the general sea clutter or be ignored as some kind of electronic echo.

But why? He turned to Kiri again.

'What's between here and Merfleur Point?'

'Nothing.' She shook her head.

'And after it?'

She looked at him. 'Witchlove Haven.'

Laird nodded grimly. If he was right, it was the same speedboat that had escaped from the *Vanneau*'s island. But that boat had fled north at the time, in the opposite direction from Witchlove Haven. But that could have been a simple deception, the speedboat could have circled back later — and Simon Mehran had arrived late for that Mehran board meeting in St Helier.

He watched the receding ferryboat, her follower now lost from sight. By the time he and Kiri could get the little *Cloth-cap* out there would be little chance of catching up, if the mystery speedboat was making for Witchlove Haven — and there would be no welcome for an intruder at the marina.

They started off down the slope again, Laird in the lead. He saw their boat bobbing where they'd left it, then heard a rattle of stones behind him as Kiri stumbled. He turned in time to catch her in his arms as she fell.

That raven-black hair brushed his face, her body was warm and firm against his own. She gasped, then her bright eyes might have been mocking him, her lips were very close — too close, and she didn't try to pull away. Their lips met, gently at first, then with a slow, mounting wanting.

'Oh, hell,' she said suddenly, shook her head, and firmly pushed him back. 'Not here, not now.' Laird heard her soft chuckle. 'Damn Belle. She said she'd bet real money it would be like this.'

'Like what?' asked Laird mildly.

'Ask Belle to explain.' She kissed him again quickly and lightly. 'Sorry, Andy. Wrong time, wrong place.'

Laird grimaced. 'I could argue — '

'Don't.' She laughed and took his hand. 'Time we headed back, or Belle will call me a liar.'

They made the return trip down the coast with the *Cloth-cap* throbbing gently through odd wisps of mist and Kiri steering with her head resting on Laird's shoulder. She slowed the speedboat as they swung in towards the blink of the lattice tower light marking Merfleur Point, then suddenly she peered ahead, frowning. What could have been a torch had flashed a pinprick signal towards the *Vanneau* island and was being answered.

'It's all right.' She relaxed again. 'Jacob and Jimmy Boullard are having a gossip.' Leaning forward, she switched on the boat's small navigation lights. 'We'd better let them know we're coming in. They're looking for an excuse to start trouble.'

The torch signals ended moments later. They reached the harbour, tied up and were ashore when Jacob West appeared out of the night, coming towards them from the direction of the Martello tower.

'Do we tell him about Peter Frere?' asked Kiri quietly.

'No.' Laird shook his head. Jacob West had his own worries, the kind of explanations involved would take time. 'Leave it until morning.'

She nodded. West reached them a moment later.

'Did you enjoy yourselves?' he asked suspiciously, leaning on his stick.

'I think so,' said Kiri cheerfully. 'I didn't hear any complaints.'

West grunted and turned to Laird. 'Want to look in at the cottage? Belle should have a pot of coffee on the go.'

'Another time.' Laird shook his head. 'It's late, and I'd better check in at the Leecom.' He thumbed out at the black line of the reef. 'All right out there?'

'Totally quiet — Jimmy is getting bored.' West considered him again. 'Will you be out tomorrow?'

Laird nodded. 'In the morning, early.'

'I'll see you then.' West left them and stumped off towards his cottage. Even from his back view it was plain that he still didn't approve of what might have been going on.

'He's going to sulk.' Kiri Vass sighed and shook her head. Then her mood changed and became totally serious. 'If Peter Frere does show up, if he will talk to the police, how much is left to do?'

'Plenty,' admitted Laird. 'But it will get a lot easier.'

'I hope so. I wish I felt sure.' Kiri laid an impulsive hand on his arm. 'I've got to keep telling myself this is all really happening, yet I know it is. Go carefully.'

She walked with him to where he had left his car. She was still standing, watching, as he drove away.

* * *

Andrew Laird had been telling a lie when he had said he wanted to get back to the Leecom Hotel. Turning the car at the junction by the Norman church, heading south on the road which passed the Witchlove Haven turn-off, he kept a wary eye on any other traffic. Everything seemed quiet enough and he slowed a little as he saw the turning. Going past it, he continued a short distance along the main road, then tucked the car in behind the shelter of a roofless, tumbledown barn.

Getting out, locking the car, he made sure of his bearings, then climbed a wire fence and started walking across rough grassland. The grassland ended at a drystone wall and, once over it, he was among trees and on the track which led to Witchlove Haven.

Laird followed the track but stayed in the cover of the trees. Now and again a twig snapped under his feet or something small, four-footed and disturbed scurried clear of him. When he reached the barrier pole across the track it was closed and padlocked down; then he saw the sentry box beside it was deserted.

From there, as the trees thinned, he moved even more carefully. At last he saw the glint of water, then the stark outlines of the marina building site. Using the shadows, refusing to rush, Laird worked his way into the site itself — then froze in the shelter of a stack of concrete pipes as he heard a clatter and a soft curse somewhere near.

Moments later a man slouched out of the darkness. Making a cursory check here and there as he went along, he had a cigarette glowing between his lips and a shotgun slung over one shoulder. Witchlove Haven had its own style of night watchman, but this one appeared no particular enthusiast.

The man stopped close to the pipes, so near that Laird could hear him humming under his breath. Suddenly the stub of his cigarette was flicked away, curving to land at Laird's feet in a shower of sparks. The man waited where he was, and another watchman appeared from the darkness.

'When do we get a break?' complained the new arrival, who also had a shotgun.

'When someone tells us, not before,' said his companion stonily. 'What's the matter? Does the dark worry you?'

'The only thing that worries me around here is Crazy Simon,' grunted the first man. 'What's so special about tonight, anyway?'

'Ask, if you're keen enough.' Laird heard a short laugh, then saw the flare of a match as a new cigarette was lit. 'Me, I just take the money and keep my mouth shut.'

They moved closer and began a low-voiced mutter of conversation. At last it ended with a shared laugh at a private joke and the men split up, going their separate ways.

Laird could move again. He took a moment to ease his cramped limbs as the watchmen vanished from sight, then thought about the little he'd heard. Something special under way could mean anything. But it was enough to inject extra caution into each step as he set off again. His target was unchanged: the natural rock ledge which edged the marina side of what had been Grunt Bay. If the mystery boat had come in as he believed, then that was where he would find it.

Then, suddenly, that priority ended. He was near the site office and chinks of light at the edges of the curtained windows showed it was in use. At the same time, the weak moonlight glinted on two cars parked beside it. One was Ray Garris's BMW, the other was the Jaguar coupé he'd seen at Mehran Gate.

Switching direction, moving silently, Laird went over. Hugging a wall, he worked round to one of those chinks of light and peered in at the gap. He saw four men sitting at a table in the office hut. He knew three of them, but the fourth had so far only been a photograph and it should not have been possible he was there.

The podgy-faced, bespectacled Matt Mehran wasn't due home from Hong Kong until the weekend. But he was there. So was his brother Simon, and both were wearing black rubber scuba-diving suits. Across from them sat Ray Garris and the fair-haired man he had been told was Erick Roder. It only lacked Paul Mehran and Diane or he would have been looking at a full line-up of the people who mattered in Witchline Shipping — and, equally important, Mehran Holdings.

Each man had a can of beer. Erick Roder was smoking a small cigar. They were talking quietly, earnestly, Simon Mehran frowning as he made a point, his brother Matt nodding in vigorous agreement at whatever had been said. It seemed to annoy Garris, who slapped a hand on the table, but after a moment Laird saw Erick Roder make a soothing gesture.

'We can do it that way, Ray.' Briefly, Roder's voice was loud enough and firm enough for Laird to make it out clearly. 'We don't need another rehearsal, we can reschedule for tomorrow night.'

Garris muttered a reply and glared at the Mehran brothers. Matt Mehran shrugged and nudged Simon with his elbow. Simon Mehran still didn't thaw, his green eyes still cold as he considered Garris. But they seemed to be in agreement. He nodded.

So they were in agreement. But about what?

Laird took a quick glance round, saw no sign of the patrolling watchmen and stayed where he was for another couple of minutes. The conversation in the hut went on, but he

285

could still only pick up an occasional fragment of a phrase or a word. Then, suddenly, Garris rose. Stubbing his cigar on a tin-lid ashtray, he went round and lightly slapped both Mehrans on the shoulder. Then, a grin on his round, pug-nosed face, he was heading for the door.

Laird shrank back further into the shadows as the door opened and light poured out from the hut. Garris emerged, then looked back.

'Get through this, and it's like Erick says, we're home and dry,' he declared curtly. 'I don't care about details, but whatever you do, it had better be right.'

Someone in the hut made a low-voiced comment. Garris stiffened.

'Don't try to be clever with me,' he snarled. 'You caused one mess already. Because you're Daddy's boy doesn't matter to me — not when I still have to clear up what's left.'

He closed the door with a slam and stumped his short-legged way across to his BMW. The car started and its headlamps swung in a swift arc as it drove away heading for the road. Taking a deep breath, Laird took another look inside the hut. Whatever the meeting had been about, it had ended. The two Mehran brothers, strangely menacing figures in their identical black rubber scuba-diving suits, were grinning as they talked with Erick Roder. Matt Mehran, even more tanned than his brother, was chewing a sandwich.

Satisfied he'd seen enough, Laird eased away from the hut. Whatever the Mehran plan, whoever was involved, a clock had begun ticking over it.

Getting back to the rock shelf and the water's edge amounted to threading through a maze of building machinery and materials. He didn't have to go far to find the speed-boat. Lying against the rock, rolling a little as she moved in the slight swell washing in, the boat was moored fore and aft by lines which led to a handy diesel-engined cement mixer.

She was big, maybe twice the size of the little *Cloth-cap*, with a large, well-equipped open cockpit. If she had ever had a name, it had been painted out. Maybe she had started life as a rich man's favourite toy. But now she had a more sinister role.

Laird stepped aboard. When he checked, he could still feel the warmth coming from her engine compartment — twin engines with that kind of control layout. For a moment, he sat back on his heels on the open deck, thinking. Then he took another glance across at the cement mixer and grinned.

Like most of her kind, the speedboat's fuel tank was located aft. He found the filler point, almost flush with the deck and with a hinged snap-up cap. Flicking it open, Laird sniffed the distinctive smell of high-octane Avgas aviation spirit.

That made things even better. Slipping ashore again, he went over to the cement mixer. Searching around, he found what he wanted — an empty, rusted paint can. Using one of the blades of his pocket knife as a screwdriver, he loosened the mixer's fuel feed-pipe and drained off nearly enough fuel to fill the can. Tightening the feed-pipe again, Laird topped the can's contents with two large handfuls of dry cement from an opened sack.

He listened. There was still only the light murmur of the wind and the steady splashing of the sea against rock. Holding the can carefully, Laird went back aboard the speedboat, bent over the opened filler pipe and poured the mixture in. Then he snapped the filler cap shut and tossed the empty can into the bay.

High-octane Avgas, diesel fuel and cement would make a devil's brew cocktail in the speedboat's fuel lines within moments of her starting up. To clear the mess and get her running again would take a long, long time.

Satisfied, Laird left the speedboat. Something moved further along the marina site, then he heard footsteps coming steadily in his direction. They were too near to run. Crouching down behind the shelter of the cement mixer, he waited. Moments passed, then one of the site guards ambled into view. The man's shotgun was still slung casually at his shoulder, but something had apparently made him suspicious. Stopping beside the speedboat, he peered down into her cockpit.

Laird rose, the man's back still towards him. Creeping forward, he raised his two hands clasped tightly together, then sledge-hammered them down on the unsuspecting watchman's neck. The man folded and went down, the shotgun clattering beside him.

Andrew Laird was already on his way, heading back to where he'd left his car.

7

The time was close to 1 a.m. and the lights of the Leecom Hotel were a bright oasis ahead when Andrew Laird at last made up his mind. He drove on past the hotel, found a telephone booth about a mile on down the road, stopped there, took out some change, fed it into the pay 'phone's slot, and dialled State Police headquarters.

He wasn't totally surprised that Detective Chief Inspector Tom Flambard was still at his desk, though not in the best of moods.

'I'm damn well closed for the night. I want to get home,' grated Flambard. 'There's a thing called sleep I've heard about, and I'd like to try it.' He sighed over the line. 'All right, what's happened?'

'I've talked with Peter Frere.'

'Talked — ' He heard Flambard make a swallowing noise. 'You mean you let him go again?'

'That was part of the deal. He says he's innocent, but he saw what happened.' Laird paused. 'I've soothed him down as much as I can. Unless something goes wrong, you'll have him tomorrow, before midday.'

'Who do we thank? Jacob West?'

'He doesn't know about it.'

'All right. I won't push.' Flambard was acid, but relieved. 'Do you need help?'

'No.' Laird let a noisy late-night truck rumble past the booth. 'But I know why the Mehrans are so nervous about things. It's big, it's offshore, and it involves a boat — that's all I know, except that it's probably off the French coast, in the Cherbourg direction.'

'Did they send you an invitation?' Flambard's sarcasm didn't cloak his heightened interest.

Laird grinned a little at the telephone mouthpiece. 'I'd know more if I could lip-read. But they've conjured up Simon's brother Matt. He's supposed to be in Hong Kong.'

'I see.' Flambard was thinking. 'There are a few things we can do. I'll make sure of them and I'll also give you fair exchange, Laird. We're still getting nowhere on the Newgrange murder and there's no trace of the two thugs who jumped you this afternoon.' He seemed to hesitate, then went on. 'But we've had a whisper from the French police about the other Mehran director, Erick Roder. It seems he knows some odd people.'

'What kind of odd?' asked Laird.

'Odd as in French major-league crooked

— they feel about him the way we feel about the Mehrans. He has the contacts, they don't know how or when he uses them.' A grim note entered Flambard's voice. 'Where are you planning to sleep tonight?'

'In my own bed, in my own hotel room,' said Laird dryly. He had an afterthought. 'Though I could use an alibi for where I've been.'

'You'll get a telephone call inside twenty minutes,' promised Flambard. 'Just be there.'

Laird thanked him and hung up. A small spider had begun weaving a night web across the door of the booth and he had to brush it aside as he left. The spider tumbled, then started again, and Laird gave it a mock salute. They were in the same kind of game.

★ ★ ★

He drove back to the Leecom, left his car in the car park, and checked his watch as he entered the hotel lobby. It was twenty minutes after one, and the clerk on duty at the reception desk gave him his room key with only a nod and a comment about the weather. Taking the lift up, Laird went straight to his room, locked the door again once he was in, then made a cursory check around. This time nothing seemed to have been disturbed; that might be either good or bad.

Still fully dressed, he lay back on the bed and considered the ceiling, thinking.

There was Peter Frere and there were the Mehrans — somehow Jacob West and his treasure brig seemed to be taking a sideshow role. Within twenty-four hours he was likely to know.

But know what?

The puzzle was broken as the telephone rang. He answered it.

'Mr Laird?' The voice on the other end was suitably bored, officially apologetic. 'Police headquarters — I've a message for you from Chief Inspector Flambard. You — uh — were here most of the evening, weren't you?'

'Most of it?' Laird gave a snort for the benefit of the listening bug in the wall socket. 'Damn near all of it. I only left half an hour ago.'

'He's grateful, Mr Laird.' The night-shift cop making the call put just the right inflection of sincerity into it. 'But it's about that appointment he made for you to come in again. Can you make it around noon, instead of 11 a.m.? He forgot about a meeting he has to attend.'

'Noon,' agreed Laird. 'I'll be there.'

He solemnly thanked the man and hung up.

In a few minutes he was undressed and in bed. In a few minutes more he was asleep. But there was a chair jammed under the room's door handle and anyone trying to come in through the balcony window would have found it had also been jammed, using the drinks trolley.

Nothing happened; he wakened only once and briefly around 3 a.m. when a group of hotel guests, noisily drunk, made their way along the corridor outside. The next time he wakened it was nearly eight, the morning was bright outside, and a gusting wind from the south was combing white spray-crests from the waves.

Both doors freed again, Laird showered, shaved, then decided against facing the hotel dining room. He telephoned down for a coffee and rolls breakfast and was dressing when he heard a knock at the door and then the click of a passkey.

It was Jo from the reception desk, balancing a tray in one hand as she entered.

'Good morning.' She put the tray down on a table and watched with a mild interest as Laird tucked his shirt into his trousers. 'How did you sleep, Mr Laird? We had some complaints — '

'The wandering drunks?' He shook his head. 'I heard them, that's all. Do you usually double up as room service?'

'We're short-staffed.' She shrugged. 'One of our waiters was in an accident yesterday — he broke his arm. 'Phone down if there's anything else you'd like.'

'I will.' Laird eyed her quizzically. 'This waiter of yours, what's he like?'

'The kind we should keep out of sight in the back kitchen,' said the girl dryly. 'I wouldn't weep if he broke his neck.'

She gave Laird a cheerful wink and went out, closing the door behind her.

Laird finished dressing and settled to his coffee and rolls. The Leecom waiter's accident could be coincidence but if the 'accident' had happened in St Helier it might be worth mentioning to Flambard later. There was more coffee in the pot. He filled his cup again, took it over to the window, and thought about his own programme as he looked out.

London was due a call: Osgood Morris would be more than interested in Frere's story that the *Rosewitch* had sailed from Jersey with two crews aboard. But, after that, the priority was Merfleur. If Peter Frere did turn up, that was a situation to be handled with care.

He heard a tap at the door again, then the click of a passkey, and turned as the door opened. It wasn't Jo. They came in without fuss or particular rush, but with an air of knowing exactly what they were doing, two large police constables in uniform, one with a hand poised casually close to his baton, the other showing a brief, humourless smile.

'Andrew Laird?' said the one with the one-off smile.

'Yes.' Laird set down his coffee cup. 'What's the problem?'

'No problem, Mr Laird.' The man shook his head. 'We'd like you to come with us, that's all.'

'Where?' Laird felt his right wrist gripped in a deceptively casual finger-and-thumb grip. The second constable had eased in on his other side.

'St Helier. Chief Inspector Flambard wants you there, right away.' The first constable had stopped smiling. 'Some help with enquiries, Mr Laird.' He followed Laird's glance. 'Don't worry about your jacket, we'll bring it.'

The other man scooped up the jacket, nodded, and Laird let them push him towards the door. The finger-and-thumb grip tightened as they went down in the lift and out across the hotel lobby, much to the interest of several guests.

'What's he done?' asked a fat woman loudly.

'Probably one of those sex attackers,' said her rake-thin woman companion. She raised her voice. 'I'd castrate them.'

The two constables stayed stony-faced. They had a police car waiting and Laird was firmly shoved into the rear before they got in.

They exchanged less than a dozen words on the drive to St Helier. The car headed straight for the harbour area and stopped at the basin where the motor cruiser *Emu* was berthed. Laird obediently got out. There were other police cars parked around, an ambulance waited nearby, and a rope cordon was keeping back the few interested spectators.

'Move,' said one of the constables. The finger-and-thumb grip was back on his wrist.

They walked the short distance along the quay to the *Emu*'s berth, and Laird stared down. There were both plain clothes and uniformed police on the boat's deck, then he saw Flambard looking up at him and beckoning. He was hauled down the quayside ladder, stepped aboard the *Emu*, and was hustled towards Flambard between the two constables.

'What the hell?' Flambard frowned as they arrived. He turned. 'Sergeant — '

'Sir.' Detective Sergeant Moisan appeared beside him, an innocent look on his thin, horse-face.

'This.' Flambard thumbed at Laird and his escorts. 'I said to get hold of him. Well?'

'I — uh — may have said to pick Mr Laird up,' said Moisan blandly. He looked sadly at Laird. 'Call it a misunderstanding?'

Flambard waved the constable away, gave a brief glare in Moisan's direction, then looked at Laird for a moment. Then, silently, he signalled Laird to follow him. They went along the deck to the cockpit door which led down into the cabin.

'Go ahead,' said Flambard tonelessly.

Andrew Laird ducked under the hatchway roof, took two steps down the short stairway inside, then froze. His mind felt numbed, he could have been sick. It was like a carbon copy of the first time he'd ventured aboard the *Emu*. The ransacked cabin was still in a littered chaos. There was blood and a body.

Except that the blood was still fresh in appearance and the dead man, lying on his back where he'd fallen, was Peter Frere.

'You can forget your meeting,' said Tom Flambard behind him. He nudged Laird on, then followed him down. They stood beside Frere's body, and Flambard gave a slight, unemotional shrug. 'Our medic says that time of death was slightly before dawn — a single stab wound into the heart. No murder weapon, but I'd give odds that we're looking

298

for the same knife that killed Newgrange.'

Laird moistened his lips. 'Who found him?'

'I did,' said Flambard. 'I came down first thing this morning — I wanted another look around.' He saw the question coming. 'Yes, we had a man on duty on the boat all yesterday. But by about ten last night we reckoned we'd finished here. He locked up and went home — blame me.'

In a repeat of what he had done less than thirty-six hours before, Andrew Laird squatted on his heels beside the dead man in the *Emu*'s cabin. Peter Frere had been killed very close to where Chris Newgrange had died, beside the police chalked markings and the dried bloodstains from the first killing. He looked at the way Frere lay, one arm flung out as if in mute protest. He'd still been wearing that old Merchant Navy uniform jacket with the button missing.

'He was out of luck this time.' The southern burr in Flambard's voice sounded harsh. 'Where did you meet him last night?'

'North of Merfleur, beside an old Martello tower.' Laird's sense of shock had begun to fade, though the sick feeling remained. He looked up at Flambard. 'I didn't see him again.'

'I know,' murmured Flambard. 'After you 'phoned, I had two men keeping an eye on things at the Leecom until daylight.'

'To keep me out of trouble?' Laird raised an eyebrow.

'If it happened, I wanted to know,' Flambard scowled. 'So they were in the wrong damned place. Was I supposed to guess?'

Laird shook his head. Somehow, despite his fears, Peter Frere had made his way back across the island, through the darkness, to St Helier and the *Emu*. But what reason had driven him to do it? Why had it mattered? Death had smoothed some of the lines from the man's thin, unshaven face. But his eyes were wide, staring upwards at the cabin roof, somehow accusing.

'Someone guessed better than we did.' Flambard's brown eyes were hard. 'I'd put money on this being a straight killing, no messing about.' He reached into his pocket and brought out a small plastic evidence envelope. 'He was still gripping this in his right hand. Maybe it means something to you.'

Laird took the envelope. It held a small gold coin, one more of the double Louis d'Ors that were being recovered from Jacob West's *Vanneau*. There were traces of blood along one edge. His mouth tightened. Peter Frere had been worrying about seeing West, returning the gold coin might have been intended to be part of the man's way of saying he was sorry.

'It matters,' he said quietly. 'Yes, I know why. But I don't think it was the reason he was killed.'

'That makes two of us.' Flambard nodded grimly. 'You're infectious, Laird. I'm beginning to get the name Mehran on the brain. We've also got a witness, though he's not worth much — he's an early-shift docker, he saw two men head away from here in a hurry, then heard a car drive off.'

'Any descriptions?' asked Laird hopefully.

'It was still dark, our docker was still half-asleep.' Flambard shook his head. 'We found him, we may dig up others.' He considered Laird again, taking the coin and putting it back in his pocket. 'I had one murder on my hands, now I have two. You wanted some rope, I gave you it. I don't like the result.'

Laird rose to his feet. 'Where do we talk?'

'Not down here.' Flambard grimaced at the thought. 'On deck will do for a start.'

They went up and leaned together on the motor cruiser's rail, facing out towards the rest of the harbour basin where life was mostly going on as normal. A small tug was churning her way out, a crane was unloading bulky, anonymous bales of cargo from a coaster, and a few gulls were floating on the greasy water alongside.

This time Laird kept nothing back. Things had gone too far. He was prepared to trust Flambard — had to trust him. It meant explaining how he'd been with Jacob West when they'd found Chris Newgrange's body. It meant explaining about West's treasure brig. It meant explaining how Kiri had had that telephone call from Frere and a lot more.

By the time he'd finished, Detective Chief Inspector Tom Flambard's eyes were narrowed, bleak and angry. Hands gripping the deck-rail knuckle white, Flambard quietly strung together six crude Anglo-Saxon oaths in a way that could have been a single word. He didn't move for almost a minute, then some of his previous composure returned.

'Now I suppose you're going to suggest that's all off the record?' he asked.

Laird shrugged. 'How much of it would matter in court?'

'You mean how much would I want any court to hear,' corrected Flambard sarcastically. He nodded to himself. 'It explains a few things — and maybe you're right about why Frere sneaked back here.' For a moment he was silent, thinking. 'Do you think the Mehrans know about this treasure galleon?'

'Brig,' corrected Laird mildly.

'I don't care if it's a bloody garbage scow. Do you?'

'If they do, it's a sideshow,' said Laird. 'Their main worry has been to stop Frere getting to me.'

'Back to the *Rosewitch*.' Flambard shook his head sadly. 'You arrive out of the blue just as they're set for something big. All right, they could tell you to go to hell, that they didn't want to know about this phoney sponsorship money you're waving — '

'Or maybe they want to keep their options open, any way they can,' suggested Laird.

'Anyway, what's the odd couple of murders?' Flambard's bitterness showed. 'You know my first problem? It's what to do with you.' He glanced past Laird. 'I could make my sergeant very happy, and throw you in a cell. Then I could haul in your pal, Captain West and the rest of that bunch, including his tame admiral — '

'But not the Mehrans,' mused Laird. 'We've got no reason, nothing that would stick.'

'So?' Flambard waited bleakly.

'For a start, someone has to tell Jacob West. After that — ' Laird shrugged ' — give me that rope again. I might be useful.'

'You might also be dead,' said Flambard

brutally. Then he sighed, turned, and leaned his back on the rail. 'You know how I spent part of last night? Checking Peter Frere's hospital file, then asking questions. I didn't get anywhere. But if it happened the way you think, I pity the poor devil.' He crooked a finger. 'I want you to come back to Rouge Bouillon with me. I want some of this in your own writing — then it goes in a drawer in my desk. Call it insurance against you being a casualty.'

'And then?'

'Go away. Help me get the Mehrans on a plate.' Flambard gave him a crooked grin. 'Any odd sins along the way will be forgiven — unless they happen to be parking tickets. I can't do a damn thing about parking tickets.'

They went back to Flambard's office, where Laird wrote and Flambard read, and cups of coffee arrived at regular intervals. When it was done, Flambard locked the pages away in the bottom drawer of his desk, then they parted. Flambard was heading back to the *Emu*, the two constables who had brought Laird in from his hotel were waiting to take him back there again. This time they were human, mildly apologetic, anxious to talk about their families, their jobs, and the weather. The younger constable wanted to know what Laird thought about health insurance. The elder told a long, rambling dirty story about a mermaid and a fisherman.

He was dropped at the Leecom car park. As the police car turned and drove away, Laird saw Jo and another receptionist watching from a window. He gave them a wave, but left it at that. Going over to the Ford, getting behind the wheel, he glanced at his watch.

More time had passed than he'd realised. It was already almost 11.30 a.m. He took a deep breath, thinking of what lay ahead for him at Merfleur Point, then started the Ford and set it moving.

The weather hadn't changed much. It was mostly blue sky overhead, but with a few white clouds being hurried along by the gusting wind. The tourists he passed were wearing sweaters, the sun umbrellas outside the roadside bars were flapping and shaking, and their customers seemed to have gone indoors. A car passed him, heading in the St Helier direction and pulling a trailer-load of sailboards. It would be exciting using them offshore — maybe more exciting than their users expected.

The wind stayed that way as he neared Merfleur. A strip of trees beside the Norman church were bending with each gust and had shed some of their leaves. But Merfleur Point was more sheltered. It looked peaceful and calm as he reached the line of cottages and the little harbour.

Maybe too peaceful. Laird looked around, puzzled, as he got out of the car and heard no barking from Benny. There was no reply when he knocked on the door of the West's cottage, so he walked down towards the harbour. The big black Zodiac boat and the yellow speedboat were tied to the quayside, bobbing a little, but there was still no sign of life.

That left the shop. Frowning now, Laird crossed over. The door opened, he went in, and there was a whine. Tail between its legs, the black dog was cowering in a corner, looking up at him nervously. There was a matted patch of dried blood on its head.

'You shouldn't have come, son,' said a weary voice.

Jacob West was standing at the fringed cords which curtained off his back shop. He seemed suddenly aged and tired, his face was pale, and he didn't have his stick.

'Jacob, what's the matter?' Laird stared at him. 'What — '

He didn't get to finish. He was vaguely aware of Benny giving a low, warning whine, a movement behind him, then a thunderburst of pain as something crashed down on his head. He knew he was falling, somehow falling into a world which seemed a spinning vortex of red on black. He heard a voice he seemed to know — a voice or a laugh. Then he lost consciousness.

Later and briefly he came round again. Pain was throbbing through his head and for some reason he couldn't use his arms or his legs. He tried to move and heard himself groan. He was in a vehicle. He could feel it pitching.

'Shut him up,' said the same voice.

'No. Don't — ' That was Jacob West, had to be. 'Damn you — '

The new blow took him in the back of the neck. This time, the world simply went black.

Time didn't have any particular meaning when Laird regained consciousness for the second time. At first, he only knew he was still alive. Whatever he was lying on was coarse and damp. When he opened his eyes everything seemed dark, as if it was night. Then gradually, very gradually, he realised he had to be in some kind of cellar, lying on a stone floor. There were lines and chinks of light from a door and somewhere else. He wasn't sure why, but he sensed he wasn't alone.

This time, he realised he was tied hand and foot. He tried to shift his position and something thin and hard grabbed at his waist.

He heard the rattle of chain links.

'Andrew.' The voice was low and soft and near. 'Andrew, can you hear me?'

'Kiri?' His head took another spin.

'Don't try moving. I'll come over — I think I can reach you.' Kiri Vass's voice was calm and controlled. 'Jacob and Belle are here.'

'Trussed like damn chickens,' grated Jacob West from somewhere in the gloom. 'I'm sorry, boy. I couldn't warn you.'

'He's an old fool,' said Belle from the same direction. 'If he'd tried, he'd be a dead old fool.'

Laird heard a brief scraping and scuffling as Kiri Vass wriggled towards him. When she arrived, his eyes had become more accustomed to the faint traces of light seeping in. He could see her face, then that her hands and feet were tied. There was a rope round her waist, angling back into the darkness.

'Where are we?' He took a guess. 'Mehran Gate?'

'Yes.' As she spoke, Kiri elbowed nearer and bent her face low over his own, peering at him. 'We're in some kind of damned basement round the back.'

'I know it.' Laird spoke feebly, his voice still a croak. 'It's their family crypt.'

'You mean we're surrounded by a load o' dead Mehrans?' grumbled Jacob West. 'Hell, the live ones are bad enough.'

'It's used as a cellar.' He felt Kiri's hair brush his forehead as she moved again. 'How long since I got here?'

'About an hour. We were brought in together.' She drew a breath of relief. 'We didn't know whether you were dead or alive — '

'Neither did I.' A new stab of pain hit his head and his neck.

She saw him wince. 'There's blood on your face, you seem to have some kind of cut on the back of your head. How do you feel?'

'Rough.' He moved, and his chain rattled again, like a dog leash. It was a thin chain, strong, padlocked round his waist, the other end leading to what he could just make out as the central stone pillar he'd seen when Paul Mehran had showed him the crypt. He gave the chain another experimental tug. 'Is everyone anchored down?'

'You and Jacob rate the chains, Belle and I have ropes. We're fixed to some old ringbolts on the back wall.'

'I had a knife in one pocket — '

'They took it,' grunted Jacob West. 'And forget about shouting, boy. They said there's no one around to hear. The house staff have the day off.'

Laird closed his eyes for a moment.

Resignedly, he said, 'So what happened?'

Between them, quiet echoing voices and vague shapes in the darkness of the crypt, they told him.

At 8 a.m. Jacob West had taken the Zodiac boat out to bring Jimmy Boullard back from his all-night guard stint on the Merfleur island. They'd returned, Boullard had driven off home, and a little later they had heard Benny barking outside the cottage. The barking stopped as suddenly as it had begun, and three stocking-masked figures had burst into the cottage.

'They had guns,' said Jacob sadly. 'Belle wouldn't let me argue with them. But at least Benny was all right — he's like you, boy. Thick-skulled. They'd just thumped him with a pistol barrel.'

They'd been taken down to Jacob West's harbour shop. Belle and Kiri had been left tied and gagged in the back room, Jacob had been told what to do — and what would happen if he didn't. They had waited like that, with no other visitor, until Laird had arrived.

'They wanted you as well,' said Kiri soberly. 'At first I thought it was because of Peter Frere — '

'No,' said Laird quietly. 'He's dead, Kiri. They got to him early this morning.'

310

It brought a shocked silence, then a oath from Jacob West. The reality of their own situation underlined, they picked up what was left of the story. Once Laird had been ambushed, one of the three raiders had left, then returned with a small unmarked delivery vehicle. They'd been bundled in, Benny being kicked aside when he tried to join them. The van had been driven off, the next stop had been Mehran Gate.

'These three men,' said Laird slowly. 'They were masked, but did you think you recognised any of them?'

'I did,' growled Jacob. 'The one giving the orders was Ray Garris. I told him what I thought of him — '

'And not much good it did you,' said Belle coldly. 'At your age, you shouldn't play heroes.'

'The other two?' pressed Laird.

'One was called Jody,' volunteered Kiri.

'That's not today's good news.' Laird was still totally puzzled, but his mind was beginning to clear; the worst of the pain in his head had dulled. Now he had to think, to try to understand. 'Why? What's this about?'

'You mean, how much do they know?' said Jacob West stonily. 'We're part of it, you're part of it. They know something about the *Vanneau*, but not a lot — they think we're

311

diving at some kind of wreck, but they're not too interested. The real concern is Peter Frere and how much we know about him.'

'But they didn't tell us he was dead,' said Belle West. Laird heard her murmur a soft curse as she reached the end of her rope tether and collided with something. There was a clatter, several things seemed to roll around the floor of the crypt, and she gave a startled yelp. 'Jacob, do something. I'm being buried by damned firewood.'

'I'm sorry, girl.' It came like a sigh from West. 'I got you and Kiri into this, didn't I?'

'Yes.' she said bluntly. 'So you can damn well get us out again.'

'Kiri.' Laird hauled himself up on his elbows to face her again. 'Won't people miss you at the airport?'

'No.' Kiri shook her head. 'I told them I was taking a couple of days off.' She stopped, suddenly tense.

Someone was moving outside. They heard the heavy click of a key, then the door swung open and bright, blinding daylight flooded in, framing two figures who paused for a moment outside then stooped to enter the crypt.

'I trust you're comfortable,' said Paul Mehran sarcastically. He shook his head as Laird, trying to get towards him, was halted by the chain around his waist. 'I wouldn't even try, Mr Laird. That's a primitive arrangement, but effective.'

The burly figure beside him grinned. Jody wiped an arm across his drooping, ginger moustache, took a step nearer, and kicked Laird in the ribs.

'Jody feels unfriendly where you're concerned,' murmured Mehran. He jerked his head and waited until the man moved back. The sunlight glinted on the automatic pistol Jody held in one hand. Taking a slow, frowning look around his captives Paul Mehran shook his head again. 'I didn't want any of this, believe me.'

'It's good to know,' said Laird acidly.

'Mostly, it's your fault, Laird.' The green Mehran eyes met his own like ice. 'You and that shambling idiot Frere — '

'So you had him killed.'

'To win time — time we need,' said Mehran unemotionally. 'Frere was beginning to remember the wrong things, but you know that, don't you?' His narrow mouth tightened. 'Exactly how much else do you know, Mr Laird?' His eyes flickered further into the crypt. 'How much else do any of you know, that's my problem.'

'Tell him to go to hell,' suggested Jacob West, then grunted with pain as Jody strolled

313

over and gave him a casual kick in the groin.

'It shouldn't have been this way.' Mehran shook his head, ignoring the interruption. 'You could say we bungled trying to kill Frere two years ago, but we decided he was harmless and after that, we left him alone. Then — ' he shrugged ' — you came along with this sponsorship story and Diane was fool enough to swallow it.' He paused. 'I presume it's a pack of lies?'

'It's something different,' agreed Laird calmly.

'The *Rosewitch*.' Paul Mehran sighed. 'For once, Simon had it right. I won't ask how or why — or even if the police know. If you say yes, you're probably lying. If you say no, it could be the same. But the *Rosewitch* — after all this time, why?'

Laird shrugged. 'Washing machines — you got careless when you dumped her cargo.'

'I see.' Mehran rubbed a shoe along the stone floor and frowned. 'That was — well, someone else.' He gave a sudden, surprising twitch of a smile. It was bitter at the edges. 'We're an old, proud family, Mr Laird. We also know how to adapt if things change. I think it will take a few hours before the police realise all four of you are missing. I don't think you can have told them much — if anything. We can risk that.'

314

'Then what happens to us?' asked Kiri Vass.

'Young woman, I haven't had time to decide that far ahead,' sighed Mehran. 'Let's say what happens to me will decide what happens to you. Meantime, make as much noise as you want, no one will hear you.'

He signalled to the silent Jody. The two men went out of the crypt, the door slammed, the heavy lock clicked, and everything was darkness again.

'Jacob,' said Belle West quietly. 'Come a bit nearer, I'm feeling cold.'

Nobody spoke after that for what seemed a long time, each preoccupied with their own thoughts. For Laird, it meant going over all that he knew, all that he'd told Tom Flambard. From a police point of view, how quickly would Flambard realise there was something badly wrong? If and when he did, how quickly could he react? He sighed to himself. Flambard was nobody's fool, but the cavalry wouldn't come charging over the hills until they had an idea what was on the other side.

'We should do something,' said Kiri Vass suddenly. 'I don't care what. We can't just sit — can we?'

She didn't spell out what she really meant. She didn't have to do that.

'There was an old motorcycle lying in here. There was some other junk,' said Laird, half to himself.

'So?' asked Jacob West acidly. 'I don't need a motorcycle — or group therapy, boy.'

'Shut up, Jacob,' said Belle quickly. 'Let's try. Kiri's right — we can't just sit and moulder.'

It was slow, it was tedious, most of the time they were inching around, feeling in the darkness behind them. They rested after a spell, then tried again, Jacob West gradually becoming the most determined to succeed.

But it was Kiri who found the small soft-drinks bottle.

'Give it here,' said Jacob firmly.

A moment later Laird heard the smash of glass and a soft curse from Jacob. He'd cut himself in the process. Murmuring happily after that, the older man fumbled for one of the largest, sharpest pieces.

'Belle,' he instructed. 'Back to back with me. Yelp if it's you instead of the rope.'

The broken glass began sawing at the ropes round her wrists. Just once, Belle West drew a quick, pained breath, then brushed aside her husband's concern. Her hands free, she nursed the circulation back into her wrists again, unknotted the rope round her waist, picked up another piece of the broken bottle, and it was her husband's turn.

Inside ten minutes they were all free except for the padlocked chains round Laird and Jacob West. It meant that once the initial cramp had passed, they could stand, could even move about. Belle hugged her husband first, then Laird. Kiri did the same, burying her face for a moment in Laird's chest.

Then she looked up. 'What now?'

The chain was tight round his waist, its length keeping him well away from the heavy wooden door of the crypt. Jacob was even further from it. When Belle and Kiri made their way over, they came back shaking their heads. The old lock would have defied anything short of a battering ram. Muttering to himself, Jacob West explored to the length of his chain, then cursed as he collided with the remains of the old motorcycle, knocking it over with a crash.

'Damn the thing,' he said, simmering down. 'What we want is a charge of dynamite.' He scrabbled noisily among the rusted metal, then sighed. 'Here — it might be better than nothing.'

A broken metal wheel spoke tinkled over the stone to Laird. One end was dagger sharp; he nursed the other end in the palm of his hand for a moment, then gave it to Kiri. He had his seaman's belt with the fighting buckle, something he knew how to use. Removing it from his waist, he saw the others were watching him.

'That's it,' he told them quietly. 'We wait till they come — if they come. Then we take our chance.'

★ ★ ★

The hours crawled past. The damp chill of the old crypt gradually ate home, and they had to fight it, moving arms and legs, talking, even forcing themselves into the idiocy of a word game. Jacob West announced he would sell his soul for a beer, then retired into a corner. Belle joined him, and the pair began singing very softly, surprisingly in tune.

Still the luminous hands on Laird's wristwatch crept round. The cracks of outside daylight began to fade, the air grew cold. Kiri Vass and Laird stayed close together, mainly for warmth. They had run out of things to say.

The first sounds of feet on gravel outside were followed by the flickering glint of a light as it played on the door. It gave them only a few seconds, but enough, as they positioned themselves on the floor of the crypt and draped the cut ropes in a rehearsed pretence of still being bound. The key rattled and clicked in the door lock, the door swung open, and the beam of powerful lantern glared in and swept around.

'All safe and snug,' said a sardonic voice. 'And don't they look pleased to see us?'

The lantern moved, the two men behind it came in, half closing the door behind them, throwing flickering shadows as one of them hung the battery lantern on a wall hook. Jody was back, his face as stolid as ever. But this time his companion was Ray Garris. The pug-nosed Mehran associate director for once was casually dressed, wearing a knitted wool jacket, denim trousers and a dark-coloured sports shirt. His eyes were small, bright and hard in the lantern light. Like Jody, he was holding an automatic pistol. Also like Jody, he stood carefully beyond the reach of the chain round Laird's waist.

'If this is a social visit, I'm not in the mood,' said Laird in a flat, level voice. 'Or did you just decide to count heads?'

Garris shrugged, mildly amused. 'Complain to the management if you feel that way.'

'We do,' snarled Jacob West from the background. 'What's going on now?'

'Outside?' Garris exchanged a glance with Jody, then nodded at Laird. 'Unfortunately, some people, including the police, are making worried noises about why your friend here

319

can't be found. They're also beginning to ask about the rest of you. We expected it, eventually — maybe not so quickly.'

'So we're popular.' Laird fought to keep tight control of his voice. One or both of the pair had to move nearer. Until that happened, he, Kiri and the Wests were helpless. He looked over at Jody. 'I thought you'd have gone helping the Mehrans with their boat.'

Jody's mouth fell open. The automatic in his hand came up, the muzzle trained on Laird, and he moistened his lips. 'What boat?'

Laird grinned at him. 'Not the one they used last night. Or didn't they find out about it?'

'They did,' said Ray Garris softly. 'They did, but we just blamed those damned fishermen Simon scared off.' He paused, considering Laird with a new deliberation. 'You've been busy. Maybe you know more than we thought.'

'Maybe we all do,' said Kiri Vass suddenly. Her voice sounded strained, unusually loud. 'What will you do about it?'

Garris shook his head, almost sadly. 'I'd say we've run out of options.'

'So you're going to kill us?' Kiri almost shouted the words, struggling up on her elbows. She sounded close to hysterics — but her freed wrists were still hidden behind her back. 'What kind of people are you?'

It was a pretence. Suddenly, Laird realised why. The crypt's door had opened wider. He sensed as much as saw a flicker of movement out in the darkness. Whoever was there, Kiri was trying to hold the two men's attention.

Ray Garris had ignored Kiri's outburst. Calmly, silently, he had been fitting a fat, bulbous silencer to the muzzle of his pistol. At the same time, Laird saw the crypt door ease fractionally wider. He took his turn.

'Run out of weever fish?' he mocked. 'Or are guns more your scene?'

'Shut up,' snarled Jody. Despite the cold night damp of the crypt, the man was visibly sweating. He glanced around. 'Shut up, all of you — you hear me?'

'Calm down, Jody,' soothed Garris. His gold teeth showed in a brief, interested, totally humourless smile. 'Good guesswork, Laird. But that fish-poison business with Frere wasn't my idea. Young Simon dreamed it up — he's full of nasty little ideas, he loved biology at school.' He shrugged and casually brought the silencer-tipped pistol round. 'It should have worked. Almost did, I suppose. One little shot from a needle. It's a pity you can't ask him about it — '

'You're a liar, Ray!' Low, intense with anger, the words cut him short. 'A liar as well as everything else.'

Garris swung round, staring, as Diane Mehran stepped into the crypt. Her auburn hair glinted like a copper helmet in the glare of the battery lantern, her broad-boned face was cold with rage and her eyes were like ice. She was holding a double-barrelled shotgun at waist level, the twin muzzles trained directly on Garris.

'What the hell are you doing here, Diane?' Garris recovered from his surprise. 'I thought — '

'You thought I'd been packed off to France for the day? That 'urgent company business' in Paris that needed a Mehran director — come back tomorrow?' Diane Mehran's head turned briefly as Jody made an uncertain move. 'No, Jody. Stay exactly where you are.' Her voice was edged with fury. 'I'm back — and this island has seen enough killing.'

'Killing?' Garris forced a quick laugh. 'Cool down, Diane. Who's talking killing?'

'I heard enough outside that door.' She took a half step forward, the shotgun rock steady. 'You wanted me out of the way. Business? Nobody I saw in Paris expected more than a letter. But about the first thing I hear when I get back is that Peter Frere is dead. Then — ' Her eyes swept the crypt

' — then I find this. Damn you, Ray. Have you gone mad?'

'Me?' asked Garris caustically. 'Your whole precious Mehran family is up to their collective neck in this, lady.' He paused. 'Whether you like it or not, that includes you.'

'You're a liar,' said Diane Mehran again.

'And you're being stupid,' snarled Garris, his temper snapping. 'How do you think all the little money miracles keep happening? You couldn't pay the grocery bills with your hotel bookings and car hires.' His voice switched to a soft, wheedling tone. 'So you just put down the gun, like a nice girl.'

No one else spoke. Their audience forgotten, Ray Garris and Diane Mehran looked at each other in a sheer battle of wills.

'Ray — ' began Diane. She moistened her lips.

'See sense, Diane,' said Garris softly.

But at the same time the muzzle of his pistol came up — and the dull plop of the silenced gun was drowned by a deafening blast from the shotgun.

Hit squarely in the chest at close range, hurled backwards, his mouth opening in a scream that didn't have time to peak, Ray Garris crumpled and went down. His body thudded on the stone floor, the pistol clattered, he twitched once, then lay still. The shotgun blast was still echoing, the battery lantern was swaying on its hook and throwing a flickering pattern of shadows, a thin haze of cartridge smoke laced the air.

Standing as if frozen, Diane Mehran stared down at what she'd done, Jody forgotten.

But the Witchlove construction man had come to life. Diving for the shelter of the crypt's central roof pillar, he brought his gun up and aimed for the auburn-haired target between him and escape.

'Jody!' yelled Laird.

Instinctively, the man half turned. Suddenly, he seemed to realise he had crossed the invisible boundary line on the floor. But Laird had already thrown himself forward, the chain round his waist rattling while he swung his leather belt like a flail. That heavy, sharp-edged buckle caught the light in a brief, vicious curve — and Jody screamed as the metal tore open the skin above one eye and ripped on across his nose. His pistol waved blindly, his other hand clutched at his face where the blood was already spurting.

'Again, boy — again,' howled Jacob West, scrambling forward, being halted with a jerk as his waist-chain tightened. 'Keep at it!'

Laird was already swinging the belt a second time, low. It curled round one of

Jody's legs and Laird instantly jerked backwards, hauling the man off balance, sending him sprawling. The pistol fired wildly, then Kiri Vass was there, springing at him, the sharp steel of the wheel spoke glinting as she used a two-handed grip to stab down with it.

This time Jody shrieked in a new mix of pain and fear as the spoke skewered through his right biceps, then jarred as it hit the stone beneath. The gun dropped from his hand. Thrashing frantically, he threw his tigress-like attacker away, slamming her into the central pillar.

Roaring his anger, Laird sprang forward. But he was beaten to it. If Kiri had been like a tigress, Belle came in like a plump, grey-haired, avenging mother bear. The billet of wood in her hand smashed down on Jody's head, then again, and again. He collapsed, cowering, shielding his head.

'No more, Belle — that's enough.' Laird had to haul her back physically. Kiri was picking herself up again, Jacob was bellowing in triumph. He kicked Jody's pistol towards Jacob, then looked round again past Ray Garris's sprawled body, and swore softly and savagely. 'Kiri, get over there — quickly.'

Diane Mehran lay slumped against the wall, the shotgun lying across her legs. She might have been resting. Her head was bowed, one hand was on her lap. But a dark stain was already spreading on the front of the grey jacket she was wearing. He had almost forgotten the single shot Garris had fired that fraction of a second before the shotgun had blasted him.

'Oh God,' said Kiri softly, then hurried past him.

Laird stopped Belle from following her, indicating his chain. 'Who had the keys to these damn padlocks?'

'Him.' She nodded at Jody, who was curled up like a ball, quivering, clutching his lacerated face.

Roughly, Laird searched the man's pockets and found keys. The second unlocked the padlock at his waist. He tossed the chain aside, then gave the keys to Belle.

'Take care of Jacob. Tell him to watch this one.' He left her, paused for a moment at Garris, and winced. The man was dead. A hole close to the size of a football had been blasted in his chest. But if that hadn't happened — tightlipped he hurried over. Kiri was kneeling beside Diane, her raven-black hair close to the older woman's face.

'I'll take her,' he said quietly and knelt down, a detached corner of his mind registering the way in which the bullet had hit Diane Mehran just under her right breast, the way in which a fine foam of blood was bubbling on her lips with each faint, shallow breath.

Her green eyes were open, looking at him. Her lips tried to shape a greeting, and failed. Gently, Laird slipped an arm round her and brought her head against his shoulder. Kiri was still close, an unspoken question on her face, and he gave her a small, negative headshake.

'Andrew.' It was like a whisper. He bent closer, and Diane Mehran's lips moved again, the words lost in another faint froth of blood. But those green eyes were still staring at him, pleading. She tried again, and he brought his head down beside her lips. They moved, forming the words, forcing them out. 'I'm sorry.'

'Don't be.' He saw her eyes still fixed on him. 'You saved us, Diane.'

Her hand moved and touched his own, as lightly as a bird's wing. Then it fell away, and her eyes dulled. Tightlipped, Laird felt for her pulse again. It had ended.

He stayed, holding Diane for another moment, then Kiri gently made him let go. He got to his feet, saw that Jacob was now over beside their captive, covering the man with his own pistol, and that Belle was heading over to join Kiri.

Maybe two minutes had passed, no more. He knew each second would remain seared into his mind. Two more people were dead, and yet it still wasn't finished. Taking a deep breath, he walked back to Jacob West and Jody. Looking up, Jacob gave a small, understanding nod.

'What about this one, boy?' He indicated the man at his feet then, stooping, rammed the muzzle of the pistol in Jody's ear. 'There's the easy way — ' The cold lack of emotion in his voice said he meant it.

'Or he can talk,' said Laird grimly. 'Sit up, Jody. Now.'

Shrugging, Jacob West removed the pistol. Trembling, Jody quickly hauled himself up into a sitting position. The blood was still trickling from the deep gash made by the belt buckle. He glanced quickly from West to Laird and apparently found no comfort in either of them.

'Is there anyone else at the house?' demanded Laird.

The man shook his head.

'What happens tonight?' Laird saw him hesitate and glanced at West. 'Jacob — '

'No — ' Jody surrendered. 'The two Mehran boys have a rendezvous with a cargo ship somewhere off Cherbourg, this side of midnight. She's called the *Sanjack*, from

Hong Kong — that's all I know about her.'

'Where's Paul Mehran?'

'At Witchlove Haven, keeping in radio touch.' The man licked some of the blood from his lips. 'Erick Roder was going over to Cherbourg.'

'Right.' said Laird softly. 'Is it drugs, Jody?'

'Yes.' It came as a reluctant sigh. 'Cocaine — a big deal. They took months setting it up.'

'That's their bad luck,' said Laird coldly, and took a step back.

'Finished?' asked Jacob.

'For now.' Laird nodded.

'Good.' Jacob West gave the faintest of smiles, then deliberately smashed the pistol barrel across the man's already damaged nose in a way that brought a fresh scream of pain. 'That's for my dog, mister. I can't stand cruelty to dumb animals.' He glanced towards his wife and nodded to himself. 'That'll do me.'

8

They needed help, help that had been much nearer than they had ever dreamed possible.

Belle and Kiri were first out of the crypt. A moment later Laird heard Belle call his name. Leaving Jacob West on guard over the captive Jody, he hurried out to join them in the fitful moonlight and saw a police car crawling cautiously up the driveway towards the mansion house. As the car's headlights caught them, the two women waved and beckoned and it accelerated in their direction.

The car stopped and a uniformed sergeant and a constable emerged warily, looking around. Then Belle grabbed the sergeant and gave him a delighted hug.

'Sergeant — bless you, whoever you are!' she exclaimed enthusiastically.

'Easy, lady!' Flustered, the sergeant freed himself and grinned at his companion. 'Looks like we found them, Bert.' He took another quick glance around, then turned to Laird. 'There were supposed to be four of you — '

Laird nodded. 'It's still that way.' He paused. 'Sergeant, how in hell did you come to be here?'

'Surveillance duty — there are cars out just about every damn where on the island tonight, on watch.' The sergeant, a heavily built man in his forties, was still uncertain but relieved. 'We thought we heard shots.'

'You did,' agreed Laird grimly.

'We called in for back-up' said the constable, looking around again, young enough to be disappointed at the apparent lack of action. 'What's been happening?'

'In there.' Laird indicated the crypt. 'Shout first before you go in — and the one with the gun is Police Honorifique.'

The sergeant grunted and carefully skirted round Belle as he led the way over. The two policemen entered the crypt and, seconds later, the constable hurried out. Jumping into the police car, he began talking quickly and urgently on the radio.

He had barely finished when they heard other cars approaching. The first to arrive skidded to a halt beside them and several police piled out. Chief Inspector Flambard was in the lead, with Sergeant Moisan at his heels. Flambard came straight to Laird.

'Where?' he asked curtly.

Silently, Laird indicated the crypt door.

'Stay right where you are,' snapped Flambard. 'That's an order.'

Other cars were arriving, more police

331

emerging from them as Flambard and Moisan hurried into the crypt. Suddenly feeling weak, Laird walked slowly to the empty car which had brought Flambard, rested his arms against it, and briefly closed his eyes. When he looked up again he saw Kiri and Belle had already been seated in the back of another car under the care of a woman sergeant. One of Flambard's men had obviously been detailed to watch him and was standing a few discreet yards away.

Shrugging, Laird took a deep breath of cool night air, enjoying the feel of the brisk wind on his face. He glanced at his watch and found it hard to believe it was already nine-thirty, that they had been prisoners for over ten hours. But that, at least, was over. Around him, some of Flambard's men were tramping off to check through the grounds; others were already coming back from looking around the house and finding nothing there.

A fresh bustle of footsteps and voices made Laird turn. Flambard was first to emerge from the crypt, followed by a limping, happy Jacob West. Then came Moisan and the uniformed sergeant, half pushing and half dragging a handcuffed Jody between them. Breaking away from the others, West headed towards the car where Belle was waiting.

Then, looking round, Flambard strode over to Laird.

'You and me, Laird.' Flambard beckoned grimly. 'Over here — now.'

They went a short distance away from the cars. Then Flambard stopped and faced him with a bleak mixture of wrath and relief.

'Two more dead.' His voice was harsh. 'If what Jacob was babbling is correct, it could have been even worse. You were damned lucky.'

'It wasn't luck,' corrected Laird quietly. 'It was Diane Mehran.'

'He said that too.' Flambard's lips pursed. 'Do we know what the hell is really going on?'

Laird nodded, watching an ambulance murmur up the driveway to park behind the other vehicles.

'They're bringing in a drugs shipment, a big one.'

Flambard swore under his breath. 'When?'

'Around midnight.'

'Off the French coast, like you guessed?'

'Yes.' Laird grimaced at the night. 'They'll collect from a ship called the *Sanjack*. She'll be waiting somewhere off Cherbourg — the Mehrans seem to have found another boat from somewhere.'

'I know that somewhere,' said Flambard, the soft southern burr edging into his voice again. 'Simon's pet power boat disappeared out of the yacht basin at St Helier this afternoon. My fault — I forgot about it until it was too late.' He scraped a thumbnail across his chin. 'Still, I took a chance or two on what we knew before. We're maybe more organised than you'd expect. So, what's the rest of it? Start with how they grabbed you.'

Laird told him, keeping to what mattered, the tiredness closing in on his mind again so that he sometimes had to search for the words he wanted. He knew Flambard noticed, but for the moment the policeman didn't comment, restricting himself to the occasional, encouraging nod.

'Good,' he said softly when Laird had finished. 'That's all we need, for now.'

In the background, two of the police cars started up and turned to leave. One had Jody and Sergeant Moisan aboard, the other carried the two Wests and Kiri. On the way out they passed the waiting ambulance, the crew out and lounging beside the vehicle, waiting their turn to be called to the crypt.

It was always that way, thought Laird. The dead had a low priority. The call wouldn't come until Flambard's men were finished in there. A picture came into his mind of Diane Mehran, the way she had looked at him and touched him before she died. The big, auburn-haired woman had saved their lives at the cost of her own. It would be a long time before he would forget. He drew a deep breath.

'What about you?' he asked Flambard. 'You were ready, waiting — '

'You mean hoping and guessing,' corrected Flambard. He shrugged. 'Thank old Admiral Boullard. He went back to Merfleur to have some kind of argument with Jacob West about the way things were happening. He didn't like what he found and had sense enough to call us.' He gave a reminiscent glance. 'All right, we were already looking for you, there were no prizes for guessing what had happened. But we'd nothing to go on. For all we knew, your safety depended on our not tipping off the Mehrans how much we knew.'

Laird nodded, trying to listen, knowing it mattered yet feeling the weakness seeping in again.

'One thing we could do was put a watch on anything that had a Mehran smell about it — though you were being held before we even started. Still, we got some dividends. We know Erick Roder flew out this afternoon on a scheduled Aurigny Airways flight to Cherbourg. We've nothing on the Mehran brothers, but we know Paul Mehran went from here to Witchlove Haven and hasn't moved since — ' He broke off suddenly, peering more closely at Laird. 'Never mind the rest. Do you feel as bad as you look?'

Laird tried to grin. 'I'll survive.'

'Would you bet on it?' Flambard looked round and signalled the nearest of his men over. 'I'll have a car take you to headquarters. Don't worry, I won't be too far behind you.'

'Thanks,' said Laird.

For once, he didn't feel like arguing.

★　★　★

They treated him well at Rouge Bouillon. A police surgeon gave him a brief but thorough checkover and put two stitches in a scalp wound he hadn't really known existed. Someone loaned him a clean shirt to replace the blood-stained one he was wearing — some of that blood was from Diane Mehran. Someone else gave him a mug of coffee and brought a plate of hot stew from the police canteen. The coffee had been solidly laced with brandy and he didn't object.

Then they gave him a cot in a spare interview room and left him alone. He lay down, glad of the chance to unwind, to let some of that weakness seep away. But plenty of other people were busy. He could hear them hurrying around outside. He heard Sergeant Moisan bellowing a few times in the background and telephones rang incessantly.

Laird dozed off, but not for long. His watch showed the time as approaching 11 p.m. when he was gently shaken awake by a policewoman. She loaned him a comb. He used it carefully on the hair around his stitches, then she led him through to Tom Flambard's office.

'Man, you look almost human again,' declared Tom Flambard. He was at his desk, looking surprisingly pleased with himself. Sergeant Moisan was also in the room, loafing against a filing cabinet, an almost friendly scowl on his long, horse-like face. They had a chair waiting for him and Flambard leaned forward once Laird had settled. 'I've packed the Wests and that Vass girl back to Merfleur with a couple of my men to keep an eye on them. Call it clearing the decks — I've no room for civilians or Police Honorifique on this little firing line.'

'What about me?' asked Laird bluntly.

'I want you with me. Life's simpler when I know what you're doing.' Flambard sat back. 'We're putting together some of the answers we need. 'Even better, Mr Jody Silk — '

'Silk?' Laird raised an eyebrow.

'That's his name,' agreed Flambard. 'But

not his nature, eh?' He glanced at Moisan. 'Suddenly anxious to help us, isn't he, Sam?'

Moisan gave an evil grin and nodded. 'Pure as the driven snow, our Jody.'

'And ready to tell anything to save his own hide,' said Flambard 'He confirms the Mehran rendezvous with the freighter *Sanjack* is fixed for just before midnight, this side of Cherbourg.' He saw the way Laird glanced at his watch. 'Don't worry, we're organised, we'll cope. Tell him, Sam.'

'We have full co-operation from the French authorities,' said Moisan and showed his teeth for emphasis. 'We've been feeding them information all day — and they owe us a few favours.'

'That includes laying on a French Navy patrol boat,' added Flambard. 'We've roped in some Royal Navy help too. Tell them the French are involved, and they'll fall over themselves to do better.' He paused. 'According to Jody, it goes like this. The *Sanjack* is carrying general cargo from the Far East to Cherbourg. She has been anchored to the south for a few days with alleged steering-gear problems, now miraculously repaired. Matt Mehran was aboard her. When were you wined and dined at Mehran Gate?'

'Two nights back,' Laird answered automatically, almost guessing what was coming.

'That was the night Simon smuggled Matt into Jersey,' said Flambard dryly.

Laird winced, remembering Paul Mehran's sudden change of mood towards Simon when he had returned that night.

'You weren't to know.' Flambard gave a faintly sardonic grin. 'What's happening right now, according to Jody, who is too frightened to lie about it, is that we've got Simon and Matt on that power boat *Devilwitch*, hanging around ready to meet the *Sanjack*. Paul Mehran is in radio contact with both craft from Witchlove Haven, with two or three hired helpers to keep him company. The plan is for the *Devilwitch* to collect the drugs from the freighter, then come back and land them at the Haven.'

'And then?'

'Jody says he doesn't know, Mr Laird,' said Moisan sadly. He sucked his teeth noisily. 'Only that Paul Mehran moves it on some time tomorrow, to the London area, using his private plane. The way he's sweating, I'm ready to believe him.'

'It doesn't matter.' Flambard's eyes were hard and bright. 'It won't happen. I'm tired of people twisting my tail. Now it's my turn.' He brought a hand down hard and flat on his desk. 'I want this cargo ship caught in the act — so do the French. I want the Mehrans in a parcel, and I want their other damned director, Roder. He'll be waiting in Cherbourg, where the *Sanjack* captain gets final payment for delivery after she docks.' It was his turn to glance at his watch, but he still seemed satisfied. 'Complicity in murder, drug-running — we'll add up the rest as we go along. But they're going to be finished.'

'Add on the *Rosewitch* sinking,' said Laird unemotionally. 'Then that crimp who drowned at Southampton.'

'I hadn't forgotten.' Flambard nodded. 'There's one aspect that might interest you — Jody again. He says any sniffing around our friend Captain West's alleged treasure wasn't mainstream Mehran. That came down to Simon and Matt more or less amusing themselves.'

'He's sure?' Laird gave a quick frown — too quick. He felt the stitches in his scalp stab as they tightened.

'Jody's version.' Moisan sucked his teeth again, but was positive. 'He says he helped them to do some diving off Merfleur, but they had to make a run for it before they found anything.' He shrugged. 'Simon always kept an eye on Frere. He heard a whisper that Frere was selling some old coins, put everything he heard together, and got interested.'

Laird nodded. But did it matter now? The

340

Vanneau and some other things had long been overtaken by what had happened.

'Basically, I'm letting Jody talk and talk.' Flambard eyed Laird shrewdly and with some sympathy, as if the dark-haired detective could read his thoughts. 'I've a change of men questioning him now . . . Whatever he says, we can build on it, or reject it later. But we're getting names.'

'Who did what, like a catalogue,' agreed Moisan briskly. 'He's certainly pulling it together for us.'

'Happen that way he keeps his own skin intact,' murmured Flambard less enthusiastically.

'What does he say about Diane Mehran?'

'Mainly that she didn't know a damn thing — and that I can believe,' replied Flambard, straightening a little. 'She was useful, as a straight, honest front. Maybe she began to have suspicions, maybe they kept on growing. But there's that Mehran family loyalty. I expect she only believed what she wanted to believe — right up to almost the last minute. Then she had to face facts.'

Laird nodded bitterly. 'You said names. What names for Frere and Chris Newgrange?'

'Names according to Jody,' cautioned Flambard. 'He says the weever-fish poison attempt was Simon's idea, with brother Matt holding his jacket. When Frere was killed this morning — that was Ray Garris, though I think Jody was probably with him. He knows too much about it.'

'And Chris Newgrange?' pressed Laird.

'Jody blames Garris again. That they really wanted Frere and killing Newgrange was a pure foul-up.' Flambard shook his head. 'I'll believe the last part. But Frere told you he saw two men, right? My money is on Garris and Jody again.'

'If I'd had more time — ' began Moisan sourly. He stopped as there was a knock at the office door. It opened, a constable looked in, and Flambard raised an eyebrow. The man nodded, then left again.

'That's it,' said Flambard as the door closed. Pushing back his chair, he got to his feet and gave Laird a small, dry smile. 'Laird, how do you feel about helicopters?'

Laird blinked, then understood.

'I suppose they beat trying to walk on water,' he said slowly.

'Sam doesn't.' Flambard gave Moisan a sad, sympathetic glance. 'He hates the things.'

Moisan grunted, but said nothing.

'We've got one waiting for us,' said Flambard. 'Probably with the meter running. Like to come with us?'

★ ★ ★

Someone handed Laird a leather jacket only a couple of sizes too large, then he was packed into a police car between Flambard and Moisan. A two-minute drive brought them to a school playing-field. Parked in the middle, rotors clunking softly in the darkness, the waiting Sea King helicopter had Royal Navy markings and a crew of three. The helicopter pilot, a young navy lieutenant named Marsh, gave an unhappy frown when they met in the glare of the police car's headlights.

'I was briefed about you, Chief Inspector — and about your sergeant.' He eyed Laird with a degree of worry. 'But an unauthorised civilian is something else. I could be breaking a few rules.'

'Happen I could be breaking my neck, lieutenant,' said Tom Flambard acidly. 'I want him along.'

'I'm like their mascot,' said Laird mildly.

'He's more like an albatross,' said Moisan. 'But we still want him.'

'I don't have to look for trouble, believe me.' Marsh sighed, considered the two policemen for a moment, then surrendered. 'All right, we're ready.'

'What about camera gear?' asked Flambard.

'My department, Chief Inspector,' said the Sea King's co-pilot. 'We've everything we'll need for the job.'

Marsh and his co-pilot climbed into the cockpit while their passengers were helped into the mid-compartment by a genial, bearded petty officer winchman. He gave them helmets, plugged their headset leads into a communication box, and had them scribble their signatures on a type-written form.

'What's that about?' asked Moisan suspiciously.

'Just a blood chit, sergeant,' said the navy man easily. 'It says night flying is hazardous and if you get killed you promise not to sue anybody.' He chuckled and waited until Laird signed beneath Moisan's signature. 'Now, gents — single or return tickets?'

Moments later the Sea King's rotors gathered speed and they rose, the lights of St Helier shrinking below them until the whole town was spread like an illuminated map, a map they were rapidly leaving behind.

'Life jackets, gents.' The winchman returned. 'Sorry, more regulations when we're over water.' There was a life jacket for each of them. Then he handed Flambard a folded chart. 'The boss says you'll want this.'

Flambard nodded and spread out the chart

344

as the winchman switched on an extra cabin light. Joining him at the chart, Laird saw Sergeant Moisan's apparent lack of interest and the start of a sweaty pallor on the man's long-jawed face.

'Pilot here,' said Marsh's voice over the headsets. 'Here's the picture, Chief Inspector. As of now our reading is 018 magnetic and we'll cross the north coast of Jersey in a moment. We'll stay at 2000 feet for the present and our speed will be around 120 knots — maybe more. We're picking up a tailwind building from the southwest that wasn't exactly forecast. Any change in what you want done?'

'No.' Flambard remembered the intercom switch, used it, and started again. 'No, Lieutenant. Your search area stands — our ship should be somewhere around two miles northeast of Alderney Island. How long will it be before we're there?'

'We've an ETA of maybe twelve minutes from now,' said Marsh easily.

As he finished, the co-pilot's voice cut in. 'Chief Inspector, I've a message coming in for you, from your headquarters. They say you'll understand. They've picked up some radio chat between an operator located at — ' He paused to check ' — at a Witchlove Haven and two apparent ships. All signals low-power, no other details.'

'Thank you,' said Flambard formally, but with a glint in his dark-brown eyes. He turned. 'Hear that, Sam?'

Moisan managed a miserable nod. As the Sea King's rotors churned their beat, a suddenly sympathetic winchman produced a sick-bag and silently gave it to the sergeant.

'You then, Laird.' Flambard beckoned him closer and tapped the chart spread on his knees. 'Here's what we've got. I told you the French are in on this. They say the freighter *Sanjack* sailed around daybreak this morning.' His finger moved. 'She was seen heading north, well to the west of the Channel Islands. What would you guess from that?'

'It's fairly easy,' declared Laird. 'She was slotting her way into one of the regular shipping lanes for Cherbourg.'

'Normal enough?'

'Yes.'

Most deep-sea freighters would head that way, in a large curve which took them well clear of the Channel Islands group with their notorious rocks and currents. After that, Flambard had to be guessing right in his choice of search area. The island of Alderney, one of the smallest and most easterly of Jersey's sister islands, was only separated by a handful of miles from Cape de la Hague on the French coast. Cherbourg was not far round the corner from the Cape.

He could picture the freighter from Hong Kong approaching from above the islands and the Mehran brothers with their *Devilwitch* heading up from Jersey to intercept her. Northeast of Alderney would be an ideal, empty patch of sea. Yet it would still be close to where that French passenger ferry would pass on her repositioning run back to Jersey, the Mehrans' cover for their return trip.

Even if that went wrong, the Mehrans had another choice — with a possible bonus. Laird looked at the chart again, frowning. It would depend on sea conditions, on the tide, on how well they knew their currents. A power boat like the *Devilwitch* was built for speed, pure and simple. That didn't make her a good sea boat — in fact, she was a poor substitute for the motor launch he'd disabled. But the narrow few miles of sea separating Alderney and France had a fierce current sweeping through, altering with the tides. Shipping was advised to stay clear or keep close to the French coast.

Yet if a boat could use that current, could ride along with it, if her crew had nerves of steel, she could add considerably to her speed.

'The French should have the *Sanjack*

located on radar by now,' said Flambard. 'But they'll keep radio silence until they hear from us.' He gave a soft chuckle. 'There are territorial waters involved and some diplomatic nonsense had to be ironed out. But we've got things agreed. That passenger ferry will appear on schedule, but she won't be empty. She'll be carrying a squad of armed French gendarmes, all probably annoyed at having to work overtime!'

The helicopter lurched, then a retching noise reached them. Sergeant Moisan was using his sick-bag, his long face a study in misery.

'Next time, sergeant, ask permission,' said Flambard without sympathy. The Sea King shuddered again as he turned back to Laird. 'The French are borrowing the Mehrans' trick. One of their fast naval patrol boats has been loitering off Cape de la Hague. She'll come in hiding behind the passenger ferry — call that their half of a pincer. The other half is a Royal Navy patrol boat sent out from Guernsey.' He gave Laird a wolfish grin. 'What do you think? Have we left anything out?'

'Only that they could make a run for it,' said Laird cautiously. Something as fast as the *Devilwitch* could sail rings round any patrol boat built.

'Then happen the Mehrans will get a clip of cannon shell up their backsides,' declared Flambard with some relish. 'That's a French idea and we've agreed.'

The bearded winchman brought them coffee in plastic cups. Outside the Sea King's side windows there was cloud moving in the same direction they were travelling, but there were breaks and moonlight enough to show the white wavecrests of sea below.

'We've got a contact that looks like our freighter,' said Lieutenant Marsh over the intercom. His voice was calm and business-like. 'Her position is pretty much as forecast. Then we've another, smaller contact moving along off the French coast. That's probably the ferryboat-load of gendarmes.'

Flambard grinned, but Laird used the intercom switch.

'Lieutenant, what's the wind speed?'

'Still building, eighteen knots, gusting well over twenty,' came the crisp answer. 'That's part of why we're bumping around a little.' Marsh paused. 'Chief Inspector, I suggest I start losing some height and reduce speed — I could use some of that low cloud.'

Laird saw Flambard glance at him. He nodded to the policeman.

'Do that, Lieutenant,' agreed Flambard.

The chunking whirr of the Sea King's

rotors eased a little, and she swayed, coming round on a new heading. His lips showing he was whistling, the winchman gave Moisan a new sick-bag while the cabin illumination faded to a soft, near-twilight glow. They were in cloud. Flambard sat like a statue, saying nothing, his face impassive again, while Laird peered at the chart in the faint light, an uncertain tendril of doubt still in his mind.

'Alderney to your left,' said their pilot. The cloud had parted; they could see a low, dark outline of land sprinkled with house and street lights. A group of lighthouses were flashing at the north end. Marsh's voice came over the intercom again. 'Beginning our approach now. That second contact to the east is confirmed as your ferryboat.'

'Let the French know we're going in,' said Flambard quickly.

'Already done, Chief Inspector.' It was the co-pilot who answered. 'Camera gear ready.'

The Sea King took another lurching swing, ducking into cloud again. As the seconds crawled by, Laird peered with a new urgency at the chart and its timetables. What he saw made him wince.

'Flambard — ' he began.

'Contact dead ahead. We've got her,' crackled the intercom, cutting him short. Suddenly they were clear of the cloud, swinging, then steadying, rapidly losing height. Down below, clearly visible in the moonlight, lay the black, beetle-like shape of a stationary ship. 'Camera stand by. Flares wait — now!'

Seconds later, first one white flare then another burst over the ship, straddling her, turning the moonlit darkness into glaring daylight. A triumphant growl came from Flambard. He slapped Laird on the back. The slim shape of a power boat lay close against the freighter's side. They were low enough to see white dots of the crewmen's faces staring up at them from the *Sanjack*'s decks.

The flares died. Just before the circling helicopter released two more to take their place there was a chance to see the lights of the French ferryboat. She was heading straight towards the freighter and already being overtaken by a much faster craft.

'Lieutenant, that 'go' signal for Jersey! You can send it,' said Flambard over the intercom. As Marsh acknowledged, the detective turned to Laird. 'That's for our people outside Witchlove Haven. They'll pick up Daddy Mehran before he can try to run.' He used the intercom again. 'Still listening, Lieutenant?'

'Every moment,' said Marsh cheerfully. There was a brief pause. 'Jersey have acknowledged.'

'We've got photographs?'

'Crisp and clear,' cut in the co-pilot's voice. There was a mild chuckle. 'Don't worry, Chief Inspector. We guarantee satisfaction and every — ' He broke off, and they heard him gasp. 'Hey that power boat! Will you look at her go!'

Laird and Flambard pressed their faces against the Sea King's compartment window as more flares lit the scene. Yet they were hardly needed. Thrusting away from the freighter like an angry wasp, already throwing up a white wash, the *Devilwitch* was on the move. Seconds later, as the Sea King made a tight turn to follow, a searchlight beam lanced across the sea from the east and caught the freighter. The French patrol boat was announcing her presence.

Immediately, the power boat's bow swung as her occupants switched her escape run from east to west. Her speed was building, her wake was spreading like a wide curl of silk ribbon.

'She's fast,' said Sergeant Moisan grudgingly, sufficiently caught up in the excitement to squeeze in beside Laird. Then he grimaced and retreated again as the helicopter lurched. 'Damn them, why can't they give up?'

Muttering to himself, reduced to the role of spectator, Flambard kept staring down. A mix of voices and static began reaching them from the cockpit area, at least one of the voices speaking French. Then, from the west, another searchlight played across the water, swung briefly, and caught the power boat. The British patrol boat was signalling her arrival. A moment later that was followed by a brief, hosing burst of tracer cannon shells as the power boat kept on in her direction. The pincer was complete.

'Now sort that out, damn you,' grated Flambard.

Someone on the *Devilwitch* did, after a few moments' hesitation when they saw her speed reduce. Again her wake took on a new curve. The next flares showed her gathering speed again, retreating southwest, heading back towards Jersey. The Sea King's flares showed the two men crouching in the power boat's cockpit, both intent on what they were doing, neither looking up.

'What are they playing at?' demanded Flambard, a wisp of uncertainty in his voice. 'How fast is that thing going?'

'Sixty knots, more in hand.' They were low enough for Laird to see the way spray mixed with the haze of the exhaust fumes as the *Devilwitch* smashed her way through a moderate swell. 'They're trying for the back door.'

'Then they're out of luck,' said Flambard

shortly. 'We can get something out of St Helier to make sure of that.' He looked back and scowled. The distance to the two pursuing patrol boats was widening. The one on the French side took its turn to fire a few rounds of tracer shell but seemed reluctant to come too far out from her own coastline. He bit his lip. 'All right, they're running for home. I suppose they could get ashore somewhere — '

'Wait,' said Laird tonelessly. Something in his manner stopped Flambard. He used the intercom. 'Lieutenant — '

'Listening,' said Marsh briskly. 'I've an update for you. The French cops are boarding the freighter — no resistance. But the patrol boats say they haven't a hope of making an interception on that thing down there.'

'Forget them,' said Laird. 'Can you tell me wind strength and direction?'

'Still from the southwest, now steadying around twenty-five knots — this time we're heading into it.'

'Check your tidal-stream data,' said Laird shortly.

'Oh hell,' said Marsh in sudden understanding. 'Wait.' They heard a brief, low discussion between pilot and co-pilot, while down below them the *Devilwitch* hammered on her way. The discussion ended, to be

354

followed by an equally swift radio exchange with the patrol boats. Then a sober-voiced Marsh spoke again to Laird. 'Yes, you're right. Do we try to warn them?'

'I think they know,' said Laird softly.

'Know what?' demanded Flambard.

'What they're risking.' Laird glanced down at the bright white streak. 'They have to know.' He used the intercom again. 'Lieutenant, where does it start?'

'On their present course, about a mile ahead.' Marsh went back to being totally professional again. 'From this height, I can see where it starts.' There was another pause, and a background murmur from the co-pilot, then Marsh returned. 'Unanimous from the patrol boats. The French commander says he can stay offshore on his side, but he's not sticking his neck any further out. Our boat says she is just about on her limit.'

'Laird!' Flambard grabbed Laird's arm with a snarl. 'What do they know down there?'

'That they're heading into a nightmare,' said Laird. He saw Flambard's total lack of comprehension. 'Do you know much about the sea?'

Flambard shook his head. Behind them, Moisan tried not to moan as the Sea King gave one of her shudders.

'They're heading back down the Race of Alderney, because that's the only way they can go,' said Laird curtly. 'Right now there's a peak tidal current heading in the same direction, giving them an extra eight or nine knots — like water going through a hosepipe.'

'So?'

Laird sighed. 'Tom, the current is from the northeast, the wind is from the southwest.'

The use of his first name seemed to emphasise things for Flambard, then the signs of a dawning understanding showed on his face. 'You mean wind and sea are meeting head on?'

'Yes.' It would do. 'Tom, you know what that gives?'

'Rough seas?' suggested Flambard uneasily.

'I'm listening. I'll tell him,' said Marsh in a flat voice over the intercom. 'There's a standard warning, Chief Inspector. Seas break heavily, dangerous heavy overfalls of water over submerged banks and rocks make powerful eddies. Even large ships should stay clear.' He sighed. 'Maybe half a mile now — it's like someone drew a line across the sea ahead. That power boat will be like an egg thrown into a kitchen blender. I'm going to try something — '

The Sea King crabbed sideways a little, still

keeping up with the fleeing boat, but now giving her passengers a clear view ahead. It was a sight which left them momentarily speechless. Both Alderney and the French coastline were clearly visible. But between them, apart from the strip the French patrol boat was guarding, the sea formed a barrier line of white, tossing rage. A battle was being fought in the Race of Alderney, a battle between wind and sea that sent great masses of water into the air, surging in a combat that used every rock and reef.

'God Almighty!' said Flambard in an awed voice that could hardly penetrate the din of the helicopter. 'They're going to try to run through that?'

'They know the alternative,' said Laird.

And the Mehrans had made their choice, had settled for the slender possibilities that existed if they could get out at the other end.

The Sea King had been gaining speed, overtaking the power boat, then racing on ahead. Just short of where the white fury began, she swung round to face the approaching *Devilwitch*. Two more flares burst below her, lighting up the scene in a final warning.

It was ignored, except that one of the men in the power boat's cockpit looked up and waved derisively.

Seconds later, her course still arrow-straight, the *Devilwitch* ran under the helicopter and met the heaving seas. Again the Sea King swung, so low now that occasional spray spattered her length, chasing while the power boat fought and heaved through the battering confusion of sea. Twice Laird saw the entire racing hull tossed clean out of the water and crash down again. Then, as quickly as it had begun, it was over.

One moment the *Devilwitch* was pitching and fighting, the next, two great lumping walls of angry water collided in an explosion of foam almost beneath her and she flipped over on her back. She vanished briefly in the fury, reappeared, rolled, and when she showed again it was as if that slim hull had been smashed in two by some giant axe.

Once more the Sea King moved in, hovering over the wreckage and firing a steady succession of flares.

One flare showed a figure clinging to a large section of boat. Then another sea swept in, figure and wreckage vanished, and there was only boiling sea.

'I don't understand,' said Flambard unsteadily. For a moment, he pressed both hands to his forehead; when he spoke there was still a shake in his voice. 'Why do it? There was no sense in even trying — was there?'

'It was what they wanted,' said Laird. 'Their choice.'

With no one else involved. His mouth tightened. The Mehran brothers would have known the kind of charges they faced if they simply gave in. They had been offered a challenge and had accepted it, probably knowing they couldn't win.

But it had been their choice.

'Signal from our patrol launch, Chief Inspector.' From the cockpit Lieutenant Marsh's voice had a hoarse note. 'Her commander requests instructions. But he says that there's not much he can do until the current slackens — he reckons at least another hour.'

'Thank her commander.' Flambard straightened his shoulders. 'Advise him we don't expect survivors. But I'd appreciate it if he makes a search when he can and recovers what he can. You'd better give the French separate thanks for their co-operation.' He gave a tired sigh. 'Lieutenant, you did your best.'

'For what it was worth,' said Marsh simply.

The Sea King swung away and began to gain height.

* * *

359

They landed back at the same school playing-field on the outskirts of St Helier. A car was waiting to take them to police headquarters and, once they'd thanked Marsh and his crew, the Sea King rose again. She was to refuel, take on a fresh supply of flares, then return to assist in the search once the Race of Alderney had calmed.

Rouge Bouillon already knew what had happened. When they got there, the welcomes were subdued. But the rest had been a success. Paul Mehran and the two men with him had been arrested with only a brief scuffle as they tried to make a break from Witchlove Haven, Mehran ready to try for the airport and his private aircraft. They were now in separate holding cells. Initial reaction coming in from the French police was a mix of satisfaction at seizing the freighter from Hong Kong, now lying in Cherbourg under arrest, and apology at the fact that Erick Roder had somehow slipped their net.

But Roder was being hunted with a total Gallic determination. Sooner or later the Mehran Holdings financial director would turn up somewhere.

Much of the rest became a clamour of telephones, a stream of telex messages, an insistence on details for immediate reports. A lot of people in a lot of places were suddenly and apparently vitally interested in the *Sanjack*. Time crawled past for Laird, mostly punctuated by mugs of coffee or by some strange face peering into Flambard's office wanting to verify one fact or another.

Though it was late, he used Flambard's telephone to make a brief call to Merfleur Cottage. Kiri answered the call on the first ring. All of them, even the dog, were fine. He told her what had happened in a few short sentences, promised he'd be at Merfleur as soon as he could, then hung up.

It was close on 4 a.m., with the headquarters building still a blaze of lights, before Chief Inspector Flambard was ready. The dark-haired policeman took a last glance through the pile of message forms which had accumulated on his desk, picked up a package wrapped in brown paper, then nodded at Laird.

They went along a corridor to an interview room where Paul Mehran was waiting under guard. As they entered it, the two uniformed men who had been there quietly left, closing the door behind them.

It was a plain room, without windows and with a minimum of furnishings. Paul Mehran sat on a wooden chair facing a simple, plastic-topped table. Silently, he looked up at his visitors as they sat down opposite him.

'You've been cautioned, Mr Mehran.' Flambard made it a statement.

'By your sergeant.' Mehran gave a faint nod. He was wearing hand-stitched denims and a tailored blue shirt. He had been left with cigarettes and a box of matches but there were only two stubbed cigarette ends in the ashtray in front of him.

But Paul Mehran had aged. Gone was the hard glint in those green Mehran eyes. He needed a shave, his face had an underlying pallor which was accentuated by those high cheekbones, his narrow, scarred mouth showed the tiredness of a man who had lost and who knew it. His whole body seemed to have sagged.

'We've some news,' said Flambard quietly.

Mehran stiffened for a moment, looking at him. What he saw in Flambard's face brought a small sigh.

'Both of them?' he asked.

'Both of them,' agreed Flambard. 'I'm sorry.'

'When can I see them?' Something like pain sounded briefly in Paul Mehran's voice.

'Later,' said Flambard.

The Royal Navy patrol boat had done its work well. About an hour had passed since it had found the bodies of both the Mehran brothers. Simon had died floating in his life

362

jacket. Matt had been caught up in some of the *Devilwitch*'s wreckage. The Sea King which had guided the patrol boat to the spot had winched everything found aboard and had flown its grim cargo back to Jersey.

'I expected it.' Briefly, Paul Mehran looked down at the plastic-topped table and his lips moved silently. Then he straightened, his hands clasped together. 'I think you understand, Chief Inspector. We are an old, proud family.'

'This proud?' Flambard produced the package he'd brought through and ripped off the outer brown paper. The sealed plastic pouch inside was still damp; it was filled with a fine, white powder. He slapped the pouch down on the table in front of Mehran. 'The Navy got some of these from the wreckage. The French seized some others on the freighter. Your sons apparently didn't have time to transfer all of them to their boat.'

'Apparently.' Paul Mehran looked at the plastic pouch, his mouth twisting a little. Then he looked up again. 'Well, I suppose at least I can say I saw some of it. That's a little better than nothing.'

'You admit what it is?' asked Laird.

'Why deny it?' Mehran shrugged. 'High-grade cocaine, uncut, 95 per cent purity guaranteed, Middle East origin. It cost us £25,000 a kilo in Hong Kong — plus expenses, of course.'

Flambard grunted. 'How much were you bringing in?'

'Forty kilos.' Mehran unclasped his hands and built a wry steeple with his fingertips. 'We had — uh — made certain arrangements with the mainland markets. I wouldn't have tolerated any of it on Jersey.'

Laird made a fast mental calculation and his lips shaped a silent whistle. From the look on Flambard's face, he felt the same way.

'Forty kilos,' he repeated slowly. 'In a single shipment?'

Mehran nodded.

'£1 million?'

'Yes. Plus expenses, as I said.' Paul Mehran was indifferent.

But high-quality cocaine guaranteed a profit of several times that amount if it reached mainland UK wholesalers. Then, from there on, cut down and adulterated every step of the way, adulterated with everything from milk powder to sifted flour, its value would keep growing again and again until it reached street-pusher level.

'How did you people manage to raise a million?' asked Laird bluntly.

'It wasn't easy,' admitted Mehran. He

shook his head. 'Some from here, some from there — a lot of it borrowed.'

'Had you shipped before?' persisted Flambard.

'No — and once would have been enough.' Mehran abandoned his steeple building and sat back, a man who didn't care much about anything any more. He looked at Laird. 'You know our financial state?'

Laird nodded.

'You would, naturally.' There was a sardonic edge to the words. 'But that shipment's profits would have changed all that. The marina at Witchlove Haven could have succeeded, would have succeeded, quite apart from anything else.' Pausing, Paul Mehran gave a faint shrug. 'When Diane and I inherited Witchline Shipping, what we really inherited was a bottomless pit of debts and bad management. Diane would never accept that, or understand it.'

'You mean she was too honest,' said Flambard grimly.

'I suppose I do.' For a moment, a crack showed in Mehran's outward indifference. He traced the stubble of beard around his chin with a fingertip and his voice softened. 'But she was always that way. I'm sorry about Diane — I think we were fond of each other, in our own fashion.' His eyes strayed to Laird.

'Her other weakness was trusting people too much. What brought you here, Laird? Was it really just the *Rosewitch*?'

Laird nodded.

'It's strange.' Mehran sighed to himself. 'The *Rosewitch* money saw us through one crisis, gave us some breathing space. There were a few small problems, of course — but I'd hoped that was all forgotten. Even when you arrived and Simon had doubts, it seemed worth a gamble.'

'Was Peter Frere your main 'small problem'?' asked Flambard deliberately.

'Yes,' admitted Mehran. 'One we botched — '

'When Simon's weever-fish idea didn't work?' Laird didn't wait for an answer. 'But you knew Frere saw too much. Where's the *Rosewitch* operating now?'

A flicker of surprise showed in Mehran's eyes, then he shrugged. 'Somewhere off Java, I think. Her new owners weren't precise about things.'

'And her new name?'

'I've no idea.' Paul Mehran shook his head with a weary indifference.

He answered a few more questions in the same way. The *Rosewitch* money had only been a temporary help. Soon things had begun sliding again. Even the Witchlove

366

Haven marina, intended to be the money-making answer to everything, had become a major headache as construction costs kept soaring. Then suddenly Erick Roder had come up with the drugs idea and some names they could contact.

'And after that, Matt went to Hong Kong to supervise it all?' suggested Flambard, the coaxing south-coast burr strong in his voice.

'No.' Paul Mehran's voice softened for a moment at the mention of his younger son's name. He picked up the cigarette pack lying in front of him, took a cigarette, but only played with it. 'He was more a hostage, until we raised the money. The Hong Kong people saw us as strangers, they wanted a personal guarantee.' He broke the cigarette in half and tossed it into the ashtray. 'We could have sent Simon, of course — he wanted to go. But Simon was always too unpredictable, Matt was more reliable.'

Flambard sat silent for a moment, then glanced at Laird and raised an eyebrow. Laird shook his head, still digesting what they'd been told. Paul Mehran might claim only one shipment had been planned but would it have really ended there? A small shipping line, based on Jersey, with all the contacts and facilities that offered, would have been too important a catch for the cocaine overlords in

Hong Kong to let slide away.

'All right.' Heavily, Flambard cleared his throat. 'You're tired, I'm tired, everybody's tired. We'll pick this up later — happen when we do I'll want names, dates, places.'

'You'll let me see my sons first?'

Flambard nodded.

'I'll think about it afterwards,' said Paul Mehran with a sudden firmness. 'Not before.' He took a deep breath, turned to Laird, and for a moment frowned. 'One thing Simon and Matt both wondered about — has that old fool Jacob West really found a treasure ship somewhere?'

'Yes,' said Laird.

'Strange,' said Paul Mehran softly. 'Very strange. Are we finished for now, Chief Inspector?'

They left him. As they went out of the interview room Laird glanced back. Paul Mehran was sitting upright, his face impassive again. But a single tear had begun running down one of his cheeks.

★ ★ ★

Rouge Bouillon could provide Laird with a cot and a couple of blankets in a spare office. He slept like a log for about three hours and woke with sunlight streaming into the room.

His own travel bag, packed, was lying on the floor beside him.

The scalp wound on his head was still a low throb, but he showered, shaved, put on clean clothes, then managed to find his way to the headquarters canteen. He was at a table by himself, eating his way through a plateful of bacon and eggs and feeling he was still just half awake, when Tom Flambard appeared and came over carrying a cup of coffee.

'Good morning.' Flambard laid his coffee cup on the table and sat in the chair opposite him. 'I thought I'd let you sleep.'

'I could have used another day.' Laird gave him an attempt at a grin. However little sleep Chief Inspector Flambard had managed, he looked fresh: he was cleanshaven and had changed his suit. 'What's happening?'

Flambard grimaced and sipped his coffee. 'Not a lot — sorting out some of the routine chaos.' He set down his cup. 'You got your things?'

Laird nodded and finished a last mouthful of the bacon.

'I sent a man out to the Leecom.' Flambard gave an awkward shrug. 'He said he packed everything.'

'Thank him for me.' Laird pushed his plate aside. He eyed Flambard in wry amusement.

'It is like someone is trying to tell me something.'

'That's right.' Flambard's brown eyes met his own. 'Happen the word is goodbye.' Reaching into the inside pocket of his jacket, the detective brought out an airline ticket and placed it between them. 'You're booked on the noon flight. You'll be in London in time for a late lunch.'

'Noon.' Laird touched the ticket with a fingertip. 'Do I get to ask why?'

'You've that right.' Flambard scowled at an inspector in uniform coming their way and the man headed in another direction. 'Look, Andrew, I reckon things are about square between us.' He sighed to himself. 'But now I've the whole mess to clear up, a lot of awkward questions to answer. You're as awkward as any of them.'

'But less awkward if I'm not around?' suggested Laird mildly.

'Happen.' Flambard nodded. 'You understand?'

'Maybe I do,' admitted Laird. 'I'm not so sure about Clanmore Alliance.'

Flambard gave a slight grin. 'You work for someone called Morris, right? I had him on the 'phone this morning. We had a long talk and — uh — I think he understands. If he doesn't, he has some problems of his own.

370

But I agreed that Clanmore will get any information on the *Rosewitch* we come up with.'

'That's fair.' Laird looked at his wristwatch. 'You said that flight was at noon — '

'Until then, I want to know where you are,' murmured Flambard. Then he grinned. 'Sam Moisan is outside with a car. We thought you might like some time out at Merfleur Point — unless you've a better idea.'

'Merfleur sounds fine,' said Laird solemnly.

They rose and shook hands.

'I can't see you off,' said Flambard. He shook his head. 'It's a pity you won't be back on Jersey, isn't it?'

'Go to hell, Tom,' said Laird.

When he collected his travel bag and went outside, Sam Moisan was lounging at the wheel of an unmarked police car parked near the main door. 'Merfleur?' asked Moisan once his passenger had got aboard. Then he surprised Laird with a wink and set the car moving without waiting for an answer.

They said very little and nothing that mattered on the drive out along the east coast road. Briefly, they both fell silent as they passed the Witchlove Haven turn-off. The half-built marina's future was just one of a long list of items that would have to be sorted out when someone got round to picking through the rubble that remained of Mehran Holdings.

A little later, the tower of the old Norman church was the next landmark that mattered. From there, Moisan more or less let the car coast until they were within sight of the group of cottages at Merfleur's tiny harbour. Grunting, he stopped the car.

'I'll wait here.' He leaned back against the seat and yawned. 'You've forty minutes, Laird — and I could use the peace.'

Leaving the car, Andrew Laird walked down the track towards Merfleur Cottage. As he arrived, he saw Jacob West and his wife sitting on chairs among the flowers in their garden. Then, barking and tail-wagging, their black dog rushed to greet him.

Apart from a visible lump on his skull, the dog seemed to have recovered. Moments later, Belle was kissing Laird and Jacob West was pumping his hand.

'We hoped you'd come over before you left.' Belle let him go with a final hug.

'You know?' he asked.

Jacob West nodded. 'Chief Inspector Flambard telephoned. Something about it being urgent you get back to London.'

'It is.' Like their dog, the Wests appeared none the worse for their ordeal. 'Talk to him if you've any problems about the *Vanneau*.'

Jacob and Belle exchanged a glance. Jacob West shook his head. 'We won't have, boy. We've had a talk — all of us. We're going to turn it over to a kind of legal trust setup. Then we can sit back, eh?'

'Less hassle,' agreed Laird. He glanced round. 'Where's — '

He saw her coming out of the cottage. Kiri Vass was wearing a short-sleeved white shirt and white trousers. Her feet were bare, as they had been the first time he'd seen her; her raven-black hair hung loose around her shoulders.

'Mind you,' said Jacob West to the world in general, 'there's still that other French ship out there somewhere. Now if we could find it next — '

Belle winked at Laird and Kiri, gesturing them away. They left the cottage, walking slowly past the harbour and along the shore. When they stopped they were near the old Martello tower hand-in-hand.

'Are you being kicked out?' asked Kiri bluntly.

'But nicely.' He nodded.

She frowned a little. 'I go to London sometimes, for a day or two — '

'I'll be there,' said Laird.

'I thought of that.' Her eyes twinkled. 'Wouldn't she mind?'

'Who?' Laird blinked at her.

'When we were in the crypt, when you were coming round, you were muttering about someone. Didn't you know?' She waited.

'No.' Laird shook his head. 'But she wouldn't mind.'

'I have someone like that, in Paris. Special — but he would understand.' She smiled at him, put her hand into the breast-pocket of her blouse, and drew out a small, linen-wrapped package. 'Maybe you should give her this.'

Mystified, Laird took the package and unwrapped it. Then he stared. It was small and beautifully shaped, a natural pendant formed by two double Louis d'Ors bound together by a pear-drop of the *Vanneau*'s black concretion.

'It's a beautiful thing — ' Suddenly he was lost for words.

'Jacob and Belle want you to have it.' She kissed him on the lips, quickly and lightly. 'So do I.'

'It's valuable — '

She glanced up at him, then nodded across at the old Martello tower. 'We've plenty more.'

Laird stared at her. 'You mean — ?'

She nodded. 'We found the real *Vanneau*

374

gold weeks ago, Andy. Most of it, anyway. It's been in there, under the floor, ever since. Jacob just kept on looking, in case there was more.' She gave a chuckle and took a breath which firmed her breasts under the white blouse. 'But this new trust will still find something, I suppose.'

'I suppose.' Laird glanced back towards the cottage. He could just make out the two elderly figures sitting in their garden. 'That pair of old devils — '

Then he laughed. It was good to have something to laugh about.

They started back towards Moisan and the police car. He still had a flight to catch.

THE END

THE INTERFACE MAN
LEAVE IT TO THE HANGMAN
BLUEBACK
WITCHROCK
LIVE BAIT
DEVILWEED
DRAW BATONS!
PILOT ERROR
THE TALLYMAN
LAKE OF FURY
AN INCIDENT IN ICELAND
PLACE OF MISTS
SALVAGE JOB
A BURIAL IN PORTUGAL
A PAY-OFF IN SWITZERLAND
CARGO RISK
ISLE OF DRAGONS
NEST OF VULTURES
THE COUNTERFEIT KILLERS
A CUT IN DIAMONDS
MAYDAY FROM MALAGA
DRUM OF POWER
A PROBLEM IN PRAGUE
CAVE OF BATS
BLOOD PROOF
BLOODTIDE

McLEAN AT THE GOLDEN OWL
George Goodchild

Inspector McLean has resigned from Scotland Yard's CID and has opened an office in Wimpole Street. With the help of his able assistant, Tiny, he solves many crimes, including those of kidnapping, murder and poisoning.

KATE WEATHERBY
Anne Goring

Derbyshire, 1849: The Hunter family are the arrogant, powerful masters of Clough Grange. Their feuds are sparked by a generation of guilt, despair and illfortune. But their passions are awakened by the arrival of nineteen-year-old Kate Weatherby.

A VENETIAN RECKONING
Donna Leon

When the body of a prominent international lawyer is found in the carriage of an intercity train, Commissario Guido Brunetti begins to dig deeper into the secret lives of the once great and good.

A TASTE FOR DEATH
Peter O'Donnell

Modesty Blaise and Willie Garvin take on impossible odds in the shape of Simon Delicata, the man with a taste for death, and Swordmaster, Wenczel, in a terrifying duel. Finally, in the Sahara desert, the intrepid pair must summon every killing skill to survive.

SEVEN DAYS FROM MIDNIGHT
Rona Randall

In the Comet Theatre, London, seven people have good reason for wanting beautiful Maxine Culver out of the way. Each one has reason to fear her blackmail. But whose shadow is it that lurks in the wings, waiting to silence her once and for all?

QUEEN OF THE ELEPHANTS
Mark Shand

Mark Shand knows about the ways of elephants, but he is no match for the tiny Parbati Barua, the daughter of India's greatest expert on the Asian elephant, the late Prince of Gauripur, who taught her everything. Shand sought out Parbati to take part in a film about the plight of the wild herds today in north-east India.

THE DARKENING LEAF
Caroline Stickland

On storm-tossed Chesil Bank in 1847, the young lovers, Philobeth and Frederick, prevent wreckers mutilating the apparent corpse of a young woman. Discovering she is still alive, Frederick takes her to his grandmother's home. But the rescue is to have violent and far-reaching effects . . .

A WOMAN'S TOUCH
Emma Stirling

When Fenn went to stay on her uncle's farm in Africa, the lovely Helena Starr seemed to resent her — especially when Dr Jason Kemp agreed to Fenn helping in his bush hospital. Though it seemed Jason saw Fenn as little more than a child, her feelings for him were those of a woman.

A DEAD GIVEAWAY
Various Authors

This book offers the perfect opportunity to sample the skills of five of the finest writers of crime fiction — Clare Curzon, Gillian Linscott, Peter Lovesey, Dorothy Simpson and Margaret Yorke.

DOUBLE INDEMNITY
— MURDER FOR INSURANCE
Jad Adams

This is a collection of true cases of murderers who insured their victims then killed them — or attempted to. Each tense, compelling account tells a story of cold-blooded plotting and elaborate deception.

THE PEARLS OF COROMANDEL
Keron Bhattacharya

John Sugden, an ambitious young Oxford graduate, joins the Indian Civil Service in the early 1920s and goes to uphold the British Raj. But he falls in love with a young Hindu girl and finds his loyalties tragically divided.

WHITE HARVEST
Louis Charbonneau

Kathy McNeely, a marine biologist, sets out for Alaska to carry out important research. But when she stumbles upon an illegal ivory poaching operation that is threatening the world's walrus population, she soon realises that she will have to survive more than the harsh elements . . .